MURDER
IN
ENGLISH PUB

BOOKS BY ALICE CASTLE

MURDER
AT AN
ENGLISH PUB

ALICE CASTLE

bookouture

Published by Bookouture in 2024

An imprint of Storyfire Ltd.
Carmelite House
50 Victoria Embankment
London EC4Y 0DZ

www.bookouture.com

ISBN: 978-1-83525-222-2
eBook ISBN: 978-1-83525-221-5

To Ella and Connie, with love

ONE

It was a fine day at the end of March when Sarah Vane parked her silver Volvo neatly and opened the rear door, undoing her little black Scottie dog, Hamish's harness. He shook himself after the long drive and gave her his favourite quizzical, head-on-one-side look.

Sarah sighed. She'd always thought of herself as a cat person – until her husband Peter had come home on day one of his retirement with Hamish in a wicker pet carrier, an adorable fait accompli in a jaunty tartan collar. The dog had tilted his head at her then just as he was doing now, a tiny creature with a big personality, who even all these months later had still not quite grown into ample triangular ears. 'A dog will keep you company when I'm not around,' Peter had said lightly. At the time, she'd thought he meant when he was on one of his fishing trips. It wasn't until after his death that she realised he didn't want her to face the future alone.

'I'm sorry, boy,' she said, smoothing Hamish's tufty head as she clipped on his lead. 'But we haven't got time for a walk now and I don't want you running away.'

Hamish did a good job of conveying hurt dignity, holding

his stout little body stiffly for all of a minute, before the cry of a gull captured his attention. They were facing a magnificent stretch of the Kent coastline, with the sparkling sea and bright blue sky on one side, and a row of pretty houses on the other. A breeze ruffled Sarah's hair as she locked the car and turned towards the middle house in the row. Hamish looked up at her, pink tongue bright against the dark coat that always looked scruffy, no matter how much his mistress tried to tame it.

'Yes, that's our new home,' Sarah said, taking in a deep breath of the fresh sea air. 'Let's go and have a look at it. Don't worry, I've got your ball safely.' She patted her pocket. Hamish woofed once and set off, stumpy tail wagging.

She still couldn't quite believe she was the new owner of this gorgeous place. According to the estate agent, it had once been a fisherman's cottage. Sarah suspected that was said about any house within five miles of the sea, but the house couldn't be more picturesque. Its forget-me-not blue front door was set between pretty latticed windows and the pocket-handkerchief front garden was bursting with colourful pink and yellow snapdragons. Beyond the red-tiled roof, cotton-wool swabs of cloud were bobbing past.

Sarah turned back towards the sea, where more gulls were wheeling far out from the shore, their cries muted by the sound of the waves. It was so enchanting. All she had to do was go inside the house, then her new life could begin. But as soon as she put one hand on the garden gate, she ground to a halt.

Hamish, snuffling expectantly at her side, looked up. Sarah sighed again. Somehow, the gate's jolly wrought-iron struts, fashioned into the shape of a slightly rusty rising sun, summed up everything that had recently changed in her life. It wasn't a set of good, solid, sensible black London railings. Nor was it original to the little cottage, which Sarah reckoned probably dated from the 1800s.

The gate had more than a hint of frivolity about it, and

Sarah suddenly felt jarred by the contrast with her own neat appearance. A sensible sixty-something woman, she wore her hair in a silvery blonde cap. Today it set off her stylish top and trousers, which in turn had been chosen to complement cool blue eyes. She was still crease-free even after the long drive and Hamish's best efforts. There was an order and professionalism about her that clashed badly with the determined quirkiness of the metal struts. For a moment, she felt adrift.

Then Hamish nudged her leg with his nose. All this hanging about wasn't his thing. 'Oh, all right,' said Sarah, reaching down to rub his ears again. She took a breath and lifted the latch. The whole point of leaving London and relocating to Merstairs was to have a bit of fun, she told herself bracingly. Yes, the gate was a tad silly – and as she passed through it, the hinges squealed in a protest that she instantly vowed to quell with a judicious squirt of WD40 – but that was seaside style for you. This house – her new home – was going to be her tiny slice of heaven on the coast. It was the retirement she and Peter had so often dreamt of in their busy urban lives, she rushing around as a GP at an inner-city practice, he lecturing in classics at one of the big London unis. It was just a shame he had never lived to see this day.

Well, it was much more than a shame, it was a howling calamity, but that was Sarah's way. A gentle understatement, covering Peter's grim terminal illness, diagnosed just after his departmental leaving party. A few short months later, Sarah had found herself at a nondescript London crematorium, receiving commiserations from the very colleagues who'd signed Peter's leaving card. She was also in sole charge of Hamish, though who owned who was probably up for debate.

With their grown-up children, Becca, a lawyer, and secondary teacher Hattie, safely off their hands, established in their careers and with children of their own, it should have been time for Sarah and Peter to start a new chapter in a long and quietly happy marriage. Now she was facing a blank page. She fumbled in her pocket for the unfamiliar keyring, bowing her head slightly as grief settled on her, as it had so often since Peter's passing.

But then she squared her shoulders, inserted the key into the lock, and opened the door. Peter wouldn't want her to mope around. Even after everything that had happened, everything she'd done. Or had to do. Hamish wouldn't let her wallow, anyway. Peter had been quite right to foist the dog on her. The Scottie, though missing Peter almost as much as she did, had got her out of the house on dark days, and his regular clamours that it must, surely, be dinner time always reminded her to feed herself too.

That made her realise how much she was craving a cup of tea after the journey. And maybe even a well-deserved biscuit. But as she walked down the narrow passageway, past the small sitting room to the even tinier kitchen, with Hamish on red alert at all the exciting new sights and smells, there was a call of 'Coo-ee' from the front door. A one-woman whirlwind was advancing towards her.

'Only me,' said a rotund figure with outstretched arms, her dyed red hair slipping out of a magenta scarf worn headband-style like a 1980s fitness-video starlet. Sarah was grabbed and unceremoniously enfolded in a huge hug.

For a moment, she stiffened, and Hamish started to growl. Then she relaxed.

'It's fine, boy, it's only Daphne,' Sarah said, her senses filled with a heady scent as she was clasped to an ample bosom. She freed herself, just in case Hamish leapt to her defence, and gave him a reassuring pat while he glared at Daphne with black button eyes. Then she turned back to her friend. 'How on earth did you get in?'

'You left the door open, Sarah. Not like you,' said Daphne Roux, arching lavishly applied black eyebrows. Daphne was nothing if not a force of nature – and had been ever since she and Sarah had met at boarding school further along the Kent coast, more years ago than either cared to remember. They were chalk and cheese, but Sarah had always loved and secretly envied Daphne's exuberance. In her GP days, her job had helped disguise innate shyness – now she was hoping some of her friend's carefree sociability would rub off on her. Daphne bent down to say hello to Hamish and he put away his growl and gave her a polite sniff. 'Anyway, I do have a spare set of keys. I let the removal guys in yesterday to unload your boxes, remember?'

With a tut at her own forgetfulness, Sarah rushed back down the passage to make sure everything was now secured.

'Oh, Sarah! You don't need to worry so much. I always leave my door open,' Daphne shouted merrily from the kitchen. 'It's not like London, you know. There's no crime in Merstairs.'

Nevertheless, Sarah closed the front door with a snap before walking back into the kitchen. She was beginning to wish she'd accompanied the removals van yesterday, instead of leaving it to Daphne. But she'd wanted to make sure the new family got themselves properly installed in her London house, and knew where to find the stopcock and so on. Now here she was in her new place where, ironically, she hadn't a clue about the plumbing. It was a sure thing that Daphne had no idea either, though she'd lived in an identical cottage right next door for years.

Now her friend was standing stock-still, eyes squeezed tight shut. Her hands were on her scarf, which was slightly askew. But she wasn't trying to straighten it. If Sarah knew Daphne – and after five decades she rather thought she did – her friend had decided she was getting a psychic message from 'the Beyond'. Daphne firmly believed she had second sight. It was all nonsense, as far as scientific Sarah was concerned, but she knew how much Daphne prized her dubious talent, and it hurt no one. 'Someone's coming through, it's very strong, it's as though they're here with us...'

'As long as you don't tell me it's Peter. You know how he felt about that stuff,' said Sarah briskly. If Peter really had been around, he would have told Daphne himself, in some very choice phrases. But the suggestion seemed to be enough. Daphne changed tack.

'No, it's not a voice, more of a feeling... just that this is going to be a very happy home for you,' she announced triumphantly, opening her eyes wide as though that settled things.

'Well, great. And are you also getting a feeling that you'd like to help me unpack all these?' Sarah said, gesturing to the towers of boxes all around.

Daphne immediately looked crestfallen. 'I thought I'd left it pretty shipshape for you, actually.'

'Shipshape!' echoed Sarah weakly. As far as she was concerned, the place was in chaos.

'Oh, I know you, Sarah. It won't take you five minutes.' Daphne swept an arm around expansively, nearly knocking over a pile of cartons. 'And look, you've got all the essentials right here,' she said, pointing to the box marked 'kettle'.

Daphne was right, things seemed much brighter a few minutes later, when they were settled round the kitchen table with steaming mugs of tea and a packet of chocolate digestives. Sarah had also found Hamish's bed and a tin of treats too, so he was happily chomping away in the corner.

Then Daphne leapt up and grabbed the nearest packing crate. 'Might as well make a start,' she said, ripping it open with such gusto that bits of cardboard went everywhere.

'Daphne, not that one,' protested Sarah. But it was too late.

'Oh,' said Daphne, lifting out a man's suit. She looked at her friend, red hair even wilder than usual as it slipped out of its scarf. 'No, Sarah! Don't tell me you've brought all poor Peter's stuff down here?'

Sarah swallowed. All at once, she wasn't the sensible doctor any more. She suddenly felt, instead, like the timid little thing she had been, when she had first met Daphne on day one at school. Daphne had seen Sarah's wobbly lip then, and taken her under her wing, and Sarah had prized her kindness and generosity ever since. Now Sarah sniffed as unobtrusively as she could. 'I know it's silly. But I just couldn't...'

Words failed her at the thought of consigning everything of Peter's to some charity shop, or even worse, a dustbin. The jackets he had loved, and worn until the elbows gave out, which she had then patched... jackets that still smelt of him, that special mixture of Imperial Leather soap and his beloved books. They'd thought he could wear these tough old tweeds while tending the pretty garden here... She swallowed.

In his basket, Hamish let out a soft whimper. It wouldn't do to upset him. Sarah grabbed the suit from Daphne, bundled it back into the box and closed up the torn flaps as best she could. 'I thought I'd... have more time. To go through everything here.'

'Of course, dear. Of course,' said Daphne, as she engulfed Sarah in her second epic hug of the day, patting her friend heartily on the back. 'But where are you going to put it all?' She twirled round, losing an earring and then stooping to pick it up from under one of the kitchen units before Hamish could pounce. He eyed her steadily from his basket, then turned away as if to say such things were beneath his notice. 'I mean... this house is not huge. I should know. My place has exactly the same footprint. There's hardly room to swing a cat.'

As Sarah was sure Daphne's enormous ginger tomcat, Mephisto, was rampaging around next door this very minute, Sarah knew this was an exaggeration. But she had been ridiculous, bringing all Peter's things down here. 'I should have made myself go through it all before... but it just seemed... very hard.' Despite her best efforts, her voice faded out. *This will never do, Sarah. Get a grip*, she told herself, always her own sternest critic.

But Daphne just sat herself down again with a flump and covered Sarah's hand with her own bigger, warmer one, and pressed kindly.

'Do you know, I think I have the perfect solution?'

'Oh yes?' asked Sarah, blinking and taking up her mug again. She'd encouraged enough people in a pickle to drink 'a nice cup of tea' in her time. She was getting a taste of her own medicine now.

'Maybe that's what the spirits were trying to tell me just now. I've bought something that's going to solve all our problems. Honestly, you're going to love this. There will be space for Peter's things, for however long you want to keep them. As long as it's not too long, that is!' Daphne finished with one of her trademark chuckles that seemed to shake her entire body, from her pink fluffy mules upwards.

'You've come out in your slippers,' Sarah said, hand to her mouth.

'Oh, don't look so scandalised. No one's going to report me to the police for that around here. Unless you do.' Daphne chuckled again. 'But seriously, do you want to hear my idea?'

'Well, yes please,' said Sarah. Though, knowing Daphne, her solution could easily be a set of magic crystals or a special incantation and Sarah would still be at square one.

'What are we waiting for?' said Daphne, slapping her hands down so hard on the table that the cups and plates danced. 'Let's go. You won't believe it till you've seen it with your own eyes.'

TWO

Ten minutes later, Sarah was staring at Daphne again, and this time her jaw was on the floor.

'You can't be serious,' she said, in her most authoritative GP voice, the one she'd had to use on the incompetent practice receptionist – before replacing her with a better one. But it was wasted on Daphne, who just clapped her hands together in excitement and smiled as broadly as the Cheshire Cat.

'Isn't it wonderful, Sarah! Don't you just love it?' Daphne gazed at the peeling pink and orange striped façade of the ancient beach hut in front of them as though she'd met the love of her life.

They were standing in front of a row of similar huts, of the type that launched a thousand seaside postcards. The rest were done out in gorgeous ice cream sundae pastels, immaculate and gleaming, and couldn't have been more evocative of the English coast. The open ones they'd passed seemed to boast all kinds of fancy extras, like fridges, bike racks, hammocks – even a sofa. All except one – Daphne's. It stood out like a bedraggled old sparrow in a flock of flamingos.

Sarah goggled at the hut, while hanging onto Hamish, who

was scrabbling in the sand at the foot of the ramshackle construction. 'The door's virtually hanging off, the paint is blistering, the wood is warped... and the colours, that awful pink and orange!'

'OK, sure, it has one or two little issues, but nothing we can't fix with a nail or two,' said Daphne, quite unfazed. 'As for the paint, I've got a few tins in my shed that'll do the job beautifully, though it's a shame to mess with such a perfect colour scheme.'

Sarah wondered, not for the first time, if she and Daphne would ever see the world the same way. 'And you've actually bought this?'

'Yep. It was a snip. Usually they go for fortunes... I suppose it was because we're only just now coming into the holiday season.' Daphne continued to gaze at it, entranced.

Sarah shook her head, deciding the buyers had very definitely seen her friend coming. Easily done, as the colours she favoured were almost as loud as this beach hut. But Sarah couldn't deny it would be useful in her present predicament. 'I'm really grateful to you for letting me move some of my boxes in,' she said, remembering her manners.

'What are friends for?' said Daphne airily, throwing her arm round Sarah's slender shoulders. 'In any case, you'll have to help me a bit first. Not just with the painting and stuff.'

'Oh?'

'Well, the estate agents did say there were a few things inside it,' said Daphne, with an unaccustomed wrinkle to her forehead. But she soon banished it. 'That's one of the reasons it was going cheap. But I dare say we can get it cleared in no time, then it'll be just lovely for the summer. Especially for when your daughters come down with the grandchildren!'

Sarah perked up at this. Family had been crucial in getting through these last few hard months. Her girls Becca and Hattie now each had a baby daughter of their own, Evelyn and Amelia.

There was nothing to beat time spent with grandchildren, especially ones as precociously talented and beautiful as hers, she thought with a totally unbiased smile. She had always wondered whether becoming a granny would make her feel her age, but it had been a blessing – especially since Peter had had the chance to meet both children briefly. 'Right, let's set to, then,' she said.

'That's the spirit,' said Daphne, rooting around in her huge squashy bag. 'Now where did I put those keys?'

Several minutes later, to Hamish's intense excitement, most of the contents of Daphne's bag were lying on the beach. He didn't seem too sure about her, but her possessions were apparently worth a thorough sniffing. A handful of old lipsticks were gathering a coating of sand, the pages of a paperback were going wavy in the damp sea air, and myriad tissues were floating this way and that on the breeze. Sarah was worn out with catching them before the dog could, and shoving them into a nearby bin. There were gentle wisps of steam coming out of her ears by the time Daphne had a last root in her bag and dragged the keys out with a triumphant 'Hurrah!'

'Honestly, Daph, you've got a luminous green plastic sea monster as a key fob, how can you possibly not have seen that in your bag?' Sarah said, in what she considered to be admirably measured tones.

'All right, keep your hair on, Sarah. It's dark inside there, isn't it?' said Daphne, throwing back her luxuriant red locks with a motion intended to be dignified. It fell short, when her scarf fell right off and hit the sand. 'Now look what you've made me do.'

The pair glared at each other for a second, then both burst out laughing as Hamish promptly leapt on the offending article. After a short tug of war, Daphne snatched it back. Somehow the women's spats never got beyond this point, before they found the situation too silly to be cross about – one of the many reasons their friendship had lasted.

'Right, well, if you and Hamish have quite finished holding me up,' said Daphne with a laughing glance at her friend. 'I'll just get this door opened, shall I?'

She fitted the key into the lock and turned, but the 'Ta-dah' on her lips quickly faded into a surprised 'Oh!'

'What is it, Daphne?' Sarah tried to peer over her friend's shoulder. But the hut, like the inside of Daphne's bag, was pretty dark. Then Daphne shuffled out of the way, Hamish started barking frantically, and Sarah saw for the first time exactly what the problem was.

Fifteen minutes later, both women were sitting on the sand outside the hut, wiping the sweat from their brows. With them was a massive cardboard box, rather like the ones currently piled up in Sarah's house – but even larger and heavier. And inside the hut were many, many more. In fact, Hamish was still rooting around, letting out the odd whine. There was something in there he wasn't too sure about.

'So what exactly did the estate agents tell you about the contents of the hut, before you bought it? And why have you never looked inside until now?' Sarah's voice was a little faint. The sun was high in the sky and, even with a frisky breeze blowing off the sea, it was getting hot. It was not, in Sarah's view, ideal weather for a pair of sixty-something ladies to be manhandling boxes out of a cramped and crumbling hut.

'I know what you're saying, Sarah. You think I've been fool-ish. A silly old woman who's been gulled into making a big mistake... ha, gulled! That's funny,' said Daphne irrepressibly, pointing at a large seagull just landing on the bin where Sarah had stowed Daphne's tissues. It regarded the women with knowing yellow eyes, gave a squawk that, to Sarah's ears, sounded like a harsh peal of laughter, then spread its wings and flew off in search of abandoned chips.

'I wish *I* could fly away. We've got our work cut out with that shed. And what on earth do we do with all the stuff? I've got enough gubbins of my own to deal with,' said Sarah.

'Let's think about this logically,' said Daphne. 'We have no idea what's in any of these boxes. They could all be full of gold bars.'

'That's logical thinking, is it?' Sarah couldn't help smiling at her friend. 'Well, this one certainly weighs enough to have a few ingots in it,' she said, kicking it with the toe of her trainer. At least she had worn sensible shoes for a day on the beach. Daphne's ancient fluffy mules, exposing the screeching scarlet of her painted toenails, were not ideal for a day as an impromptu removal man. But now she was removing her slippers entirely and trickling the nice warm top layer of sand onto her toes.

For a second, Sarah felt disapproving. Then she realised that was ridiculous. Why shouldn't Daphne relax and enjoy the beach? And why shouldn't she, come to that? She wasn't in London any more, rushing through her appointments to hurry back and tend to Peter. No, she was living her new life – one of ease, apparently.

She took a deep breath and settled herself more comfortably against the hut. Hamish was still busy inside, she could hear him scrabbling around, but he surely couldn't be doing any harm – the place was already a total mess. That left her free to take in the sight in front of her.

The golden sands of the beach stretched down to a frilly line of waves, playing a game of catch-me-if-you-can with two children, one of around seven and a chubby little toddler. Suddenly a bigger wave sneaked up on them, knocking the baby off tiny feet. Sarah could hear the indignant roar and see the

panic of the older child, trying to pick up the wet, yelling creature, before it was swept out to sea. Sarah struggled to her feet,
ready to save the day – then the young mother swooped, picking
up the little mite and leading the crestfallen older child away.
No need for Sarah to get involved.

Daphne, watching Sarah with an amused smile, shoved her
toes back into her mules. 'Come on then, let's be having you.
Can't be idling away the whole day, you know. We've got work
to do. Let's see what's in this box first.'

With that, Daphne set about ripping open her second
carton of the day. There wasn't a gold ingot in sight, but it did
contain a ladies' pure silk square scarf patterned with horseshoes, jumbled in with some men's trousers, a number of high-
visibility jackets and, at the bottom, pair after pair of heavy
work boots, which must be what had made the box so difficult to
shift.

'Right, if it's all clothes, it's going to be easy,' said Daphne
brightly. 'I know just the place. Fantastic antique shop, with a
few rails of second-hand things. Run by quite a dishy chap, too.
You'll love him, Sarah. Let's see what's in the next box.'

Sarah ignored the mention of the 'dishy chap'. Daphne
ought to know she was hardly in the market for that sort of
thing. 'OK, but let's leave it in the hut, instead of dragging it
outside, shall we?' said Sarah.

They both stepped back inside, to find Hamish sitting
sheepishly next to a mound of chewed bits, pulled off one of the
cartons. He wagged his tail when he saw Sarah, and gave that
odd whine again. 'Well, Hamish seems pretty sure we should
open this one next,' said Sarah.

'Oh, fine,' said Daphne, helping the dog out by tearing the
top to shreds. 'More clothes. But that's funny, there seems to be
a sort of trunk inside, at the bottom,' she said, peering down into
the box. 'No wonder this one weighs a ton, too.'

Hamish was now pawing at Sarah's trousers, almost as

though he was trying to tell her something. 'Do you want your ball?' she asked him, fishing it out of her pocket. But for once, he ignored his favourite toy, and kept on staring from her to the trunk with what Sarah was sure was a worried expression on his little face. She went over to have a better look. 'Let's get rid of all the cardboard from the sides, then see what we've got,' she said sensibly.

Once they'd done that, there it was – a large, oblong trunk, much like the ones they'd both had at school. Hamish sat, whining gently, and looking from one woman to the other.

'Honestly, I don't know what on earth he's trying to tell us,' said Sarah.

'Oh, simple, Hamish thinks this really could have gold bars in it,' said Daphne cheerily. 'I'm getting a good feeling about this,' she added, rubbing her hands together.

'All right then, go for it,' said Sarah.

Daphne set to eagerly, unbuckling the strap around the middle of the trunk, and then popping the two latches, one after the other.

'I bet it needs a key,' Sarah couldn't resist saying. Daphne just tutted, then lifted the lid, as Hamish started barking fit to burst.

Immediately, both women heartily wished the trunk had been locked. With a shocked gasp, they clutched each other and automatically took a step back, away from the terrible sight before them, not to mention the sudden stench. For, curled up inside the confined space, almost like a baby in the womb, was all that remained of a very dead elderly man.

THREE

While Daphne ran up and down the beach, screaming and gathering quite a crowd of onlookers, Sarah took several deep breaths, trying to collect herself and fight the dizziness that threatened to overwhelm her. She knew she was on the verge of fainting, which wasn't going to do anyone any good.

After a couple of minutes, she felt her pulse steadying and her vision cleared. She picked up the whimpering Hamish, clipped on his lead and tied him up outside the hut. Then she fished an unused tissue out of her friend's abandoned handbag, put it over her nose and mouth, and made herself duck back inside. She tried to survey the corpse with practised calm, telling herself sternly she was a professional – albeit a retired one.

The deceased was a white male, not much hair, but reasonable teeth, judging from the mouth, which was lolling rather horribly. And he wasn't that old, Sarah realised with a jolt. Not much older than her, at any rate. The petechiae, or red spots, still visible in the rheumy open eyes, told their own story. The poor man had been strangled. There was certainly no need to fumble for a pulse or start CPR. Sarah did, however, get out her phone and dial 999. And then she took a quick picture. It was an instinct, nothing more, but she had a feeling it might come in handy for the police.

Just then, Daphne poked a distressed face round the door of the hut. 'Sarah! What are you doing? How can you stand being in there? Come away immediately.'

Sarah didn't need to be asked twice. She got up carefully and backed out of the hut. The passageway between the boxes looming on all sides seemed to have narrowed, now she knew the horrible secret lurking within the trunk. She had a moment of irrational dread that she might get trapped in the hut with the body. But the next minute, she was through the door and out in the open again. Hamish was thrilled to see her, dancing this way and that on nimble paws as she untied him, wagging his little tail until it was a blur.

She breathed in the clean seaside smell of salt and seaweed, leaning against the side of the hut. Though she prided herself on being an old hand with bodies, as her duties had included certifying the occasional passing of patients, she had not often had to attend such a *delayed* deathbed scene. And murder was – pretty much – a new one on her.

'Gosh, this is all so *ghastly*,' said Daphne, with a voice that suggested at least a pinch of horrified relish. 'Who'd have thought something like *that* would have been in my hut?'

Sarah, now mercifully feeling a lot better, started to think hard. 'Exactly who did you buy it from, Daphne?'

Daphne paused for a moment. 'Oh, well, there's no need to say it like that, Sarah.'

'Like what?' Sarah was genuinely puzzled. 'I just think there's a good chance that the previous owner knows something about that, erm, trunk. Wouldn't you say?'

'Oh. I thought you were implying that I'd made a stupid mistake...' Daphne said.

Sarah thought privately that buying a hideous beach hut

complete with mouldering corpse could certainly be classified in that category... but it was her turn to put an arm round her friend. 'Come on now, Daph. Don't take it to heart. After all, it's not as if we did the murder ourselves, is it?'

Immediately Daphne broke free of her embrace. 'What on earth are you saying? *Murder?* In Merstairs? No. It isn't possible!'

Sarah shrugged. 'I'm afraid it is. Just ask yourself how that man shut himself in the trunk, Daph. Anyway, I wonder where they are? It seems like ages since I rang.'

'Who?' said Daphne weakly.

'The police, of course,' Sarah said in a low voice, trying not to attract any more attention from the little knot of onlookers. They were thinning out now, realising there was no chance of seeing the dead body Daphne had been shouting about. Not while Sarah was standing right by the entrance with Hamish, who was directing forbidding looks at anyone edging too close to his grisly find.

'Oh but Sarah, I should have called Mariella. Why didn't you say?'

Sarah looked at Daphne blankly. Mariella was Daphne's daughter. When Sarah had last seen her, a year ago, she had just finished a cookery course and was about to start work at a local restaurant. Not the first person Sarah would think of ringing in an emergency like this.

'Don't look at me like I've gone mad, Sarah!' Daphne snapped. 'The café thing didn't work out. Mariella's a trainee constable now. It's tough, juggling everything with the kids, but she's doing brilliantly. She can sort everything in a trice for us.'

'Oh, I'm sorry, Daphne, I had no idea Mariella was with the police,' Sarah said. And indeed, Daphne had been much too busy running up and down the beach screaming to mention her useful law enforcement contacts.

Sarah now wished she hadn't been so efficient, especially

when she heard the swish of a vehicle coming to a halt on the road just behind the row of beach huts, followed by the slamming of car doors.

The sound of boots crunching on sand and a burble of police radios heralded the arrival of two very solid-looking police constables, both in stab vests. Sarah had seen such sights regularly in the big city, and normally wouldn't have thought twice about it. But here, against the backdrop of cheery painted beach huts, with families building sandcastles and sunning themselves, the hefty size-tens of the policemen, kicking up the sand as they went, seemed terribly out of place.

'So, ladies, what's all this then? Something about a body?' said the taller of the two policemen, with a tiny, amused glance at his colleague which told Sarah he was pretty sure a pair of silly old dears were getting their knitting in a twist about nothing.

'This way, officer,' she announced, in her most businesslike tones, handing Hamish's lead to Daphne, despite his protests that he really needed to be showing their visitors this new development himself. Once inside the hut, Sarah didn't venture too close, she just pointed out the obvious cause of the problem. This time the look the officers exchanged was a lot more circumspect.

But, when she heard the shorter policeman ask his companion how he thought death could have occurred, Sarah decided she could learn nothing useful from remaining inside with the duo. It was clear at least one of them didn't have a clue. Outside, the sun was really beginning to beat down. Daphne was sitting near the hut with the disgruntled Hamish. She was just putting away her phone. As the proper authorities were now in situ, Sarah decided she might as well try to get things back to some sort of normality.

'How about a sandwich, Daph?'

'Oooh, I could never eat again, not after what I've seen

today,' Daphne said, shaking her head and sending coppery hair flying everywhere. 'How could you even suggest such a thing, Sarah? Anyway, I've just rung Mariella. She's on shift, luckily, so she'll be popping over.'

'Oh, well that's great,' said Sarah. Daphne's daughter could only be an improvement on what she'd seen so far of the Merstairs constabulary. 'I'd still like to get Hamish away from the scene of the crime, it's quite unsettling for him. And I know what we've just seen has probably killed your appetite – but I think we need to keep our strength up, Daphne. It must be well past one by now and we were moving boxes for ages before – well, you know. If you really don't want anything, I'll just nip and get a roll. I can see a little café over there.' She slung her bag over her shoulder. 'If you're sure?' she asked again quickly, just for form's sake.

'Hang on,' Daphne called her back. 'Well, perhaps something small... if I really must... actually, they do a marvellous bacon butty at the Beach Café. Just a couple of those, and a sweet tea, as I've had a shock. Maybe one for Mari, too. And a tiny slice of cake, just in case,' Daphne finished, managing to look as though she was being very restrained.

Sarah hoped she had enough in her purse to cover what had suddenly turned out to be a slap-up lunch. But Daphne was right. They needed it, after that terrible shock.

But did she really want to wrap herself up in cotton wool and hide from sights such as the one they'd seen this morning, horrible though it undoubtedly had been? No, thought Sarah. A quiet retirement, of the sort Peter had wanted, was all very well. She would have loved that, with him. But he wasn't here any more. She still had plenty of life in her yet. And if she could be useful, then she would be.

FOUR

After twenty minutes of queuing for bacon butties (and all the extras Daphne had demanded), Sarah was feeling every one of her years. She'd had to tie Hamish up outside the café and he had made his feelings plain about missing the shenanigans no doubt going on in the hut, and being excluded from all the yummy smells in the café as well.

But once she got back to her friend, she looked around in surprise. Daphne had found an old rug – Sarah couldn't help hoping it wasn't from one of the other boxes in the hut – and was sitting in lonely splendour, facing the sea, which was now as flat and still as a painted blue line, beneath the even bluer sky. The hut door was firmly shut, with only a tiny strip of crime scene tape across it, like a badly wrapped Christmas present.

'Where are those policemen?' Sarah asked.

'Oh, they said someone would be along soon. An urgent message came in on their walkie-talkie things and they were off.'

'Really?' Sarah was astonished. 'But what could be more urgent than a dead body in a trunk?'

'Search me,' said Daphne, holding her face up to the sun.

'Have they taken the body with them?'

'You mean, did they do up the trunk and drag him away through the sand? No, they didn't,' said Daphne, closing her eyes and looking as though she hadn't a care in the world.

'So they've just left a corpse in your beach hut? Great. What are we supposed to do now?' Sarah was baffled.

Hamish busied himself standing guard at the door of the hut, while Sarah scratched her head. In London, instead of a measly piece of tape, the entire hut area would have been cordoned off and a SOCO team would have been on their way. Daphne would emphatically not have been allowed to use the structure as her own personal sunbathing post. 'Did they at least say when they were coming back?' she asked.

'Not a word.' Daphne was now busily pushing up her sleeves, the better to tan her arms. 'But that's good news.'

'How do you work that out?' asked Sarah. She certainly wouldn't have wanted to have a decaying body in her property for a second longer than necessary. But she supposed Daphne was a little less aware of the health hazards it presented.

'Well, this way, we get some time off from emptying boxes,' Daphne said, opening one mischievous eye. 'Don't worry, Mari will be along in a bit. She'll sort it all out.'

With a sigh, Sarah dropped down onto the sand and perched on a corner of the rug. 'Well, that's great. But you know, I really think we should move just a little further away for our lunch.'

'Ha! And I thought I was the squeamish one,' said Daphne.

'We can leave Hamish,' Sarah said. 'He's quite happy making sure the hut doesn't get away. And we can plan what to do next.'

'After lunch, you mean?' said Daphne vaguely. 'As soon as Mariella gets here, I just want to leave. That dead body is playing havoc with my psychic vibrations,' she added with a shudder.

With a sigh, Sarah started gathering her friend's things up – hairbrush, scrunchies, slides, insect spray – just to speed matters along a little. 'I'm sure it is,' she said. 'But we'll have to make a statement, of course. I'm surprised those two policemen didn't ask us any proper questions.'

'Oh, they asked me a few things while you were getting the butties,' said Daphne airily. 'And I expect Mariella will go over the rest. Just for form's sake. After all, we don't really know anything.'

Sarah, trying not to feel disappointed that she'd missed out on the constables' interrogation, shook her head. 'Of course we do. We know a lot. We were the first people on the scene. Well, after the murderer, of course.'

'I wish you wouldn't say that,' said Daphne. 'It must have been some sort of horrible accident.'

Sarah looked over at her friend, wondering what kind of accident would cause someone to squish into a trunk and strangle themselves for good measure. But she let it go.

'Here, this spot will do,' Daphne said, sinking down abruptly, leaving Sarah to shake the sand out of the rug, spread it out and arrange the sandwiches neatly on top of the bag.

'You'll feel better when you've eaten something,' said Sarah, passing a bacon roll to her friend. Daphne might think she was in shock, but actually she was showing all the signs of low blood sugar. She'd be a lot less irritable once she'd taken a few bites. Sarah tucked in herself and instantly felt better.

After they'd munched in companionable silence for a few minutes, Sarah spoke up. 'I hope Mariella gets here soon.'

'Oh, she'll do her best,' said Daphne. 'But they're very under-resourced, the police here. Not that it's usually a problem, it's so quiet and peaceful.'

Hmm, thought Sarah. Not from where she was sitting. 'Well, they've got quite a big case on their hands now,' was all she said.

'I suppose so,' said Daphne, a frown line appearing between her pencilled brows. 'Poor Mariella.'

'She and those colleagues of hers need to find out who that poor man is. He'll have worried relatives somewhere... someone will be missing him,' said Sarah.

'Yes,' said Daphne doubtfully. 'Though they can hardly be that bothered, can they? Or he wouldn't still be in there.'

Daphne had a point. But Sarah was silent, her mind ticking away. If the man in the hut really had no family to care about him, all the more reason for her to get involved. 'Well, if Mariella and her team are too busy to do anything, then I suppose it will have to be the next best thing, won't it?'

'What do you mean?' Daphne asked idly, eyes straying towards the food bag hopefully. 'Any crisps in there?'

'No, you didn't ask for them. I can make some enquiries. I've done it before, in London. Sometimes you have to act a bit like a private detective, helping people get access to the right sort of housing, educational support, that sort of thing. This wouldn't be so different.'

'Maybe,' said Daphne. Then she brightened up. 'Well, I could be really useful, too, with my connection to the Beyond,' she said, failing to look modest.

'Well, let's see how things go. How's your sandwich?' asked Sarah.

'To be honest, I'm still feeling a little delicate,' Daphne said, taking a massive bite.

Sarah scanned the horizon for Mariella. She then checked on Hamish, who was lying down outside the hut. He thumped his tail on the sand as she smiled fondly at him. What a good boy he was, staying on guard. She would have hated any of these kiddies playing so innocently nearby to see that awful sight.

'So, shall I tell you what we should do first, to sort things out?' asked Daphne, who was cheering up a little more with every morsel she ate.

'Look, it's probably better to keep this quite low-key at the moment...' Sarah started to say. But then she thought again. If she was going to be making discreet enquiries, Daphne's local connections could be priceless. With her warm, outgoing nature, she must know virtually everyone in Merstairs. 'What do you suggest?'

'Simple,' said Daphne. 'We'll have a séance.'

Sarah tried not to look as unenthusiastic as she felt at this bright idea. 'You know, I think we could just start with the estate agents. Once we've had a chat with your Mariella,' she said gently.

'Oh. Really? How dull,' said Daphne crossly.

'Yes. But the agents will know where the previous owner is. And then, bingo, we've got our killer. Hopefully before too many people start suspecting it's you.'

Daphne dropped her butty into the sand. 'Me? What on earth do you mean?' she asked, her voice as high as her eyebrows. 'No one will think I had anything to do with that... that awful thing. Will they?'

FIVE

The look on Daphne's face would have been comical – but the situation really wasn't funny. Sarah was absolutely sure most people would assume her friend was a murderer. She owned the beach hut, after all.

'I'm sorry, Daph. But you *are* the most likely person.'

'What? Surely you don't believe I did it? Oh come on, Sarah...' Daphne fanned herself with the paper bag, spraying crumbs everywhere. 'This is a nightmare.'

'Well, *I* don't suspect you. But I'll be in the minority.' Sarah shrugged.

Daphne gaped, then she waved her hand dismissively. 'Oh, phooey! This isn't one of your squalid London murders, you know,' she smiled. 'This is Merstairs! Everyone knows I wouldn't hurt a fly. And only good things happen here.'

'Tell that to the dead chap in the trunk,' said Sarah concisely. 'Ah, that looks like your daughter now.'

Striding across the sand was a tall, determined-looking woman in her early thirties with what could only be described as a plume of bright red hair. She reminded Sarah so strongly of a young Daphne that for a moment she wondered if she was seeing double, or peering into the past. Daphne's hair might be receiving some chemical assistance nowadays, but it had once been every bit as naturally vivid as her daughter's. Unfortunately, the closer Mariella got, the crosser she looked. Oh dear, thought Sarah. It looked like they were in for it now.

* * *

Ten minutes later, the beach hut was finally as festooned with police tape and SOCO officers as any crime scene in London – and Mariella had *almost* finished telling them off.

'You know, finding a murdered man is not exactly what we intended when we got up this morning,' said Sarah, trying to calm things down.

'Are you telling me Mum wasn't poking her nose in for a change?' Mariella replied.

'Most certainly she wasn't,' said Sarah, rushing to her friend's defence. 'She was very upset when we found the body, and it was entirely by accident.'

'Well, now you've found it, just leave it be,' Mariella said sternly. 'None of your Tarot card readings to find out more. Promise me, Mum. Otherwise there will be endless talk – you know how people gossip around here.'

Daphne for once looked quite abashed, and murmured something that sounded like assent.

'Now, I've taken a brief statement from you, Mum. How about you, Sarah? Presumably nothing to add?'

'Just that the man was definitely murdered,' said Sarah, packing away all the traces of their lunch into the paper bag.

Mariella, who'd been sitting on a corner of the rug, straightened up at this. '*What?* Tweedledum and Tweedledee – um, my colleagues – they didn't mention murder. I thought it was a natural death.'

'Nothing very natural about doing up those trunk clasps

from the outside,' said Sarah with a shrug. 'Unless the man was a contortionist or something.'

'Poor Gus. He wasn't that,' said Mariella thoughtfully.

'Gus? Was that his name? You knew him, then?'

Mariella clapped a hand to her mouth, for a second seeming uncannily like her mother. 'Gosh. I shouldn't have said that. Forget I spoke.'

The effect on Daphne was electric. 'Gus? You mean it's *Gus Trubshaw* in there? The landlord of the Jolly Roger? But we all love Gus! Sarah, he's the nicest man! Makes everyone feel so welcome... *made*, I suppose. A kind word for everyone. Well, when he's not losing his temper and barring people. I didn't really get a good look before, it was all too...' she tailed off in horror.

'Yep. It's Gus, all right,' said Mariella. 'But don't you go saying a word, or I'll be in big trouble,' she added vehemently. 'Not a single syllable to anyone, mind.' She stared at both the women.

'Your secret is safe with me. I don't know a soul here anyway,' said Sarah.

'Who, me?' said Daphne, looking the picture of innocence.

Mariella gave her mum one more hard glance and then took out her phone. She started striding up and down the beach, setting up interviews left, right and centre. Things were getting moving.

* * *

Once the pathologist had arrived to examine the body, gone into the hut, and come out some time later giving Mariella a grim nod of the head – which Sarah presumed meant agreement that it was a suspicious death – the SOCO team photographed the inside from all angles. Mariella then supervised the removal of the body, which she achieved with minimal disruption to holiday-makers. Then she hurried off, no doubt with a very busy evening ahead. The beach quickly seemed to get back to normal – but the hut was still taped shut, out of bounds. Sarah folded their picnic blanket while Daphne wrangled her possessions back into her handbag. Then they stood up and looked at each other.

'This wasn't quite the introduction to Merstairs that I had in mind for you,' said Daphne ruefully. For once her mobile face was thoughtful and still. 'After all, you've had enough of death, what with poor Peter... and all that.'

Sarah rather agreed. *All that* had not been great. But she found herself comforting Daphne. 'Not to worry. It isn't as though you planted the corpse there for us to find. And anyway, thinking about it all is going to be a distraction from my own worries.'

For a moment, she looked down at Hamish, sitting patiently by her side, now that he'd lost hope of getting back into the beach hut. 'I don't know about you, but I think Hamish has had enough for one day,' said Sarah. 'I want to take him home and get him properly settled in. But tomorrow, shall we do as I suggested?'

Daphne looked at her blankly.

'Go and talk to the estate agents?' Sarah reminded her.

'Oh, do we have to?'

'To me it makes sense,' said Sarah. 'You bought that hut, and recently, complete with corpse.'

'Don't remind me,' shivered Daphne on cue.

'But you see what I mean?' Sarah persisted. 'Did the estate agents know what the hut contained? Is that why you got it for such a bargain price?'

'OK, I get it. Well, I suppose we can give it a go in the morning,' Daphne said.

'Are you worried Mariella will be annoyed?'

'Oh, pfft,' said Daphne. 'She'll never know. Anyway, it's outrageous, the way she tries to tell me what to do these days.'

'Well, she is with the police,' Sarah reasoned.

'But her own mother? That's a bond far above such worldly concerns,' said Daphne, with that spiritual look on her face again. Sarah shook her head, and the little trio retraced their steps back to their cottages, Hamish's tail wagging as he enjoyed the late afternoon sunshine on his tufty back.

As they walked down the esplanade people were out on the sands in force, playing rounders, making sandcastles, lounging on towels or sitting on little fold-away chairs and staring out at the twinkling sea. Gus Trubshaw's passing didn't seem to have made much of a dent on things, and that seemed sad.

But the thought only served to spur Sarah on. Gus Trubshaw wouldn't be forgotten, any more than Peter would be. Not if she had anything to do with it.

SIX

The next morning, Sarah woke up with a start. She'd been having the most horrible dream, that she was in Daphne's claustrophobic, overcrowded beach hut... and someone was doing their best to suffocate her. As she struggled to clear her mind of the awful vision, she opened her eyes, only to see Hamish's furry face peering down at her, from his vantage point sitting heavily on her chest. No wonder she'd had such an awful nightmare.

'Hamish, do get off,' she said, grabbing his solid little body and putting him down firmly on the floor. Next she looked at her bedside clock, and groaned. Only 7 a.m.! Back in London, that had always been getting-up time, but then she'd had a busy schedule, sorting out the practice, making sure Peter was OK and not in too much pain... Hamish had clearly not got the memo that things had changed and she was now a lady of leisure. And little Scottie dogs were definitely in retirement now, as far as their services as alarm clocks went. But Hamish was deaf to her strictures. He gave two or three excited barks and pawed at the eiderdown. In his world, it was high time for them both to be up and about.

She must remember to shut the door to her room more firmly, she told herself, resolutely blocking out the fact that she'd already put a bed for Hamish in the corner. His reassuring presence, snorting and chasing seagulls through the night, had actually been a great comfort and taken her mind off the empty space on Peter's side of the mattress. Until, that was, the dog had made her dream about the beach hut killer.

The sight of a tower of boxes still left in the sitting room dampened Sarah's spirits when she got downstairs. How was it that, no matter how many of the dratted things she emptied, there were still somehow more to go? Maybe they reproduced at night, when she and Hamish were asleep, she thought, cheering herself up with the ridiculous notion.

She flicked on the kettle and got down a favourite mug. She'd unpack in her own good time, and then this cottage would really feel like home. The kitchen was already more welcoming, she decided, since she'd found her jolly red and white checked tablecloth. All she needed was a cup of tea and a slice of golden toast with her favourite chunky marmalade to set her up for whatever the day might bring.

* * *

Once her breakfast plate and mug were washed up and the kitchen was as neat as she could make it, she and Hamish collected Daphne for the short stroll into Merstairs proper. Sarah enjoyed watching the crisp spring breeze ruffle Hamish's black fur as he padded along the coastal road, with Daphne pointing out the sights, including the yacht club near the harbour, the fishing boats out at sea and the ruined castle in the far distance. When they turned off the esplanade into the high street, Daphne suddenly let out a loud 'Aha!' and stopped dead in front of the estate agency. Hamish, who had been told by Sarah they were going on a lovely *long* walk, felt most ill-used.

'All right, boy, I know, but we've just got to pop in here and then we'll, um, probably be going back to the beach,' Sarah said placatingly, running her hand along Hamish's coat as she covertly inspected the premises.

Daphne didn't seem to feel the need for stealth, and pressed her nose up against the glass, peering at the staff tapping away at their computer terminals. She was about to yank the door open and sail in, when Sarah grabbed her arm. 'Wait a minute, what are we going to ask? We should have planned what we were going to say on the walk, but I was too distracted by that gorgeous view. I think we should be a bit careful. We don't want to come right out with...'

But it was too late. Daphne simply threw open the door, and stood on the threshold, exclaiming, 'Which one of you lovely people sold me a dead body?'

SEVEN

Daphne's question was greeted with a deafening hush. A lady who'd been on the phone cut the call discreetly and the other agents looked at Daphne, stupefied. Then a door opened at the back of the office.

'Daphne, lovely to see you! Come through, come through,' beckoned a man in his fifties, his salt and pepper hair and slightly shiny suit giving him the air of a bargain basement George Clooney.

'Oh, Michael! Of course, it was you,' said Daphne, striding forward.

Well, thought Sarah. It wasn't the approach she would have chosen, but she couldn't deny Daphne's fearless ways got results. She followed Daphne and the estate agent into the back office with Hamish, who sat down and did his best 'good dog' impression, ears pricked. Having shut the door, the man held out his hand to Sarah. 'Michael Benchley, top estate agent of this parish, for my sins.'

Sarah took a seat in a designer chair that looked comfortable and was anything but. 'So, you sold the beach hut to Daphne here?' She put her head on one side, unconsciously mimicking Hamish.

'Wonderful, isn't it? I expect you've come to see if we have any others on our books. Well, I'll certainly have a look for you, though I can't promise anything...' Michael said importantly, looking intently at his screen as his fingers rattled over the keyboard.

'Let me stop you, um, Michael, I definitely don't want anything like Daphne's. I don't know if you've heard, but—'

'There's a dead man in it,' Daphne broke in.

Sarah put a hand over her eyes.

'A dead man?' Michael Benchley's eyebrows shot up, he drew back a tiny bit in his chair – but somehow he didn't look nearly surprised enough at this headline news. Sarah watched him with interest.

'You've already heard,' she said, and it wasn't a question.

Benchley just harrumphed, weighed Sarah up with a glance, and then spoke.

'Yes. Poor old Gus. He was such a character, always ready with a joke.' Benchley shook his head. 'Barred me once, remember, Daphne? I'd asked for prawn cocktail crisps. Said I'd have to go to Whitstable for fancy rubbish like that. He loved to keep things traditional. Had my mugshot behind the bar in his Wall of Shame.' He chuckled. 'Next day it was all forgotten. I never ordered crisps again, though. Yes, in a place like this, news travels fast.' He spread his hands. 'And now tell me, what exactly can I do for you ladies?'

'I would have thought that was obvious,' Sarah said, before Daphne could butt in. 'We'd like to know the identity of the hut seller.'

'But Daphne, I mean Miss Roux, already knows that,' said Benchley, back to the bluff George Clooney act. 'It would have been on the exchange and completion documents she signed.'

Sarah looked at Daphne, who immediately started to

rummage in her handbag, as though the deeds were miracu-
lously going to materialise there. 'Documents, yes of course,' she
mumbled. Then she put her head up again. 'I have no idea
where they are, though.'

'But you'll have the records to hand here, I'm sure,' said
Sarah, turning to Michael with one of what Peter used to call
her 'professional' smiles.

'Well, data protection, you know.' Michael was all evasive
charm, from his widely spread fingers to the blinding white
smile in his perma-tanned face.

'There can't be any suggestion of infringement, though, can
there? If Daphne is the legal owner of the property.' Sarah sat
back, making it clear that she was willing to wait as long as it
took.

With an exasperated glance, Michael started prodding his
computer again, though his fingers didn't float over the keys
nearly as efficiently as they had when he'd thought a sale might
be in the offing. Hamish lay down with a little sigh. There was
clearly going to be quite a wait before his mistress saw sense,
and took him back to his vital sentry duty at the beach hut.

EIGHT

Back at the house later, after a solid afternoon of unpacking with Hamish's 'help', Sarah was more than ready for a square meal. She straightened up – with a little difficulty – from the cupboard where she'd been stowing her best casserole dishes. Thanks to all the shenanigans since she'd arrived yesterday, there hadn't been a moment to get to the shops, so there was nothing for it. She'd have to head out again.

She brushed the dust from her hands onto her trousers, slightly regretted it, then shrugged. That was the great thing about Merstairs. Though a well-heeled place, it was still a holiday resort when all was said and done. If she didn't want to get changed, she didn't have to. She strode to the front door and rattled Hamish's lead. Within a couple of seconds, he'd bounded up, tail whirring like a little helicopter. Once outside, she debated asking Daphne if she wanted to come too – but she squared her shoulders and walked on. It was time she started being brave and discovering her new home for herself.

The walk into the centre of town didn't take long, even with Hamish doing his best to investigate every tussock of tough seaside grass with self-important thoroughness. As Sarah pulled on his lead, the streetlights came on and twinkled over the dark mass of the sea. The swish and sway of the tide was hypnotic. She was almost sorry when they reached the first of the little shops along the parade.

Now the question was a simple one: where to eat. Not *what* – Sarah had set her heart on a proper Merstairs fish and chip supper. But where should she find her catch of the day? There was a large pub on the corner, the Ship and Anchor, with loads of pretty window boxes bursting with flowers, and another, smaller inn a few doors up. A swinging sign emblazoned with a large skull and crossbones announced that this one was called the Jolly Roger. The image would usually have been made less threatening by the enormous grin on the skull's face, but thanks to Sarah's find in the beach hut, it just made her shudder. She wouldn't have fancied pub grub tonight anyway, but the discovery of poor old Gus Trubshaw put a tin hat on that idea. There was a police car stationed outside. Sarah wondered whether Mariella had interviewed the staff yet, or whether Tweedledum and Tweedledee had got that job.

Luckily there was no shortage of little cafés and takeaways, all bustling with happy customers oblivious to the day's dramas. There was a lovely Italian on the corner with a red and white striped awning and pavement seating, wafting wonderful aromas of oregano, basil and garlic. A couple of doors down was an Indian takeaway, and Sarah sniffed appreciatively at the rich mix of garam masala and cumin drifting from its doorway. Next to that was a Thai place, and Sarah made a mental note – she was very fond of a creamy green curry made with rich coconut milk.

There was only one thing that was going to hit the spot tonight, though, and she walked on until she smelt the uniquely delicious tang of freshly cooked chips. The café was in a perfect little spot. It was set back from the seafront, sheltering next to a souvenir shop on one side and a baker's on the other. There were chairs positioned outside, like the other places, but they were a bit fancier, made of scrolled wrought iron and painted an appealing lavender colour. The sign above said 'Marlene's Plaice' in elaborate loopy writing and Sarah felt herself smiling at a pun which her old London self might have winced at. But tonight she was ready to embrace everything about her new home – except the body in the trunk, that was, she thought with a shudder.

She went in, just to check that one of the tables outside was free and that Hamish's excitable presence wouldn't be a nuisance. Immediately a woman in a pale mauve apron, matching the signage outside, bustled forward. 'Can I help you, modom?'

Sarah was irresistibly reminded of Maggie Smith playing the very grand dowager countess in *Downton Abbey*. Fish and chips was pretty ordinary fare, but this lady was obviously determined to make everything as posh as possible.

'Just fish and chips for one – and maybe a bowl of water for Hamish here? Is outside all right?'

'Take a seat, modom,' said the lady, as expansively as if she were offering a front-row spot at a coronation. 'Ai'll be with you shortly with our hextensive menu.'

'Wonderful,' said Sarah, hurrying through the door before too much of a smile could peep out.

She sat down outside, facing the magnificent view, and settled Hamish with his tennis ball to chew. When the menu appeared, it offered all the usual fish supper variations – though each was described in laborious detail and promised to be 'garnished with fresh salad in season'. Well, Sarah was all for eating her healthy veggies. Heaven knew how many patients she had chivvied into upping their intake over the years. When the food came it looked and smelt wonderful – though the promised salad turned out to be a sad leaf or two of lettuce. Sarah wasn't fussed, though she did wonder what everyone at the practice would say if they could see her tucking into this plate of deep-fried delights. Oh, who cared? This was perfect.

Just as she was spearing a particularly delectable-looking chip with her fork, a woman strolled by, then did a double-take and stopped right next to her table. 'Oh, you're the lady from the beach hut, the one with the... trouble.'

Sarah looked up in surprise. Forty-something, dark-haired, pretty, motherly and smiling from ear to ear. Ah yes, it was the lady from the beachside café who'd served her the bacon butties yesterday.

'Trouble? I suppose that's one way to describe it,' Sarah said wryly, swallowing and blotting her lips with a paper napkin from the dispenser on the table. This could be a great opportunity to find out even more about what, or rather who, she and Daphne had discovered. 'Did you happen to know the, er...?' She didn't want to use the word 'body', it sounded a bit too clinical. But luckily the lady seemed to know exactly what she meant.

'Well, course I did. Everyone in Merstairs knows... *knew* Gus. Life and soul of the party, he was. Do you mind?' she said, pointing to the empty chair next to Sarah.

'Be my guest,' said Sarah, and Hamish obligingly got up and shuffled round to make room, taking his ball with him.

'What a cute little girl,' the lady said, patting Hamish on the head.

'Well, boy. But yes,' said Sarah, avoiding Hamish's eyes. 'So, poor Gus, then?'

'Yes, gave us all a stir, it has! Everyone's talking about it. First time anything like this has happened in Merstairs, right enough.'

'And on my first day, too,' said Sarah mildly.

'Come from the big city, did you?' said the lady. 'Normally it's quiet as the grave down here. Oooh, shouldn't have said that, should I?' She clapped a hand to her mouth. 'My name's Hannah. Hannah Betts.'

'Sarah Vane.' The two women shook hands over Sarah's rapidly cooling chips.

'Carry on, love, eat up,' Hannah said airily. Sarah, unable to tuck in with her normal gusto when she was being watched, cut off a tiny piece of fish and chewed carefully before asking, 'So, you actually knew him well?'

'Well, I said so, didn't I?' Hannah said, her pleasant face suddenly shuttered. 'And I know the last owner of your hut, right enough. Charles Diggory, him what has the antiques shop a couple of doors down.'

Sarah supposed this was meant as a great revelation – but in fact this was the one useful piece of information they'd managed to glean from Michael Benchley earlier. 'Yes, it's not my hut, but I'd heard about the owner,' she said carefully.

Hannah looked momentarily disappointed that she wasn't first with that particular nugget of gossip, but then plunged on. 'Well, everyone knows Charles. But it can't be anything to do with him, nice enough chap and ooh, those eyes,' said Hannah, with a shake of her dark curls. 'Given everyone quite a turn, it has, this whole business. If you can believe it, my café's been swamped ever since. Queues round the block, with all these folks gawping at your hut,' she said, cheering up a bit. 'Thinking of getting my niece in tomorrow if it's still as busy. That's my Betsy.'

Sarah nodded vaguely. 'Oh yes? Um, back to poor Gus...?'

'Oh *him*,' said Hannah, waving her hand dismissively, as though the poor man was far less important than the mini-boom he was causing, not to mention her staffing dilemma. 'Well, you see it's my assistant that really knew him best. Mavis, from down the road?' she jerked her head to indicate a spot not so far from the esplanade.

'Erm. Would it be possible for me to chat to Mavis at some

point? It's just that, having found him...' It was Sarah's turn to wave her hand.

'Of course, of course. You're going to feel a bit funny about it, aren't you? Not your beach hut though, you said? Belongs to that Daphne Roux then, does it?'

'Yes. You're a friend of Daphne's?' Sarah said eagerly.

'She gave my mother a Tarot reading once. Fair dos, she didn't charge Mum a penny for it, she's a kind lady, I'll give her that. But Mum was right off her custard creams for a week. Not sure I hold with all that stuff,' Hannah sniffed.

Sarah felt a sneaking sympathy, but she turned the conversation. 'What days does Mavis work?'

'Thursdays, dear. Try around three. Betsy'll be glad of a hand, I dare say.' Hannah got to her feet. 'I'll leave you to it then. Bye girlie,' she said to Hamish, who looked most affronted, then she walked briskly away.

Sarah, staring out at the blackness of the sea, and munching on a now rather chilly chip, wondered about all she had been told. Hannah had mentioned this Charles Diggory man, but was somehow sure he had nothing to do with the body in the beach hut. She had definitely known something about Gus, the corpse, as well, but didn't really want to talk about him for some reason. She'd palmed Sarah off with this Mavis instead.

Well, Hannah might have thought she'd put Sarah off the track, but Sarah was made of sterner stuff. She was happy eating cold fish and chips – but she'd be even happier when she got some piping hot information out of Mavis at the café. She might leave Hamish and Daphne at home, though, much though she loved them both. Then she felt a bit guilty, and broke one of her own cardinal rules by sneaking Hamish a chip under the table. He licked the salt off her fingers gratefully, instantly forgiving her everything.

NINE

The next morning, Sarah folded back her crisp white lace-edged duvet and got up with a big stretch. Then she opened the curtains onto a view which she was sure would never pall. Yesterday's cotton-wool swabs of cloud had all but disappeared. The sky was clear and bright, the sea below it glittering as though the surface had been strewn with jewels. Even the odd dead body wouldn't put a crimp in her mood, she decided, as she wrapped her dressing gown around herself and padded down the stairs, the dog frolicking around her heels as she went.

Sarah was looking forward to tackling Mavis at the café on Thursday, but what could she do today to advance what she was beginning to think of as her investigation? She was thoughtful as she crunched the last of her delicious toast and drank her tea, and by the time she'd picked up Hamish's lead she'd made a decision. She would take the bull by the horns, and engineer a meeting with this Charles Diggory, the chap who ran the second-hand clothes shop.

From Daphne's description of him, Sarah had an inkling he might be some kind of Lothario – but that was no reason for her to feel nervous. She was sure she'd come across worse. And she hardly needed to worry about having her head turned, not in her situation, she told herself stoutly. The fact that he might well be a murderer was surely more alarming.

But it was vital that she did what she could to clear Daphne's name. Time was ticking by, and the police seemed to have made no real progress, even with Mariella on the team. So she told herself not to be a nervous Nellie about asking this Charles man some forthright questions, like why he'd landed poor Daphne with his accursed beach hut. She shut her front door with a snap and then breezed into town. She spotted a little group practising what looked like Tai Chi on the beach, then she came to the clothes and antiques shop. She peered into its windows. They were full of stuff she wouldn't have given houseroom for a second – large clocks, gloomy oil paintings and a selection of nautical-looking brass instruments which would surely be useful only to a nineteenth-century sailor.

The door, when she tried the handle, had one of those old-fashioned bells that announced her presence with a jingle. She stepped forward cautiously, Hamish at her heels, snuffling as he went. The place was dark, after the bright sunshine outside. Thank goodness, it lacked that musty aroma of old clothes – and possibly unwashed bodies – that second-hand clothes stores so often had. She stepped over to inspect the rails of fine linen suits, then saw an array of hats on a shiny table, all in pristine condition. Peter would have looked wonderful in one of those.

She was just turning a straw boater in her hands, remembering long ago holidays, when a discreet cough behind her almost made her drop it.

'Can I help you with something?'

The voice was cultured, amused, and when Sarah swung round, she saw the man's face fitted it perfectly. This must be Charles Diggory. He had a curved, slightly beaky nose, a high forehead and piercingly blue eyes. He wasn't conventionally good-looking, as Daphne had led her to believe, but he certainly had something. In fact, he looked like a hawkish, very tall cross between two of Sarah's fictional heroes, Sherlock Holmes and Lord Peter Wimsey.

'Oh! Well, now that you mention it, um, I suppose – your hut?' she said nervously.

'My... hut?' his eyebrows arched in surprise. 'Do you mean *hat*?' He looked towards the boater in Sarah's hands and she put it down as though it was on fire.

'No, no. Your beach *hut*. Over there,' Sarah said a little desperately, gesturing towards the door, the street outside, and the beach beyond it. There was a silence, then the man spoke again and some of the tension in the room broke.

'Oh yes, *that*. The beach hut. Silly me. But forgive me, you don't look like the bucket and spade type,' he said, raking her with a glance.

'Um, no,' said Sarah, realising it had sounded as though she wanted to buy the hut, not interrogate him about its contents. But perhaps she would find out more if she didn't correct his assumption? 'Er... it would be for my grandchildren,' she said with a smile she was pretty sure was unconvincing. 'It'd be so great for them.'

She hoped he wasn't going to chime in with the usual cliché about how she couldn't possibly have grandchildren, not at her age... There then followed another pause, which this time stretched for long enough for her to feel something surprisingly like disappointment. Then Hamish at her feet lurched forward, the better to get the scent of this apparent new friend. 'And of course my dog would love somewhere to store all his precious tennis balls,' Sarah added, blessing the Scottie for his timing.

At once, the man unbent, quite literally, stooping from his great height to pet the little creature. Hamish immediately whipped over to show his fluffy underbelly, and wriggled with unashamed pleasure at the tickles that followed. Honestly, thought Sarah. She and Hamish needed to have a long chat about dignity as soon as they got home. But if he managed to win this man over, then maybe it was all to the good.

Sarah waited, with growing impatience, for the love-in to finish. Then the man stood up straight again with a sigh. 'What a great little fellow. I'd love to bring my dog to work.'

'Oh? Why not do that, then?' And stop making a fool out of mine, thought Sarah.

'Difficult, with this place to run. And not the sort of pooch you can trust with valuable antiques,' he sighed, looking round the shop fondly.

'Each to their own,' Sarah said simply, seeing only tat. 'So, the hut?'

'Oh, didn't I say? It's not for sale any more. I got rid of it... erm, found a new owner recently, someone who... well, let's just say the estate agent seemed to think she'd have a lot of clutter to store.'

Sarah knew he was referring to Daphne. She thought he had a cheek calling her belongings clutter, given they could barely move for all the ancient bric-à-brac in his shop. Hamish was currently involved in a staring contest with a stuffed stag's head on the wall and she had just almost tripped over a row of wooden tennis racquets in their original presses.

'Oh, I see,' said Sarah, trying to look disappointed. 'Well, I'm still interested in finding out more about it. I was just wondering how long you'd owned it for, whether you'd sublet it. You know, things like that. Um, in case it comes back on the market.'

'Now why on earth would I tell you my life history? You'll be wanting my inside leg measurement next, I presume?' he said, in a distantly amused tone.

Sarah bit back a retort at that, though by the looks of things it would be a sizeable tally of inches. He towered over her in the dark shop interior, and she was by no means short. She decided she'd have to come clean. 'Surely you must have heard what happened at the hut?' she said at last.

'I'm really not sure what you mean,' he said dismissively. He was getting a little testy, Sarah realised. Yet he must be putting on this show of blissful ignorance. From her brief experience of Merstairs, news seemed to travel at the speed of light. There was no way he hadn't already heard.

'I mean... about the body in your beach hut.'

There was a silence, as the man's jaw sagged and his eyes seemed to lose focus, and he gazed from Sarah to Hamish and back again. Hamish woofed encouragingly, then locked eyes with the ancient deer again. He was almost sure he was about to get the upper paw. Finally, Charles Diggory spoke.

'What on earth are you saying? It's got all mod cons, if that's what you're talking about.'

'Well, only if you consider that mod cons include a festering corpse,' said Sarah, in a quietly reasonable voice.

And, with that, all the colour drained out of Charles Diggory's face.

TEN

Sarah leant over the counter in the Jolly Roger, just down the road from the antiques shop. Charles was sitting at a banquette seat by the window, with a shellshocked look about him. How was Sarah to have known he'd been away for two days buying more of his blessed antiques, missing all the Merstairs drama? She'd been seriously worried for a moment back then that he might topple over like a tall tree in a storm. If she'd had any doubts over his innocence, she surely had to banish them now. Unless, of course, he was just a superb actor.

She'd attempted to take Charles to the other pub, the Ship and Anchor, as it was a little closer, but he had insisted on coming to the Jolly Roger despite his weakened state. There was a chalkboard on the pavement with a little drawing of a pirate ship firing a cannon at a larger vessel, announcing that an array of sandwiches and snacks was available.

Once they were inside, there was no sign of anyone serving. She supposed that wasn't so surprising, as Gus Trubshaw had been the landlord here. She'd seen the police car outside yesterday evening, presumably carrying on questioning the rest of the team and the regulars. But the front door had been open just now, so they must be ready for business. Anyway, getting Charles Diggory a restorative drink after his shock was as good an excuse as any for Sarah to come and have a look at the place Gus Trubshaw had once called home. She hadn't felt like popping in last night, but it was different during daylight – and perhaps easier with a man in tow, even if he looked as though he might swoon at any second.

Now she leant even further forward, almost banging her head on a wooden fish caught in artful netting hanging down from the light fittings. Some interior designer had really grabbed the pirate theme and run with it, she thought ruefully as her eye ranged over the various skull and crossbones flags, fishing nets, plastic seagulls and treasure chests that were dotted around. Either that or it was evidence of the late Gus's fabled sense of humour. Behind the bar was a row of postcards, and a sign saying 'Wall of Shame', with a variety of snapshots pinned beneath it. And sure enough, there was one of Michael Bench-ley's attempts at a Clooney grin.

Suddenly, there was movement through the door that must lead to the kitchen. A member of staff bustled towards her. Sarah's first thought was that he was a pleasant-looking middle-aged man, then she realised her definition of middle age was stretching like elastic as she got older herself. His salt and pepper hair and comfortable shape suggested he was in his sixties. Beneath heavy glasses, his brown eyes looked tiny and raw and his nose was pink. He was clutching a tissue in one clenched fist.

'Not waiting long, I hope? What can I get you?' he said with a faint Scottish accent, throwing away the tissue, washing his hands briefly, and then taking a glass and buffing it somewhat haphazardly with a cloth. The way he felt for things before he picked them up told Sarah those glasses were for a very strong prescription. Now he peered at her, reminding her irresistibly of a mole. A very sad one, at that.

'I've just brought Charles in for a restorative, really,' Sarah said, nodding her head towards her companion, sitting listlessly on the banquette, with little Hamish at his feet. She was assuming everyone in a small place like this would know the proprietor of the antiques shop. The man squinted over to where Charles was sitting, evidently trying to make him out. 'He was a bit shocked on, um, hearing the news.'

'About Gus, you mean. Aye, everyone's heard right enough.' He sniffed again, then seemed to rally, and held his hand out to shake hers. 'Trevor Bains,' he said.

'Hi, and I'm so sorry for your loss. I'm Sarah Vane. Gus was your business partner, I'm imagining?'

'And the rest,' said Trevor, pulling a fresh tissue out of a box on the bar and dabbing his eyes. 'Twenty years, we were together,' he said, almost in a whisper. He took down a photo from behind the bar. It showed a much younger Trevor, and a Gus who was bursting with life, both beaming fit to bust at the camera.

'Oh gosh,' Sarah said again. 'You look so happy – made for each other.' For a second her chest constricted as she remembered all the pain of Peter's passing. 'I really feel for you. It must have been an awful shock. But, um,' she wondered how to phrase it, 'he'd been missing... for a while?'

Bains's head came up. 'Yes. He was on a hiking trip, in Canada. He went every year. He must have got back this time... and had an accident.' He shrugged and covered his eyes.

Sarah made sympathetic sounds, and tried not to look too sceptical. It seemed Daphne wasn't the only one who wanted to pretend people ended up dead in trunks by chance. Or perhaps Trevor hadn't been told everything yet by the police.

He took a breath and continued. 'Aye, Gus always loved getting back to nature, living in a tent, the full bit. I could never stand it, I get bitten to shreds by all the bugs, and as for sleeping on the ground, don't get me started,' he added with a shudder.

'You must have missed him, though,' said Sarah.

'Yes. But it always did him the world of good. And he sent me postcards...' He gestured vaguely towards the row behind him, showing views of Niagara Falls, the Rockies and Quebec. He picked up one of a handsome Mountie and handed it to Sarah. She turned it over. 'MISS YOU XXX' it said simply in block capitals. The only flourish was a little curlicue on the final X. She put it on the bar.

'Do you mind if I look at the others?' she asked.

'Sure,' Trevor said, getting them down and handing them to her. 'Gus always said he needed the break, to recharge his batteries. This place can be full on,' he said, looking round. 'He loved the peace and quiet out there.'

'My husband was the same,' said Sarah wistfully, looking through the cards. The messages were all similar, short and to the point, but with lots of kisses. 'He used to go off fishing.'

'Oh aye?' said Trevor sympathetically. 'Gus loved to do a proper digital detox, you know, old school. "Only ring me in an emergency," he used to say. Of course, I can never ring him again, now,' he said, reaching for a fresh tissue. 'I don't understand any of this, really I don't.'

Not for the first time, an expression of bafflement crossed his face. Sarah got the distinct impression she wasn't dealing with an intellectual powerhouse. 'Anyway...' He took a deep breath. 'Got to keep the business going somehow. Gus wouldn't want to see us all out on the street. What can I get you?' He tagged on a professional smile, which for Sarah was more heartbreaking than his tears.

'I'll just have a fizzy mineral water, and er, Charles will have a brandy, in the circumstances. We were going to go to the other pub, but he wanted to come here,' Sarah said more quietly.

'The other pub? You mean the Ship and Anchor?' Now Trevor Bains grew very still, his mild tearful eyes suddenly staring through the thick lenses. She wasn't sure quite what she'd said, but it had obviously struck the wrong note.

'Um, yes. But as I say, Charles insisted.'

'Aye. Aye, Charles and Gus were chums,' Bains said gruffly. Sarah was mystified at what had upset him moments before. 'A double is probably just what the doctor ordered,' he said, getting down a glass and bumping it against the optic before getting the angle right.

'Oh, er, yes,' said Sarah, realising belatedly he didn't mean it literally. In fact, she wasn't sure if there was any therapeutic value in spirits after a shock – though the taste was often enough to distract people from whatever had upset them. She handed over her cash and took the drinks to the little nook where Charles was sitting. 'Here we are. Have a sip,' she said, placing the glass in front of him.

Charles picked it up, waved it towards her in salute, and drank it down in one. Then he gasped, wiped his watering eyes and looked at her properly for the first time since her bombshell in the shop. 'Well, that's better. But I just don't understand – Gus, gone. How on earth did this happen?'

'That's just what I'd like to know,' said Sarah, picking up her own drink. 'What sort of person was he, anyway?'

Charles went quiet for a moment, and gazed straight ahead, as though seeing his old friend behind the bar. 'Oh, he liked to keep things traditional. I think the décor is more Trevor's, ah, thing. He was the life and soul, was Gus. And his jokes.' He shook his head.

'I've heard he was funny,' said Sarah.

'Yes, yes he was,' said Charles, falling quiet again. And then a smile tugged at his lips.

'What are you laughing at?' Sarah asked, intrigued.

Charles coughed. 'It seems inappropriate, in the circumstances. But I've just remembered the last joke he told me. Right here, just a few weeks ago.' Once again his mouth twisted into a smile, almost against his will.

'Come on, then. Tell me.' Sarah's expectations were low, but she supposed this might help Charles come to terms with Gus's death.

He looked at her, and then shrugged. 'All right then. A doctor rings his patient. "I've got good news and bad news." The patient says, "What's the good news?" "You've got twenty-four hours to live." "If that's good, what on earth is the bad news?" says the patient. 'I forgot to tell you yesterday," says the doctor.'

Sarah couldn't help it, she laughed out loud. She had a weakness for doctor jokes – and now she had a clearer picture of Gus. She could just imagine him, hanging over the bar, holding court, getting to the punchline, and then roaring while his regulars joined in.

Over by the bar, Trevor Bains clattered some glasses noisily and Sarah suddenly felt how wrong it was to be giggling away. She stopped abruptly and they both wiped their eyes, though she suspected Charles's tears might not all be of mirth. 'Well, that is a good one. But it doesn't get me any further on with what actually happened to poor Gus. That's the most important thing at the moment. And you're the person best placed to be in possession of the facts.'

Charles looked at her blankly for a second, then he chuckled. 'Oh I see! You think I did it. You think I'm some sort of Bluebeard, filling my secret hut with dead bodies...'

Sarah squirmed uncomfortably under his gaze. What he said was true. He was, so far, her main suspect. And it made sense. He'd owned the place right before Daphne, therefore he must be responsible for the contents. 'Are you suggesting there's some other reasonable explanation?' she asked as mildly as she could.

'There is, actually.' Charles picked up his glass and signalled to Trevor Bains for another. Bains didn't see, so

Charles stood up and waved his glass in the air until the gesture finally registered and Trevor brought over a refill. 'And can I get you one, too?' Charles asked Sarah, somewhat belatedly.

'I'm fine,' Sarah said quickly. 'What were you saying about the hut?'

'Oh yes, the blessed hut. Well, what about our friend over there, for instance?' he said in a low voice. 'Surely even Trevor's a more obvious suspect. They say it's always your nearest and dearest...' He winked and nodded his head at Bains, who was back polishing the glasses again, unaware that he was being shoved into the frame by one of his regulars.

Sarah, fresh from her own bereavement, felt inclined to reject the idea out of hand. Anyone could see the poor man was devastated. And, for reasons of her own, she hated the idea that people always suspected the victim's loved ones. 'Maybe, but he's genuinely grief-stricken. Just look...' She gestured discreetly in the direction of the bar, where Trevor was blowing his nose on a tissue. He looked shattered.

'You're taking a lot of interest in all this, aren't you?' said Charles slowly. 'How long have you been in Merstairs?'

'Since Monday morning, actually.'

'And you've come down here to, what, enjoy a comfortable retirement, I imagine? So perhaps do that – leave all this to the powers that be.'

Charles's expression was not unsympathetic. But he had inadvertently hit on a tender spot. Again, she felt a sense of kinship with Trevor Bains. His plans, like hers, had been thrown up in the air by fate.

She sat up a little straighter. 'The thing is, I am involved. I discovered the body,' she said, overlooking the role played by Daphne and the excitable Hamish for a moment.

'So that gives you a right to meddle?' Charles raised his brows, amused.

Suddenly his patrician air got under Sarah's skin. She was

used to people trying to patronise her. The occasional pompous patient, NHS managers, even colleagues who'd got too big for their boots and, of course, a bevy of senior doctors and consultants, at medical school long ago. They usually found out the error of their ways.

'I think the police round here could do with all the help they can get,' Sarah said crisply. This was probably unfair on Mariella, who seemed highly competent – but she was just a fledgling officer, in her first year on the job. The constables she'd referred to as Tweedledum and Tweedledee, and who had missed the glaringly obvious cause of Gus's death, were actually her superiors. It didn't bode well.

'So you thought you'd step in, sort things out before the clod-hopping local bobbies make a terrible mess of things?' Charles assessed her with those heavily lidded eyes.

Sarah had the grace to laugh at that. 'Something along those lines, I suppose.' She shrugged, and raised her glass to her lips.

'Well, I must say... it makes perfect sense to me.'

Sarah spluttered. 'What?'

He handed her the last couple of napkins from the dispenser on the table. 'Why not? As you have so rightly and quickly guessed, the budget for our local constabulary is not what could be called healthy. And more importantly, once the news of your... discovery gets into the local press, it could have a catastrophic effect on businesses like my own. The last thing we need, as we swing into high season, is the notion that a murderer is stalking the streets of Merstairs.'

Sarah blinked. 'Well, I'm surprised you think it's such a good idea. Given that you are, as you pointed out yourself, my main suspect at this point.'

'Ah, but I won't be for long, I do assure you.' Charles sat back and crossed his arms, looking quite satisfied with proceedings.

'How do you work that out? You don't deny you're the owner of the hut?'

'Past tense, dear lady. I *was*. And then I sold it, as I've said. You'll find the new owner is a lovely woman but also, by all accounts, an odd bod. Should shoot right to the top of your list of shady characters.'

Sarah couldn't help frowning. She had only been in Merstairs for a couple of days but was already getting the impression that Daphne was known as something of an eccentric.

'The person who bought the hut from you is an old friend,' she said loyally and firmly. 'Besides, she hasn't been able to put anything in it, let alone a body, because it is still full of your stuff. That trunk had been there for some time, left for reasons of your own. Perhaps because you wished to pass on the problem of disposing of a dead body.'

Charles sat up a bit in the booth, and inadvertently brushed up against a plastic sea urchin perching on the top of the seat. He pushed it away and tutted. 'What you don't know – and why should you? – is that I myself bought the hut complete with all its contents. And I only got it a couple of months ago. Then I immediately sold it on.'

'Oh!' This was, indeed, news to Sarah. So Charles had barely owned the place long enough to stash a body in it. 'I see. But isn't it a bit odd to buy it and then sell it so quickly?'

'It may be.' He shrugged languidly. 'But I did it anyway.'

'Why?' Sarah asked baldly.

'I'm not sure I need to explain myself to you,' he started, then seeing her determined expression, the fight seemed to go out of him a little. He drummed his long fingers on the table, then seemed to come to a decision. 'All right. I don't want to remain on this list of yours for longer than I need to. I bought the hut as a favour, you see. I didn't really need it, so I immediately decided to sell. The season was just about to start gearing up, and I knew I'd probably get the best possible price if I popped it straight back on the market. The buyer seemed to think she'd got a bargain. That's the long and the short of it.'

Charles sat back as though he'd got everything off his chest, and it was now clear he was as innocent as a newborn babe. Sarah wasn't so sure. She narrowed her eyes at him.

'But who did you buy the hut from? And do you know why they were selling it?'

'Ah,' admitted Charles a little ruefully. 'That's where things start to get complicated.'

'Complicated? Why?' Sarah put her chin in her hand.

'Well, you see, the "who" part is a little ticklish.' Charles swirled the last remaining drop of his drink round in the glass, then gulped it down.

'So? Do you have a name?' Sarah persisted.

'You just don't let things drop, do you?' Charles said. 'A bit like that dog of yours.'

Sarah glanced quickly at Hamish, sitting under the table. He had his tennis ball clamped in his widely grinning jaws, and woe betide anyone who tried to get it away from him. She couldn't help smiling at the parallel, before Charles burst into speech again.

'I suppose there's no real harm in telling you. I bought it from my wife, you see.'

ELEVEN

Sarah tried to ignore the slight swooping sensation in the pit of her stomach, as she sat in the Jolly Roger with Charles Diggory and processed what he had just said. He had bought the beach hut containing Gus Trubshaw's dead body from his wife.

Sarah had only known the man for two seconds. It was ridiculous, feeling disappointed in him already. That usually came later, in her experience. Not that Peter had ever let her down, she told herself, glossing over her late husband's aversion to washing-up and his apparent inability to understand that putting the bins out was not a once-in-a-lifetime experience.

She didn't want to overanalyse things, but she had been enjoying chatting to Charles, even if their discussion had been about corpses and conveyancing. They hadn't been flirting – not at all. But it was still a surprise to hear he was spoken for all along.

She looked at him questioningly, and he cleared his throat before speaking again.

'Um, well, actually she's my *ex*-wife. The beach hut was part of our settlement... honestly, sorting out the financial aspects of our split seems to have taken twice as long as the marriage itself.' He smiled at Sarah, showing very white teeth. Why was she suddenly reminded of the big bad wolf? 'Just thinking about all that makes me feel like getting another drink. What shall I bring you?'

'My round,' said Sarah firmly, feeling it was a good idea to get some distance. Somehow the pub, complete with its odd assortment of nautical decorations, was suddenly feeling every bit as claustrophobic as Charles's antique shop.

Behind the counter, Trevor Bains was polishing another glass, scrutinising it carefully from behind those chunky glasses. No wonder this place was spotless, despite the man's eyesight and all the pirate memorabilia. As Sarah approached, he smiled mistily.

'Another mineral water for you? Or will it be a G&T this time?' he said, once she'd ordered Charles's brandy.

Sarah stopped to think. She'd been intending to go for more water… but a gin did sound tempting.

'Nearly lunchtime after all.' Trevor shrugged, pointing in the general direction of a clock with a stuffed parrot on top of it. The hands were bones, inching round the clockface in a rather macabre way that fitted in with the whole pirate theme, but seemed a tad grisly under the circumstances.

'Oh, go on then, you've convinced me,' Sarah smiled.

'No, I've just got you to understand your own needs. Aye, you get to know a bit about human nature working here,' grinned Bains.

'I bet you do,' Sarah said.

Running a bar must be a little like being a GP, she thought. You saw a lot of people who wanted to make their problems go away, one way or another. In her view, alcohol was never going to be the solution. But maybe a good barman could dispense wisdom as well as booze. Bains didn't seem like the fizziest Prosecco in the fridge, but perhaps what he lacked in intellect he made up for in common sense. He put the drinks on the bar, and made to turn away. Sarah was keen to keep him talking, though. It seemed like too good an opportunity to miss.

'You know Charles quite well, I take it? If he was, um, Gus's friend and so on?' Sarah said tentatively, with a little movement indicating the table where Charles sat, apparently now absorbed in his phone.

'Oh yes,' said Bains, raising his eyebrows, saying nothing in a way that spoke volumes.

'Do you know anything about his ex?' Now why had she said that? She should be trying to find out more about Gus, and any possible clues to why he'd ended up dead in a hut. Her cheeks burned. But Trevor Bains didn't seem to notice a thing.

'Charles's ex?' Was it her imagination, or was his voice unnecessarily loud? She risked a glance back at the booth, but the man in question seemed as fascinated by his mobile as ever.

'Forget I asked,' she said quickly. 'What I really meant, well, it's difficult to say this, but do you know of any reason why poor Gus would have ended up dead?'

'Sorry. I can't...' Trevor Bains put down his cloth and rubbed a tired hand over his eyes. 'Everyone loved Gus, he had such a way with the punters. Sure, he banned people sometimes – but he unbanned everyone before he left. I only keep that rogues' gallery up for a laugh,' he said, though he looked a lot closer to tears than a good chuckle. 'Just going to check a barrel...' He choked on his words and walked off quickly through the swing door to the kitchen.

Sarah kicked herself. She shouldn't have pushed her luck. Just then, a lanky young man of about twenty bustled in. A junior member of staff, Sarah guessed. He had a tea towel slung nonchalantly over his shoulder and his white shirt was rolled up to the biceps, displaying a rather sinister tattoo of a snake curling around his arm. There were matching snake rings on several of his fingers, and a serpent earring dangled from one lobe. His face, however, was round and cherubic and Sarah had the sudden conviction that the 'cool' inkwork and edgy jewellery were designed to give the lad a hardman image his big blue eyes and still-chubby cheeks did much to dispel. He loped over to her and braced a hand on one of the beer taps. The snake writhed as he flexed his muscles and Sarah had to suppress a smile.

'All right?' he said sharply, then noticed her drinks were already on the bar. 'Anything else? Or are you just here to ask questions? We've had enough of that, these last couple of days, with the police. Poor Trev. As if he hasn't got enough problems, with the trouble Gus caused with the Ship and all that.'

Sarah instantly pricked up her ears. 'The Ship? Is that the Ship and Anchor, down the road?'

'Might be,' said the youth truculently. 'What's it to you? Are you another one who's going to abandon the Roger, then, and go for all that gastropub nonsense? Pah,' he said with a sneer. 'Just because they got the brewery down a penny on the barrel. You'd think people would have more loyalty, small place like this,' he said, the snake on his arm wriggling as he ran a cloth up the beer taps. The taps themselves were intriguing, decorated with pictures of what looked like a friar with a saintly expression, holding a pint pot aloft. The wording above said *Merstairs Monk.*

'Oh, I-I wouldn't dream of going to the Ship,' Sarah said quickly.

'Quite right too. Trev needs all the custom he can get, now Gus's out of the picture,' the lad said, almost as though daring her to disagree.

'Of course he does. It's an awful business,' she said, gathering up the glasses. 'I'm so sorry. You're his, um, assistant, are you?'

'Nephew. Albie Cartwright. And yeah, I'm helping him out. It's been a lot. Not that it's any of your beeswax,' he said, polishing the space where Sarah's glasses had stood as though erasing all trace of them – and her.

She went back to her seat, her mind working overtime. Albie Cartwright seemed to have a lot of time for his uncle. That was not surprising, Trevor Bains appeared to be a nice man. A bit vague, but kind. And at least Sarah knew a little more about the pub rivalry now, though something so trivial could hardly play a part in a murder. No, the mystery was surely why Gus Trubshaw, a man who seemed to put the 'jolly' in the Jolly Roger, with devoted employees and a heartbroken partner, had not been found for so long.

In London, people could, and did, slip through the cracks. There'd been a horrible case not that far from her and Peter's house – the sad demise of a man in a social housing block had gone unnoticed for months. But surely there should be scant chance of such a thing happening here in Merstairs, where everyone seemed to know each other's business? And yet Gus Trubshaw, apparently such a popular and well-liked man, running a thriving local business, had vanished for weeks.

'Here,' a shout from Albie behind the bar cut into her thoughts and she turned round and retraced her steps, eager to hear whatever the boy might have to add.

'I'll just say one thing,' he said in a low, would-be menacing tone, flexing his snake-ridden biceps as he braced himself on the bar. 'You might not want to tangle with his ex,' he said, nodding towards Charles.

'His... ex-wife?'

'Yes, Francesca Diggory.'

'Why ever not?' Sarah took a sip of her drink and the tonic bubbles shot up her nose, almost making her sneeze.

The boy gave her a sour look. 'Well, in a place like this... no one gets the better of the mayor.'

TWELVE

Sarah rocked back on her heels. So Charles's ex-wife, Francesca Diggory, was the mayor of Merstairs, no less! That must make her quite a bigwig, in a small town like this. She was beginning to feel that everyone was seemingly connected to everybody else in Merstairs, by a web of invisible ties, some of which were beginning to seem rather sinister.

'Right. Thanks for the info,' said Sarah, mustering a smile for Albie, who shrugged and carried on leaning on the spotless bar, a strange look in those wide blue eyes. Sarah had thought him guileless only a couple of minutes before. Now she wasn't so sure. He seemed pleased that he'd disconcerted her. Well, she'd see about that. She squared her shoulders and wandered back over to Charles's table with the drinks, apparently without a care in the world. She put the double down by his elbow – realising he was racking up quite a tally, without showing any signs of intoxication.

'Just going to take Hamish out for a quick breath of air. Back in a second,' she said lightly.

Charles looked up briefly and smiled, his mind still clearly on whatever enthralling tidings were on his phone.

Sarah walked the little dog out quickly, and they strolled as far as the corner. She hauled him away from the chalkboard in front of the other pub, the Ship and Anchor, before he could cock his leg against it. Looking back at it, she couldn't help but admire the beautifully drawn picture. It showed a ship in full sail, while a pirate boat with a skull and crossbones flag sank into the deep. Someone had taken great care over it. Then she stood surveying the real sea, magnificent and ever-changing, while Hamish snuffled about happily. But she wasn't thinking about the impossibility of counting the shades of blue in the restless waves that kept crashing onto the beach. Her mind was on Charles Diggory alone. Why hadn't he mentioned the fact that his hut had been owned, very recently, by no less a luminary than the mayor of Merstairs herself?

Why on earth would a mayor want a hut anyway, Sarah wondered. Surely this Francesca had some sort of grace-and-favour residence, or was that a bit medieval? Even if she lived in an ordinary house somewhere, it was hard to believe she'd be so short of space. Not everyone had as much stuff as Daphne, nor lived in such a tiny cottage.

Being mayor of a place like this must be all about civic pride, making sure the beaches were scrupulously clean and the municipal flowerbeds were well-stocked with bright blooms. One thing it should emphatically not be about was concealing dead bodies in glorified sheds.

Once she judged that Hamish had had enough fresh air for the moment, she returned to the pub, where Charles scarcely seemed to have noticed her absence. She sat down and sipped her drink until Charles finally looked up and crinkled a smile at her. Then he put his phone on the table and spread his palms, apparently ready for a serious chat.

'So. You know I'm divorced... but you haven't told me about your situation,' he said with a meaningful look. It took a second or two, but Sarah suddenly realised he was flirting with her.

Immediately she was all fingers and thumbs, and nearly sloshed her gin and tonic over the table.

'Oops, sorry,' she said, as he reached into his pocket for an immaculately laundered linen handkerchief. 'Listen, don't ruin that, I've got some tissues here,' she said, fishing a pack out of her bag and efficiently mopping up the spill.

'Was that a tactic to avoid my, er probing?' Charles said. Then he shook his head. 'No matter. None of my business, I'm sure.' His smile was charming and wry, and Sarah let her gaze fall, feeling a bit silly. His lovely handkerchief was still lying there, pristine on the battered, now rather sticky table. Delicately stitched into the fine linen, in a marvellous shade of midnight blue, were two initials, curling round each other like bindweed. It was exquisite work. But the letters, though. Surely that wasn't a C and a D, as you would expect? Just as Sarah leant forward to get a better look, Charles's hand came slapping down on the handkerchief with a surprising turn of speed and it was spirited away into his jacket pocket.

Just then, the bar door was thrown open and a rangy woman stalked in, her narrow face intent. She looked like Princess Anne in a towering temper, an effect amplified by the horsey headscarf tied under her chin – which must be so hot on a lovely spring day like this – and her bunchy below-the-knee pleated skirt. For a moment, Sarah felt a tiny flash of recognition, but then it was gone and, try as she might, she couldn't get it back.

The woman scanned the bar, which was still half-empty, and then her snapping dark eyes locked onto Charles's. 'I thought I'd find you here. And this is your latest, I presume?' Her accent was exquisitely posh and her tone was as cold as her words.

Charles spread his hands like a man who was as innocent as the day was long, while Sarah looked on, agog. There were no prizes for guessing this was Francesca Diggory, the mayor. She was not wearing a chain of office, true, but something about her high-handed manner meant the insignia was priced in.

Sarah flushed uncomfortably under the woman's scrutiny, as dark eyes wandered over her, totting up her potential threat value, and then looked back at Charles with a 'really, couldn't you do any better?' expression on her face.

Sarah wasn't sure whether to be offended at having been taken for a 'bit of stuff' in the first place, or for now being so transparently dismissed as substandard in the floozy department. She decided it would be a lot better for her self-esteem if she just extracted as much comedy value as she could from the situation, so she took a tiny sip of her drink and settled back to enjoy the show. It seemed the mayor was by no means finished with Charles.

'And have you forgotten?' Francesca Diggory said to Charles contemptuously as he did his best to look devil-may-care in his seat.

He shrugged his shoulders and looked up at her blankly. 'Forgotten what, Francesca?'

'It's your turn to pick up the twins. Half-day at school today! Our grandchildren, you know,' Francesca explained to Sarah.

'Oh my Lord...' Charles clapped a hand to his forehead, directed a deeply apologetic grimace at Sarah, and scuttled out as fast as he could. She watched him go, hoping he wasn't even going to think about getting behind the wheel of a car. The pub door banged shut behind him.

Francesca Diggory gave Sarah another hard stare and was clearly about to turn on her heel and charge away too, but Sarah realised this could be an unmissable moment. She needed to find out more about poor Daphne's beach hut, and now that she knew what Francesca Diggory was like, she might never have the nerve to approach her again.

'Actually, um, mayor, I wondered if we could have a word?

Do sit down. Would you like a drink?' Sarah offered, only for Francesca to shoot her a look that would have been quite useful stripping the paint off Daphne's beach hut. 'Fine. Well, the thing is, I'll get to the point. I was only talking to, um, Charles about a discovery that I made on Monday in one of the beach huts...'

Francesca cut through Sarah's uncharacteristic burblings like a red-hot knife through butter.

'Oh, you were the one at the beach that day? I thought it was that loopy mystic woman.'

'That's my friend Daphne.' Sarah bit her lip. 'But yes, that was the hut I was talking about. And, now that you mention it, I'd like to ask you this question. Did you *know* it had a body in it when you sold it to your ex-husband?'

THIRTEEN

Much to Sarah's surprise, her no-holds-barred query elicited Francesca Diggory's first smile since she had walked into the pub. She even sat down and relaxed a little in her seat, until her headscarf came into contact with the plastic sea urchin behind her and she yanked the offending object off and threw it onto the next table in disgust. Luckily the booth was empty, but Sarah was fairly sure she would have hurled it no matter what. Suddenly she realised what had given her that jolt a while back... but Francesca was speaking again and, despite herself, Sarah found the subject matter intriguing.

'Let me tell you a little something about Charles,' Francesca said, taking a breath and laying her hands flat on the table as though she had nothing to hide. 'We're not divorced, actually. Whatever he may tell you. He just never bothered to get that piece of paper, and I suppose I never pressed him. Why worry, when a, well, loose arrangement suits us better?' She directed a hard stare at Sarah, to see how she was taking all this. Sarah did her best to assemble an expression of polite interest, nothing more. 'Well, you can see for yourself Charles is hardly a details man,' Francesca went on. 'The number of times he's forgotten to pick up little Calista and Max! If our daughter only knew...'

Sarah found herself mesmerised, against her will, by the woman. Her brown eyes were now gleaming as she went on to list the many, many faults of her ex-husband – or rather, estranged husband, Sarah supposed, given their legal situation. 'He really can't help it, you know. Unreliable? Yes, completely. Feckless? Some would say so. Unfaithful? Well, obviously.' Francesca gestured towards Sarah, and then cut off her protests. 'Cruel? Maybe he is.' Francesca shrugged. 'But I've known him, what, forty years at this point. Despite it all, everything he's put me through, I do try to keep his little secrets.'

'So are you saying these "little secrets" of yours extend to corpses on your property?' Sarah asked mildly.

Francesca looked Sarah up and down again. It seemed to be the woman's speciality. Then she gathered up her handbag, patted her strange headscarf and said tersely, 'Well, they'd hardly be secrets if I told, would they?'

With that, she would have swept off – except that she had to work her way out of the well-padded booth seat. By the time she'd finished, her cheeks were clashing with the cherry hue of her scarf and Sarah was hard pressed not to laugh. She looked up and saw Albie Cartwright grinning at the sight from behind the bar.

'Don't you have better things to do than stand around gawping, Albert? Aren't you supposed to be working on my Jaguar?' Francesca barked as she sidled free at last.

'Got to help Uncle,' he mumbled at her. 'Be round when I can.'

With that, Francesca gave a final, deeply disapproving sniff, directed primarily at Sarah and Albie but encompassing everyone in the pub, and flounced out, banging the door behind her.

Sarah looked towards Albie again, hoping to exchange the

kind of bonding smile you swap when an ordeal is over – but the boy was clattering about getting glasses out of the washer, and didn't spare her a glance. There was something about the determined way he was hunching his shoulders that made her think he was deliberately ignoring her, though.

Oh well, she thought. She stared into her drink, watching the tonic bubbles rise and burst. The suspects in this whole business seemed to be acting in much the same way, making themselves obvious, then disappearing just as fast. She wouldn't trust Michael the estate agent further than she could throw him. And then Charles, who'd seemed at least gentlemanly, turned out to be the type who'd forget his own grandchildren and leave them crying at the school gates.

What sort of a person did that? Just imagining her own beautiful grandchildren's crushed faces, as they waited at pick-up time in an empty playground, made her feel furious. Meanwhile Francesca was clearly ruthless... but was she ruthless enough to kill?

A quiet cough broke her train of thought. It was Trevor the bereaved barman, gently wiping her table down. Surely it wasn't necessary to linger so long on a simple job? Particularly not when the bar was finally beginning to fill up. She looked enquiringly at him and he gave a faltering smile, eyes still bleary after his latest bout of weeping.

'Should you be working, so soon after... everything?' she couldn't help asking him.

'Not much choice. Single-handed – or as good as.' He shrugged, directing a look at Albie, who was loping around the tables and chairs. 'He tries... shouldn't be here really, he should have gone off to art school, but he blotted his copybook a while ago with some silly graffiti nonsense. Och, this keeps him out of trouble.'

Sarah glanced over at the boy. He was supposed to be collecting glasses but it looked as though he had stopped to gossip with a group of boys his age who had just come in. As Sarah watched, he passed one a small packet, and took something in exchange which he pushed down into the pocket of his jeans. A second later, he'd sauntered back to the bar. 'Anyway,' said Trevor with a bit of a gulp. 'It takes my mind off things.'

Not very successfully, thought Sarah, but she knew there was merit in keeping busy. It had certainly helped her just after Peter had passed away. She turned from the thought quickly. There was so much to find out here, if she was going to straighten this business out for Daphne. And for poor Gus Trubshaw himself, of course.

'Everyone seems to have had a hand in that hut belonging to my friend Daphne. Who'd have thought the mayor owned it, and really not so long ago either,' she ventured, half-hoping Trevor would tell her something damning about Francesca Diggory. But in fact, when he spoke, he went off at quite a tangent.

'Just a thought, but have you tried the Scouts?'

Sarah couldn't help biting back a smile. 'Well, I've heard some odd suggestions in my time, but this one really takes the woggle. I think I'm a little old,' she said.

Trevor looked blank for a few seconds, then he smiled. 'Ha, no, I didn't mean it quite like... I just thought...' Here he straightened up and, seeming to forget he was holding a wet washcloth, raised it to his brow then rapidly put it down again. He sighed, then continued. 'Well, when the hut belonged to the mayor, there were various groups that were allowed to use it to store equipment, the litter pickers, the Tai Chi lot... and that included the Scouts.'

'Oh I see...' said Sarah, her mind whirring. Groups? That could mean a very large number of potential suspects. While she was grateful for the information, she couldn't help but feel her self-imposed task had just got that much more difficult. And there was one other thing. 'So why the Scouts particularly? If lots of different groups were using the hut?'

'Och, no reason,' said Trevor mildly. 'Why, look who's just walked in. Bill Turbot. The head of the Scout troop.' Sarah couldn't be sure, but was that a meaningful look Bains was giving her from behind his thick glasses?

The man who had just strutted through the door paused in the entranceway, taking up space, gazing round as if to assess his audience. He seemed to shine with vigorous health, from his well-brushed brown hair to his shiny deck shoes. Although he was wearing everyday clothes, a polo top and casual trousers, Sarah had no trouble at all instantly imagining him in khaki shorts, blowing a whistle and ordering small boys around.

'Ah, mein host,' he said, as Trevor took up his station at the Merstairs Monk beer taps again and blinked at him expectantly. 'The usual please. My little lunchtime pick-me-up.'

This reminded Sarah she'd been in the Jolly Roger for what seemed like hours. She was in danger of becoming quite the barfly, she thought to herself with amusement. But Hamish was still perfectly happy at her feet, enjoying all the interesting smells of beer and strangers, and besides, this could be a perfect opportunity to work out exactly what Bill Turbot might have been up to in the beach hut.

As he took his first pull of the pint Trevor placed in front of him, Turbot looked around the room again. Sarah couldn't work out if he was looking for someone who wasn't there yet, or whether he was just deciding who to go and talk to. As he continued to scope the place out and she carried on watching, their eyes met. Sarah looked away immediately, then checked back. Turbot was still staring at her, with what, if she wasn't mistaken, was quite a lascivious look on his face.

Perhaps it was the sea air, but there was definitely something strangely frisky about the men of Merstairs, thought Sarah. First Charles, now this chap. She looked down briefly, checking her understated top hadn't suddenly lost a few buttons or become see-through. But no, it was as meekly floral as ever. Meanwhile, Turbot had picked up his pint and was advancing towards her, a strange smile on his face. From having been keen to question him on his doings in the hut, Sarah now realised she was feeling a distinct reluctance to have anything to do with the man.

FOURTEEN

Just as Sarah had begun to think there was no way of stopping
Bill Turbot joining her at her table, short of getting up and
making a run for it with Hamish, there was a commotion at the
door and in came Daphne like a breath of fresh air, complete
with swirling tissues, slipping scarf and giant bag crammed with
goodness-knew-what.

'Coo-ee,' she chirruped, catching sight of Sarah and then
tripping up slightly on the welcome mat. Bill Turbot changed
direction abruptly and went over to the bar, where he seemed to
be leafing through the stack of postcards Trevor had left there
earlier. Then he slunk away to the far side of the pub.

Trevor, who'd just been helping Albie get in some boxes of
crisps from outside, smiled as Daphne waved vigorously at him.
He didn't seem to have too much trouble recognising her –
perhaps helped by today's lime green outfit.

'Well, who'd have thought I'd find you propping up the bar
on only your third day in Merstairs?' Daphne said, jogging
Sarah's elbow and nearly making her spill the last of her drink.
'If I hadn't seen the usual note on Charles Diggory's shop door
saying he was in here, and guessed you might be with him,

talking about Peter's suits, I'd be none the wiser. You're a dark horse and no mistake.'

Sarah merely raised her eyebrows. 'I'd have thought it would be easy enough to find me, for someone with your skill set.'

For a second Daphne looked blank, then she realised she was being teased. 'Oh, the Beyond, you mean? I've been too busy for the spirits this morning, Mephisto almost got the postman's arm. There was quite a to-do.'

Sarah could only imagine. Daphne's cat's main aim in life seemed to be maiming as many unsuspecting people as possible. He had always treated Sarah with grudging respect – although the scent of Hamish wafting from next door might change things, she realised – but any passing tradesmen were fair game.

'Luckily I got my letters before Mephisto went for him. He left a big envelope for you as well, I just happened to notice.'

Immediately Sarah felt a warm glow. It was bound to be a card from one of her daughters, hopefully with some artwork by her fabulous grandchildren inside. Her new fridge could certainly do with some wonky drawings of sunflowers or houses with severe subsidence to brighten it up. 'Lovely. Let me get you a drink, Daphne.'

'Oh, thanks Sarah. I'll have a Dubonnet and lemonade.'

'Do they still make that?' Sarah asked.

'It's very fortifying. Full of herbs,' said Daphne stoutly. 'A lot more medicinal than that mother's ruin you're drinking.'

Sarah went over to the bar. When Trevor turned to serve her, she asked for just a tonic water, and then enquired rather gingerly whether they had any Dubonnet. To her surprise, he produced the distinctive dark bottle she'd last seen in the 1990s. When he topped it up with a dash of lemonade and dropped a curl of lemon peel into it, it looked quite an attractive drink, its ruby shade glowing.

She took their glasses over, noting that Bill Turbot was still

sitting in the corner of the room, determinedly not looking her
way. What on earth was all that about, she wondered. He
clearly had a problem of some sort with Daphne. Maybe he'd
fallen foul of Mephisto? She couldn't help smiling at that idea.
Her friend's marmalade bruiser was certainly more than a
match for most men.

She slid the Dubonnet in front of Daphne. 'Don't look now,
but do you know that chap?' she said, nodding discreetly in the
direction of Bill Turbot.

'Who? What? Where?' Daphne's voice was like a foghorn,
and she stuck her head up out of the booth like a meerkat
surveying the desert for threats. The scarf wobbling away atop
her red curls didn't help matters at all.

'Shh... That chap over at the other end,' Sarah whispered.
'He's got his back to us now but apparently he's—'

'Oh *him*,' said Daphne, and again her voice was so loud that
Sarah was surprised that every drinker in the bar didn't swivel
round and have a good look, too. 'He's that weirdo, Bill Some-
thing-or-other... it's a fishy name, too, which when you think
about it is hilarious,' Daphne said with one of her full-bodied
laughs.

'Bill Turbot,' Sarah confirmed very quietly.

'That's the blighter,' Daphne all but shouted back, slapping
the table in glee.

Mopping up the spilled Dubonnet occupied them both for
a few minutes, with Daphne emptying out the contents of her
handbag in search of a tissue, while Sarah, having exhausted
her own stock earlier with Charles, went to the bar and got a
cloth from Trevor, who was watching proceedings with
interest.

'Now that all the excitement's over,' said Sarah firmly to
Daphne when she'd sat back down, 'perhaps you can tell me
exactly what it is about this Turbot man that's so awful?'

'Oh goodness, where do I start? Well, you know how the

teachers used to warn us, back at school, that some men weren't safe in taxis?'

At the time, Sarah and Daphne had just rolled their eyes. Their teachers were all hundreds of years old, how could they possibly know the first thing about handsy men? Whereas Sarah and Daphne, as adolescent schoolgirls, would always be more than a match for the most predatory of suitors.

But putting a man who wasn't safe in taxis in charge of young people was no laughing matter. 'How on earth did he get to be the head of the Scouts, if that's his reputation?' Sarah frowned.

'Don't ask me,' said Daphne with a shrug. 'But sometimes that happens here. No one volunteers, you see... and I suppose even Bill Turbot is better than having no Scout troop at all. Well, maybe. Anyway, I didn't come here to talk to you about that. You'll never believe it, but I've found something out.'

Sarah looked over at her friend in surprise, and realised Daphne was positively radiating excitement, from today's floaty silk throw to her acid yellow dangly earrings. 'What on earth is it?'

'Well, it was my book group meeting last night, so of course I asked around a bit, just to see what everyone had heard about our discovery, you know,' said Daphne blithely.

'Don't you think it might be a bit dangerous to gossip about it like that?' said Sarah as mildly as she could. 'After all, there is a killer lurking around here somewhere. What if they don't like the idea of you asking lots of questions?'

Daphne drew herself up to her full height. 'Well, for one thing, Sarah, I absolutely never indulge in idle chit-chat. You should know that, if anyone does. As I was saying to my Mariella only yesterday, you'll absolutely never catch me spreading rumours – not like Mrs Freedman at number 46.'

With that, Daphne sat back, an expression of outraged virtue on her face. Sarah realised she'd get nowhere if her friend took umbrage. 'Daphne, how about getting out of here and seeing about some lunch? I'm beginning to feel as though I've taken root in this pub, and as for Hamish, it's high time for him to stretch his legs again.' Sarah was also acutely aware that, although no one was looking in their direction, there were ears everywhere. If she could get Daphne to tell her the news out in the open, with fewer people within eavesdropping distance, so much the better.

Hearing his name, Hamish uncurled himself from the comfortable little cushion he'd been snuggling up to. Looking down and realising it was one of Daphne's scarves, Sarah scooped it up quickly and folded it neatly before presenting it to its rightful owner, hoping there weren't too many suspicious doggy hairs on it. Daphne just looped it round her neck without a thought, and the pair left the pub, Sarah waving to Trevor as she went. He raised a hand sadly in return as she closed the door.

As she stood on the pavement, blinking in the bright spring light, Sarah realised she'd hardly ever spent so much time in a bar. Well, Merstairs was certainly full of firsts, she thought, as she and Daphne linked arms and bowled along the seafront. As they turned, she caught sight of the pretty hanging window boxes outside the other pub, the Ship and Anchor.

'What *is* the problem with that place?' asked Sarah.

Daphne followed her glance. 'Oh, not the Ship! Really, Sarah,' her friend said, as though she'd said something dreadful. Then she went on. 'Just look at their chalkboard – typical of the way they're always having a go at the Roger.'

Sarah looked at the sign again, and suddenly the sinking of the pirate ship in the picture made sense. She couldn't help smirking a little at the passive-aggressive attack, though. It was rather clever.

'That young barman mentioned the Ship has gastro meals. It sounds nice,' she said.

'Barman? Oh, you mean young Albie. He was quite wild at one point – he even got into trouble with the police – but he seems to have calmed down now. He's been helping Trevor out recently. But he surely can't have been recommending the Ship? They're dreadful sharks, always trying to do the Jolly Roger down. Gus and the Ship landlord, Alan Wragg, couldn't stand each other.'

'Why not? I mean, I can see they're business competitors, but surely they could get on?'

'Oh, Gus was all about being a traditional pub. He thought the Ship was really pretentious. "Quinoa with everything," he used to say. And the rivalry has only got worse since he's been gone.

'That was the great thing about Gus,' Daphne continued. 'He didn't waste time having a go at the opposition like that. He was usually such a joker – apart from the times when he lost it a bit and banned someone – but there was one thing he was serious about. He always wanted to get the price down for customers, and that put him at loggerheads with the brewery. That's what people want, affordable drinks – not fancy dining, and silly pictures,' Daphne said sniffily.

Sarah said nothing, but she actually quite liked a nicely cooked meal, with or without quinoa. And those window boxes, bursting with pink begonias and blue lobelia, were really attractive. She'd like to see what the place was like inside. If it had fewer plastic lobsters dotted about the interior than the Jolly Roger, so much the better. Then a sudden gust of wind blew her cap of hair about her face, and little Hamish whined. He was nearly getting swept off his feet.

'Where shall we go and eat? Somewhere out of this breeze, preferably – and dog-friendly, too, please,' Sarah said to Daphne as her friend held onto her scarves and flowing silky cardigan.

'Let's pop into the Mermaid Café,' Daphne said after a

moment's thought. 'It's quite sheltered as the cliff overhangs it above. We'll be snug as bugs there, won't we Hamish?'

Hamish grinned obligingly at Daphne, and Sarah was relieved. It seemed he was accepting her as a fixture, which would make everything easier. 'Good boy,' she told him encouragingly and gave his ears a stroke. He really was shaping up to be quite a treasure. 'And while we're walking, you can tell me whatever it is that you heard at your book group last night.'

Daphne opened her mouth to reply when there was a horrible hissing sound. Suddenly Hamish, who'd been plodding along so sedately a moment ago, was yanking her arm off in his bid to get over to the other side of the road in record-breaking time. 'Hamish? What on earth is going on?' Sarah yelped as she was towed in his wake.

Once they'd crossed – there was no traffic, mercifully – Hamish came to a grinding stop outside a rather dusty-looking shop, and barked as though his life depended on it. Sarah couldn't see what on earth the problem could be. She tried peering this way and that through the windows, but visibility was severely reduced by the amount of grime on them. Then Daphne came puffing up by her side.

'What on earth do you think is going on in there?' asked Sarah. 'What is this shop, anyway? There's no sign anywhere, and I can hardly see in.' She tried wiping away some of the dirt, but only succeeded in getting her fingers mucky. 'This is serious, Daphne. I think there might be something really bad in there,' she said, really alarmed. 'I've never heard Hamish bark like this in my life.'

FIFTEEN

As Sarah peered at the shop in consternation, and Hamish yapped his head off at her side, Daphne tutted. 'Honestly, there's no need for all this fuss. I can just open up and show you around.'

'What do you mean?' asked Sarah, eyes wide.

'Well, it's my shop, silly. My Tarot emporium. And I imagine Hamish is just very excited to be at the threshold of the Beyond.' With that, Daphne rattled in her bag and produced her enormous bunch of keys, before selecting one and opening the door with a flourish.

'Oh!' Sarah said. 'You did say you were thinking of getting a place a while back but I thought you must have decided against it,' she added, a little miffed that she was so out of the loop. 'Anyway, it doesn't explain why Hamish is going so crazy.'

'Oh, just excitement, I expect,' said Daphne blithely. 'He knows he's close to the spirit world. Anyway, I had to go ahead. Popular demand, you know. Welcome to Tarot and Tealeaves.' With that, she stepped over the mound of unopened post lying on the mat, and disappeared into the dusty interior.

'But if you have this shop, why do you need the beach hut

for storage? There must be plenty of room here to keep things,'
Sarah said, being pulled inside by an eager Hamish and looking
around curiously.

Although it had an air of musty disuse, there was no
doubting what Daphne's shop was intended for. There were
huge blown-up pictures of Tarot cards on the wall – Sarah
noticed the Lovers and the Wheel of Fortune – and there was a
small consultation area with seats around a table, upon which
was positioned a large crystal ball. This could also have done
with a good dusting, if not a hefty spritz with some window
cleaner. If you could actually see through it, she thought, it
might provide a better portal to the Beyond.

'Oh, I couldn't possibly jam this space up with unnecessary
items,' said Daphne. 'It's sacrosanct.'

Sarah wheeled round, looking at the crowded shelves
drooping in the middle under the weight of books, many of
which seemed to be about something called the Arcana. There
were also tottering piles of paperwork littering the tops of two of
the three filing cabinets – the third seemed to have a bundle of
cloth on it.

'You're impressed, I can tell,' Daphne went on, clasping her
hands to her heart. 'Oh, I'm so thrilled. I was worried you'd
think it was really silly.'

Sarah was glad she'd bitten her lip. Daphne was always a lot
more sensitive than she looked. 'Of course it isn't silly, Daph. If
you've got the custom, then it makes sense to have a, um, nice
place for people to come to...' she said, rather tailing off, unsure
she would classify this shop as that, exactly. Though it wouldn't
need that much work, she decided, to bring it up to scratch.
'Where does the tea part come in? Is there a café area?'

'Yes, here,' said Daphne, with a ta-dah movement, indicating a corner with a couple of tables and some comfy-looking
chairs. 'And here are all my teas,' she said, flinging open a
cupboard. Immediately, five or six packets of loose-leaf tea fell

out. 'Oopsie,' she said, kicking the spillage under one of the tables. 'Would you like a cup?'

'Erm, not at the moment, thank you,' Sarah said quickly. 'I just wonder what Hamish was barking about? And what on earth that strange hissing noise was.'

They both looked at the little dog, who was now sniffing around the base of the filing cabinets like a demented hoover – something that would be extremely useful in this place, thought Sarah.

'Oh, that was probably Mephisto,' said Daphne.

'Your cat? But he's at your cottage, isn't he? I thought he was chewing off the postman's arm this morning.'

'Well, it was just a warning nip, really,' Daphne said airily. 'Anyway, Mephisto is a law unto himself, he moves in mysterious ways,' she explained with half-closed eyes as she went over to the filing cabinet with the bundle on top, then whipped off the fabric to reveal the enormous back view of a sleepy cat. It was Mephisto, his stripy orange girth overspilling the cabinet in all directions.

Hamish, of course, had just had his worst suspicions confirmed, and started barking fit to bust. Mephisto turned round – a difficult operation at his size – and opened one lazy green eye. He surveyed Hamish, now jumping up and down as though on springs, treated him to a look of deep disdain, and promptly went right back to sleep again.

'Good gracious! However did he get in?' Sarah asked, while pulling Hamish back before he could topple the cabinet with his scrabbling. For a moment, she had visions of Mephisto galumphing down the street and letting himself in with his own key.

'Oh, you know what he's like. He's a puff of smoke, impossible to contain,' said Daphne fondly.

Sarah decided that if Mephisto was a puff, it was probably of the cream variety. She looked around – and then spotted the cat flap in the shop door. Mystery solved. Even so, it was quite a walk from Daphne's cottage, and it wasn't entirely clear what was in the trek for the cat. Then, as Sarah looked over at one of the piles of papers, she spotted the characteristic chewing and scrunching that suggested a few mice had taken up residence in Daphne's ancient tax returns. Well, if Mephisto could keep their number down, then good luck to him. He was definitely an extraordinary creature.

'Shall we give this place a bit of a spruce-up?' Sarah said to Daphne. 'And you can tell me your news. I can tie Hamish up outside.' Although he had quietened down nicely, he was still sitting at the base of Mephisto's filing cabinet, bristling with anticipation, as though hoping the cat would somehow fall off, right into his jaws. Well, Sarah had news for Hamish. If that happened, he would be flattened.

'A spruce-up? But I did the spring cleaning only a little while back... it must have been before Christmas,' said Daphne in surprise. 'It won't need doing again for ages. Don't tell me you're turning into one of these hygiene freaks,' she said disapprovingly. 'I really can't afford to be constantly messing with the vibrations in here.'

Though she wondered if there was a doctor in the country, retired or not, who didn't prefer cleanliness to these levels of allergen-rich dust, Sarah decided to abandon the topic. 'In that case, shouldn't we get on and find some lunch and we can talk then about what you found out last night? It's lovely seeing your shop' – she tried to make this sound sincere – 'but time is cracking on and if you don't need a hand here, I should probably get on with my own boxes back at home.'

'OK, let's make a move. Mephisto gets cranky if his afternoon nap is interrupted. Now, bye-bye to my beautiful boy,' Daphne cooed to the huge cat, giving him a lavish stroke which dislodged a thick cloud of fur.

Down at the base of the filing cabinet, Hamish sneezed, a

long-suffering expression on his little face. Inhaling his neme-sis's ginger fluff might be the closest he was going to get to his quarry today – but he lived in hope.

Sarah and Daphne were soon outside again, with the shop locked up and Mephisto apparently more than happy to be left in charge. Hamish had his nose pressed up against the window, and was loudly pretending that if they were still in the same room together, he'd be showing the cat who was boss.

Just then, there was a discreet cough behind them. Sarah wheeled round, only to be confronted by the two policemen who had initially investigated Daphne's beach hut.

'Hello, ladies. We'd like you to accompany us to the station,' said the shorter of the two. His tone made it clear this was an invitation they could not refuse.

SIXTEEN

'You want us to go to the station? But why? We're not catching a train,' said Daphne, adjusting her scarf coquettishly and smiling at both policemen.

'I don't think that's what they mean, Daphne. I think they want us to go to police headquarters,' Sarah said tensely under her breath.

'Oh, how exciting,' said Daphne, clapping her hands together in glee. 'I've always wanted to get a proper look at Mari's office. She's never let me come and sort out her feng shui, you know, to make sure her desk is facing in an auspicious direction.'

'Looks like it's your lucky day, then, love,' said one of the policemen, and the other chuckled heavily.

* * *

After a short journey in the police car, with Daphne waving to half the town while Sarah shrank in her seat, mortified at the notoriety they must be courting, they arrived at the small police station. Hamish got out and shook himself thoroughly, giving

Sarah a look as if to say the day was not turning out as he'd planned.

'You and me both, boy,' said Sarah quietly. She squared her shoulders, while Daphne bounced out of the car and bustled straight into the squat redbrick building, calling out for Mariella.

A burly man in his forties stepped forward. 'Are these the bid— erm, ladies?' he asked the two constables, who nodded. Sarah was pretty sure he'd been going to say 'biddies'.

'I'm Detective Inspector Blake, in charge of this investigation,' the man continued importantly, his chest puffed out and his hands behind his back, peering at them with eyes like currants in a doughy white face. 'Thank you for popping in.'

'I didn't realise we had a choice,' said Sarah crisply.

'Can I see Mariella now? She's my daughter, you know,' said Daphne excitedly.

'Ah... I see. I wasn't aware of the connection,' DI Blake glared at the two PCs. 'I'm afraid she wouldn't be able to question you even if she was here – conflict of interest – but if you'd like to leave your, um, dog with our receptionist and follow these officers to the interview room they'll take an official statement, Mrs Roux and Mrs...?'

Daphne burst in. 'It's Ms.'

'Mrs Mizz?' The inspector appeared confused, looking at Sarah.

'No, *I'm* Ms. Ms Roux,' Daphne said firmly.

'Right. Well, Ms Roux and Mrs...?'

'*Doctor,*' Daphne burst in.

The man looked round quickly. 'Where? Who asked for a doctor?'

Sarah and Daphne looked at each other. This could take all day.

'No, Inspector Blake. This is *Dr Sarah Vane,*' Daphne said, enunciating every word slowly and clearly, while Sarah smiled a little self-consciously.

'Ah. Right. Well, get on with it, you two,' he snapped.

Sarah and Daphne looked startled.

'No, no, not you... *them*. Dumbarton and Deeside,' Inspector Blake said, waving an arm at the constables.

Sarah, realising where Mariella had got her 'Tweedledum and Tweedledee' nicknames from, smiled, before catching sight of Dumbarton's scowl.

'This way, ladies,' Deeside said, ushering them into a cheerless interview room, painted a drab green and containing only a table and four hard-looking chairs.

'Ooh, this is just like *The Sweetie*, isn't it, Sarah?' said Daphne, her eyes gleaming.

Sarah looked at her blankly, thought for a moment, and then something clicked. 'Oh yes, the tough detectives! We used to watch it on the quiet at school. *The Sweeney*...'

'You got me bang to rights, guv,' said Daphne in a terrible fake Cockney accent while Dumbarton and Deeside looked on, supremely unimpressed. Then Daphne pirouetted towards the mirror on the back wall of the room. 'This is two-way, isn't it? Coo-ee! Mariella, are you there?' she shrilled.

'Um, it's just a mirror. If you could please sit down, madam,' Deeside said, wiping a bead of sweat from his brow as Daphne finally subsided into a chair.

Dumbarton got out his notebook and flicked through to find a clean page, as Daphne spoke up again. 'Hang on, aren't you supposed to be doing this, *beeeeeep*,' she said, letting out an earsplitting squeaking noise.

'Daphne! What on earth?' said Sarah, jamming her hands to her ears.

'It's the tape, silly. That's how they always start it. "For the benefit of the tape, interview with Mrs Mizz and Dr—"'

'If you've quite finished,' said Dumbarton, now looking

rather pinched around the nostrils. 'We won't be taping this as you aren't under arrest. Yet.' He glared at both women. Sarah squirmed in her seat. Immediately, there was a knock on the door.

'Here, you're needed out in reception,' said another officer. 'Some dog's eaten the ham out of your sandwiches.'

'You two, stay put,' said Deeside as the men rushed away.

'Oops,' Sarah said. 'Perhaps I should go and sort this out.'

'They've told us not to move. I must say, being interrogated is not nearly as fun as it looks on telly,' Daphne remarked.

Just then, they heard footsteps coming to a halt outside their half-open door. 'Shh,' Sarah said quickly to Daphne.

'So you're sure?' came the voice from outside – it sounded like DI Blake. 'The newspaper he was lying on, it dates back to six weeks ago?'

'That's right, sir, it was the *Merstairs Marketeer* freesheet from the twelfth of February, it's delivered all around here,' came Mariella's eager voice.

'And why isn't Dr Burns telling me this?'

'He's had to shoot off, sir, stabbing down in Ramsgate,' Mariella said.

'*Dr Burns must be the pathologist,*' Sarah whispered to Daphne.

'Huh, that's typical, just when I need him,' said Blake tetchily. 'But it doesn't help us much. Anyone could have saved the paper just to make it seem like the murder was on February twelfth.'

'They could have done,' said Mariella. 'But Dr Burns says the body has lain undisturbed on it for at least six weeks. He can tell due to larval development.'

Daphne looked at Sarah in confusion. 'You don't want to know,' Sarah whispered.

'So that takes us up to...' It sounded as though DI Blake was struggling with the maths.

'Just about now, sir,' said Mariella kindly. 'Shall I get Gus Trubshaw's partner in, sir? Trevor Bains? Interview him about the newspaper?' she asked.

'What? No, no. Tell Deeside to get onto it. As for you...'

'Yes, sir?' the eagerness in Mariella's voice was plain to hear.

'Tea. Two sugars. My office. Now.'

With that, they could hear Blake's heavy tread receding down the corridor.

'Yes sir,' said Mariella in a resigned voice.

Sarah and Daphne looked at each other. 'Your Mari needs help,' Sarah said to Daphne in a low voice. 'We've got to sort this out for her sake. Not to mention...'

'What?' said Daphne, sitting up straight all of a sudden.

'Well, we need to find the real culprit – just in case they decide they do want to charge us with something,' Sarah said, and the women stared at each other with round eyes.

SEVENTEEN

After Dumbarton had reappeared and gone through the laborious business of taking down every word of the women's impressions of their grisly discovery in the beach hut, and they had then signed everything, Sarah and Daphne were finally allowed to collect a smug-looking Hamish from reception and make their way back to Merstairs proper.

'Well, I don't know about you but I'm bushed – and starving. I'm going to go straight home for beans on toast and put my feet up,' said Daphne.

'I couldn't agree more,' said Sarah, who could see that Hamish badly needed a post-prandial nap. 'Shall we meet for lunch tomorrow and discuss everything?'

'Why not?' said Daphne. 'I'll pick you up at twelve thirty.'

* * *

Daphne was as good as her word the following day, rapping on Sarah's door at half-past twelve on the dot, and the pair walked into town companionably, with Hamish frolicking ahead,

pouncing on unsuspecting clumps of weed and woofing at the
seagulls far above him in a sky as blue as Charles Diggory's eyes.

'I'm ravenous,' said Sarah. 'There's something about all this
sea air that really whets the appetite. And we did miss our
lunch yesterday. I still haven't heard your news from the book
group – and we've got to talk about the police station, too.'

'Tell you what, we didn't make it to the Mermaid Café then,
so let's go now. It's just the place,' said Daphne. 'As soon as
we're settled I'll tell you everything. It's along here, out of the
wind. We can sit outside and Hamish can have a bowl of water
all to himself.'

It was nice that Daphne was taking to Hamish, Sarah
thought, as they sat down and then looked at the laminated
menu card. She wasn't going to waste away in Merstairs, that
was for sure. Eventually she decided she'd opt for the goat's
cheese salad. When the waitress pottered out to take their
orders, Daphne went for a club sandwich, and they both
ordered mineral water.

It really was a fine spot to survey the beautiful coastline,
nestled into the rock which formed a sort of embrace around the
little café, giving it lots of shelter. Today, the sea was a mass of
restless waves, whipped by a wind that was sending shreds of
cloud flying across the blue sky – but Sarah couldn't admire it as
she should. She was itching to have a proper discussion. It was
pointless trying before Daphne had her food in front of her,
though.

The smiling waitress soon deposited the contents of a
groaning tray on their table and both ladies tucked in. Sarah's
goat's cheese had just the right level of tartness, and the salad
was crisp and well-dressed. She sipped her mineral water and,
once they'd both made good inroads into their meals, she spoke
about what was on her mind.

'So what do you think, then, about what we overheard in the
police station yesterday?'

'The stabbing in Ramsgate? Can't say I'm surprised, it's not like here...' Daphne started.

'Not that!' Sarah said quickly. 'What the pathologist said, about Gus being found lying on the *Merstairs Marketeer* newsletter from mid-February. I was thinking about it last night. That really dates the murder.'

'Do you mind, Sarah? I'm trying to eat,' said Daphne, taking a big bite of her sandwich.

'All right, but this is important. I don't think the police believe we're responsible, not now they know you're Mariella's mum, but we still want to help Mariella out, don't we? You heard how that Inspector Blake was treating her,' Sarah said firmly.

'So how will this help things?' Daphne said a little indistinctly as she chewed.

'We'll have to bear in mind the time of death, sometime after the twelfth of February, when we talk to people. It'll help with the process of elimination,' Sarah said enthusiastically.

'Well, if you say so,' said Daphne with a moue of distaste. 'Anyway, are you ready to hear what I discovered at my book club meeting the other night?'

'Of course, yes,' said Sarah, remembering Daphne's hints that it was a pretty key piece of information.

'Well, you'll absolutely never believe it, but Charles Diggory had bought my hut from, guess who, only his ex, Francesca!' Daphne waited for a reaction, then, not getting one, added a little tetchily, 'You know, she's the mayor of Merstairs.'

Sarah suppressed a groan. After waiting so long, this was all the reward she was going to get – a nugget of news she'd already gleaned herself. 'Yes. I met her yesterday in the Jolly Roger, before you got there.' Suddenly Sarah had a flashback to Charles Diggory's flight from the pub, to fetch his poor neglected grandchildren. She hoped they'd been OK when he'd eventually turned up.

'You could sound a bit more interested,' Daphne huffed as she set about her club sandwich. 'Mariella was quite right. She said people are never as grateful as they could be, when she rang me this morning to say that Gus Trubshaw had drugs in his system. She'd gone out of her way to get the pathologist, that Dr Burns, his favourite type of latte before he went off to Ramsgate and he didn't even say thank you.'

'Wait... what? Some sort of analgesic had been administered ante-mortem? Are you sure?' Sarah tried to make sense of what she'd just heard. Surely the body in the beach hut had been strangled. She'd spotted tell-tale signs... but then again, she had been retired for a few months now. Could her medical skills be rusty already?

'Well, I don't know the jargon, not like some people.' Daphne was still a bit ruffled, but Sarah's expression of acute interest was beginning to mollify her. 'But that's the gist of it. According to Mari.'

Sarah grimaced. 'She might want to keep things like that under her hat.'

'Oh of course,' said Daphne airily. 'Mariella's the soul of discretion. I was so glad when I heard she'd got the job, from Sharon on the till in the minimarket. She'd got the news from Mariella's next-door neighbour only a few minutes after Mari found out, she hadn't had a moment to ring me herself as she'd had to dash off to get the kids.'

Daphne took a huge mouthful of her sandwich and Sarah loaded some salad onto her fork, thinking all the while about the pathologist's findings, and Mariella's eagerness yesterday.

'Is Mari enjoying being with the police?'

'Oh yes,' said Daphne. 'She's hoping to make the move into plainclothes soon – you know, CID. But she's got a way to go. She started training just when Peter... well, you know. You weren't really in a fit state to discuss it all with.'

Sarah digested this. She felt she'd always been up to

listening to other people's news. But it had been a terrible time. Particularly towards the end. She closed her eyes firmly, to shut out the picture of Peter pleading for the help he knew she shouldn't give him.

'This must be her first really big case,' said Sarah. 'We could be so useful to her, get all this cleared up, and hopefully move her on to the next stage in her career. Then you'd have your hut back – and I wouldn't have to give Peter's clothes to Charles Diggory.'

Daphne was all concern. 'I know it's hard for you to part with Peter's things. But even if we put them in the hut, it would be just delaying the inevitable...'

Sarah picked up her glass again and blinked rapidly. 'Anyway,' she said as firmly as she could. 'You must want that hut for storage yourself, Daphne, otherwise why buy it?'

'Well, Mephisto needs more space in the cottage to spread his whiskers, and I can't risk Tarot and Tealeaves getting disorganised, obviously.' Daphne shrugged. 'By the way, Mari told me specifically to warn you not to get involved! She said the last thing the Merstairs police need is amateurs meddling. I must say, I thought that was a bit much myself,' Daphne said a little more crossly. 'You're so self-contained and controlled, you'd never be the meddling type. And me, too! As if I'd ever poke my nose in where it's not wanted.' She shook her head. 'Excuse me, you need to do up your shoelaces,' she said loudly to a teenage boy wandering past. 'You could have a nasty fall.' His glare suggested he welcomed her intervention every bit as warmly as her daughter did.

Sarah smiled. This was just the sort of thing Mariella had to say, at this point. She would doubtless come round to the idea. Because if the Merstairs police were as overstretched as they had seemed yesterday, then it looked like Mariella and her colleagues needed all the assistance they could get.

EIGHTEEN

By the time Sarah and Daphne had finished their lunch, it was almost time for Sarah's next rendezvous. She looked at her watch. It was just shy of a quarter to three, the time Hannah Betts had told her Mavis was due to clock on for her usual Thursday shift at the Beach Café.

'I think I should be making a move,' she said, a little reluctantly as Hamish was asleep, with his head heavy and warm on her toes. 'Chatting to Mavis could be a great source of information, Hannah Betts said so. I hope she wasn't just fobbing me off.'

'Oh well, I suppose you'll find out,' said Daphne lazily. 'I might just stay here for a bit. Do you want me to keep an eye on Hamish?'

Sarah was sorely tempted. It seemed a shame to wake him. But she knew he was still just that little bit iffy about Daphne.

'I think it would be good for him to have a little walk,' she said diplomatically. 'We'll come back once we've had our chat with Mavis, though. Hopefully you'll still be around.'

'Well, that's if I don't get the call to go into the shop

urgently. I just never know when one of my clients will need me,' Daphne said with a pious look.

Sarah remembered the levels of undisturbed dust at the little store but said only, 'OK then. See you soon, I hope.'

With that, she gave Hamish a gentle stroke. The little dog opened one eye, as if to register disapproval at this interruption to his well-deserved nap time – but then his innate sense of adventure won through and he bounced to his feet as though he'd been waiting for the off the whole time.

'Good boy,' said Sarah. Off the pair went down the road, keeping up a jaunty pace as they crossed over and onto the beach. Sarah's progress immediately slowed down. She'd forgotten how much she hated getting sand in her shoes. Today's were open-toed, in celebration of the fine spring weather, so soon she was shipping almost a beachful in each shoe. There was nothing for it but to take them off, which she did rather precariously by standing on one leg after another, still hanging onto Hamish's lead. She didn't want him dashing away and chasing any children's balls – or children, for that matter. He was turning into a very good dog but still prone to puppyish overexcitement at times, as his sudden scenting of Mephisto had shown yesterday.

Sarah had read recently that the ability to stand on one leg was a useful indicator of general underlying health. While she didn't really agree with these fad diagnoses, which popped up even in the reputable newspapers she and Peter had always favoured, she was rather proud she could carry out this flamingo-like procedure while also hanging onto a dog without any trouble at all.

Of course, she spoke, or thought, too soon. A pretty little Chihuahua high-stepped past Hamish and immediately he yanked on his lead like a rocket heading for the moon. Sarah, who had just about got her second strap undone, was pulled sideways and toppled unceremoniously onto the sand. Mercifully, it was soft and dry, and her landing was by no means painful. The only injury was to her dignity. But, as she was lying there catching her breath, and realising she had to get on Hamish's trail before his romance with the Chihuahua got serious, a large arm came down towards her, her hand was grabbed and she was hoisted unceremoniously back to her feet.

Sarah brushed herself down, blushing furiously, and looked up at her saviour. Of course, it had to be Charles Diggory, with an inscrutable look on those patrician features.

'Well, if it isn't Sarah, the lady with all the questions. I saw you taking a tumble there. I'm afraid that was my Tinkerbell who caused your chap to bolt.'

'Tinkerbell?!' Sarah was breathless after her fall, and even more so after being yanked to her feet again, but the little dog's name caused her to snort with laughter in a most unladylike manner. She tried to turn it into a cough but the look Charles gave her suggested he wasn't fooled for a moment. And an answering gleam of amusement lurked in those compelling blue eyes.

'Named by my ex-wife, er, shortly to be ex anyway. We have joint custody.'

'Of course you do,' said Sarah. From the little she'd seen of Francesca Diggory, it had been clear she wasn't giving up anything about Charles without a fight. 'It must be difficult,' she added. 'No one wants to part with a dog, I quite see that.'

She'd had her moments with Hamish initially, almost cursing poor Peter for landing the dog on her, but she couldn't imagine life without the little scamp these days.

'Hmm. There are times,' said Charles tersely, turning this way and that, clearly in search of his own dog. Sarah scanned the beach worriedly, too.

Suddenly Sarah remembered his grandchildren, and her shock that a man could be so callous – and self-absorbed – as to forget his own flesh and blood. 'Did you pick up the little ones all right, yesterday?' she asked.

'What?' asked Charles, confused. Then his face cleared. 'Oh, that. I'm afraid that was Francesca's idea of a joke. When I got there, I was told that they'd been collected an hour before by their mother. Frankie does like her fun.' It was said lightly, but the prank clearly stung. 'Now, where have those dogs got to?' said Charles, scanning the horizon.

There was no sign of the two reprobates anywhere – but there was a bit of a commotion going on over by the café. 'What do you bet that's something to do with our dogs? I vote we go and investigate,' he said, seeming relieved to be off the topic of his grandchildren – and his estranged wife.

'Yes. Yes, good idea,' said Sarah. She was castigating herself for letting Hamish give her the slip. She should have just put up with sandy shoes. He was much too young and silly to be running about on his own. Goodness knew the trouble he could get into. And that was without being led astray by an obviously out-of-control toy dog.

With a worried look at the melee developing, she started to stride forward, her sandals in one hand. But the beach wasn't that easy to walk on. The wind had brushed the sand up into peaks and troughs, and she kept stumbling as she rushed onwards. Without Charles occasionally grabbing her elbow to steady her, she would have come a cropper several times. It was kind of him – and his hand was certainly warm on her arm – but she wished he'd kept his silly little dog on a tighter leash. Then Sarah wouldn't be worrying what Hamish was up to.

It was almost as alarming as losing sight of a toddler. All those tricky shopping trips when her girls were small and wilful, and their one mission in life was to escape, Houdini-like, from their pushchairs to cause their mother's heart to stop beating momentarily. She'd thought those days were over, but here she was again, replaying it all with a dog. Well, thank you Peter, she couldn't help thinking, completely contradicting her earlier gratitude. No one had these anxieties with a cat.

But when she reached the knot of people over by the hut, she was surprised to see that it wasn't a badly behaved Scottie holding people's attention. Indeed, Hamish was sitting tidily on his haunches, watching like the rest of the crowd, as Tinkerbell the tiny Chihuahua flatly refused to get out of a child's pram. The little girl owner was in hysterics, while her exasperated mum kept trying to tip the pooch out. But Tinkerbell was keeping her balance against all the odds, sitting up as straight as any Disney princess on her rightful throne and showing the whites of her eyes to the poor beleaguered mother.

Just when it looked as though the mum was going to have to bodily eject the dog, and probably get bitten for her pains, there was an ear-splitting whistle from beside Sarah. Charles had summoned Tinkerbell. Tinkerbell immediately transformed herself from sulky royalty to slavishly obedient pet. She leapt down from the pram and trotted over to her master on matchstick legs as though winning the obedience round at Crufts dog show. Charles immediately swept her up and tucked her under his arm.

'I do apologise, dear lady,' he said with a bow to the mother, who went from red-faced crossness to blushing forgiveness in seconds. Even the infuriated child was much mollified at being able to reinstall her doll in the pram, and carry on with her morning walk unimpeded by imperious doggies.

'Well! After all that, I'm ready for a cup of tea. Shall we?' Charles said, sweeping his hand towards the Beach Café.

Sarah was in a conundrum. She had an imminent appointment at the café. She could see a waitress who must surely be Mavis bustling around the tables, and this was her golden opportunity to ask her about the hut and its horrible contents. But did she really want to do all that in front of Charles? For one thing, he was still her prime suspect.

NINETEEN

After a moment of indecision, Sarah allowed herself to be guided towards the café. Hamish, trotting along beside Sarah with many an excited glance and sniff at Tinkerbell under Charles Diggory's arm, was obviously keen to keep the acquaintance going. Sarah was beginning to get the ridiculous notion she was going along with this to suit her dog's romantic plans. It was absurd. But she soon found herself being ushered into a shady seat under one of the canopies stretching out from three sides of the café building. The place really had the loveliest view of the sea. It meant her feet were still in the sand, but this far from the tide it was the white powdery kind, and warm from the sun despite the breezy day.

'We could almost be on the French Riviera, couldn't we?' said Charles, looking at her through half-closed blue eyes as he stretched out his long legs and sighed in pleasure.

Just then, a family with a red-faced, truculent teenager walked by. 'Aw, Muuum, you promised I could have my phone back if I watched Lizzie this morning. Come on, Muuum, a deal's a deal,' the boy whined, while his little sister grizzled loudly and his mother did her level best to ignore both children.

Finally she turned on the boy. 'We've come here to have fun, and don't you forget it,' she shrieked at him.

Sarah and Charles exchanged a laughing glance. It wasn't that Sarah didn't sympathise with the poor mother's struggles – it was just that nowadays she allowed herself to enjoy the comedy in life when it struck her. Goodness knew she had been serious for long enough.

A pleasant voice at her elbow distracted her from her thoughts. 'What can I get you two?'

'Er, Mavis, is it?' said Sarah, looking up into a pair of twinkling eyes. 'Um, I'd love a tea... but also I was having a little chat with Hannah the other day...'

Immediately Mavis's friendliness vanished. 'Was you?' she said.

'Yes, nothing about you... or rather, it was about Gus.'

'Gus? Here, you're not from the papers, are you?'

Sarah quickly reassured the woman. 'Of course not. I just wanted to ask you about the beach hut. The orange and pink one.'

Mavis looked from Sarah to Charles. '*His* beach hut, you mean?'

Charles coughed. 'Well, I sold it, you know...'

'Oh yeah. To that Tarot lady, the one with the laugh and all the hair, that's right, innit?'

It was now Sarah's turn to cough. Then she asked gently, 'I wonder why Hannah thought you knew who might have been using the hut for storage?'

'Ah, I see. Yeah, well that's because of the Merstairs Tai Chi group.'

'Oh, right... in what way?'

'I'm in charge of the equipment, see... and I asked the mayor if we could stash it in the hut... it were well known that she had the space. It's only a few ribbons and whatnot we use.'

Sarah remembered how dramatic they had looked against

the backdrop of the sea, when she'd seen the little group moving in harmony. 'So... you carried on using it, even after the hut changed hands?'

'Well, yeah. My key still fits, right? And it's not like anyone told me it kept being sold. Like musical chairs, it's been.'

Sarah was keenly aware of Charles, at her side, taking in all her questions – and the answers. But it might be her only opportunity to press Mavis, so she carried on. 'And did you see anything in the hut? Anything that... worried you?'

'If you're asking me if I saw a dead body and just ignored it or put some ribbons on it, then you're as cuckoo as the Tarot lady,' Mavis said. 'I saw nothing. Just a bunch of boxes, weren't it?'

Sarah thought hard. 'Does the group meet every day?'

'Just once a week, usually. We have the odd bit of time off... my sister Jules broke her leg, middle of February, so we didn't meet until she had the cast off, ooh, end of March it would be,' Mavis said grudgingly.

Sarah tried not to look too excited about this snippet of information, and pressed on with another question. 'What about a silk scarf? Did you ever see one of those in the hut, a square with horseshoes...'

Both Charles and Mavis were goggling at her now, but only Mavis spoke. 'That'd belong to the mayor, obviously. It used to be her hut, didn't it? Did you want to order something, or was it just the questions?' She moved from foot to foot, obviously yearning to be gone.

It was a shame. Mavis had seemed so friendly at first, but Sarah had now seriously got her back up. Asking about the murder didn't seem to go down too well with anyone. Charles was looking distinctly frosty too. Still, it had to be done. Otherwise, the killer might escape justice, and Sarah couldn't have that.

'I'd love a pot of tea,' said Sarah, with as cheerful a smile as she could manage. 'Charles, what will you have?'

'Sounds good to me,' he said with a shrug, his tone off-hand.

'Two teas, then,' said Mavis, jotting it down in her little order book. 'Nothing to eat?' Her tone was disapproving.

'I've just had a huge lunch...' Sarah started apologetically.

'Two slices of your most delicious cake,' Charles broke in, smiling away Sarah's protests. 'I'm sure we need a bit of sugar after all that, erm, fuss with the dogs,' he said to her.

Sarah didn't dare contradict him, after bringing up Francesca's scarf, which was tantamount to an accusation. She hid her pink cheeks by looking under the table, where a love-struck Hamish was gazing adoringly at Tinkerbell. But the Chihuahua had her back to him and was looking unimpressed with the way her day was shaping up.

'So, Sarah,' Charles said, raising his eyebrows. 'I'm not sure I buy this quiet retirement story any more. What is it, actually, that brings you to Merstairs? Are you really an amateur sleuth, or are you just trying to get away from something in London?'

'Ah now, that's quite a question,' said Sarah, not sure she liked the tables being turned on her. In her job, she'd always had a huge amount of leeway to fire enquiries at people. Anything was fair game, from bowel movements to alcohol units – a figure that should always be doubled to get anywhere close to the truth, in her experience. It was novel for her to be on the receiving end. 'Do you know, sometimes I'm not entirely sure?'

Charles nodded, as though acknowledging the way she had ducked out of answering, but just then the tea arrived so he couldn't press her further. With it came two huge slabs of delicious homemade coffee and walnut cake, the shiny icing on top studded with a pattern of nut halves while a fluffy buttercream oozed between the layers. After the fuss of pouring, adding milk, stirring and allocating plates, Charles raised his cup to her.

'Well, here's to a very happy time here, no matter what you've come to do.'

Sarah took a sip, and decided to come clean. Or clean*ish*. 'I'm not sure I really have a mission here, I just needed... a new start.'

'Aha. Escaping the past. Yes, I suppose we all do that sometimes.'

Sarah was rather stung. 'I don't think I'm trying to escape, exactly...' she said. And then she realised there were elements of recent events she did want to evade, if at all possible. 'I'm just trying to enjoy my retirement.'

'Well, that's wonderful. Of course, some of us haven't quite retired yet,' Charles said ruefully.

Sarah wasn't sure you could call it work, running a shop full of antiques but empty of customers. Yet it wasn't Charles's fault that Merstairs didn't seem to be crammed with curio collectors.

'I suppose divorce – or not-quite divorce – is expensive?' she asked.

'Ouch, yes,' said Charles, disappearing behind his teacup. Sarah immediately felt bad. Perhaps that had been a bit near the knuckle. But when Charles replaced his cup in the saucer, he was smiling again. 'Well, now you're here, and so evidently interested in the hut and all who sailed in it, perhaps I should show you around the place properly?'

'Around the hut? I think I've seen about as much as I want to of that. Besides, when I last saw it, it was cordoned off with police tape,' Sarah said firmly.

'No, not that. I meant Merstairs, in all its glory,' Charles said, waving towards the beach, the esplanade and its line of shops facing the sea.

Sarah felt she'd pretty much covered the basics in the last few days, but she tried not to look as sceptical as she felt. Charles was very charming, but he was still definitely in the frame as far as she was concerned. Did she really want to traipse around the place with a potential murderer? And also, she'd been out the whole day. She really was yearning to get back to her cottage and get to grips with its organisation. Heaven forfend that she end up like Daphne – much though she prized her friend – with a chaotic house, chaotic shop... and of course a chaotic hut, complete with a dead body.

'That's so kind of you... I've got to get back home really, for Hamish, you know...' she said vaguely, hoping that Charles would read into this some essential dog maintenance activities that could only be achieved under her own roof. 'But another time that would be splendid!'

Her tone was perhaps a little over-bright, because the look Charles gave her was not entirely convinced. He shrugged gracefully, though, and to her relief did not try to pin her down. At least, she thought the feeling she was getting was probably relief.

All that was left on her side of the table was a plate of crumbs and a drained cup, so she delved in her bag for her purse, but Charles immediately forestalled her.

'No, no. This one's on me. The least I could do, after Tinkerbell was such a pixie and got your good boy into trouble.'

As Hamish was still making goo-goo eyes at Tinkerbell under the table, Sarah wasn't sure this was entirely justified, but she accepted gracefully. 'Well, thank you so much. And see you again soon, no doubt.'

At this, Charles just gave a slightly wintry smile, then redirected his gaze to the waves which were now pummelling the shore. It seemed he was rather peeved she'd turned down his invitation. Sarah decided she'd made the move to leave at just the right time. Things were suddenly getting decidedly chilly.

TWENTY

A few short hours later, Sarah was sitting at her pristine kitchen table, enjoying another well-deserved cup of tea. There was a lopsided crayon picture of Hamish on the fridge, a house-warming present that had come in the post courtesy of little granddaughter Evelyn. Sarah had even picked a few snap-dragons from the front garden. They now sat in pride of place on the table, in a small alabaster vase Peter had bought her on a trip to Italy.

Now, apart from Peter's clothes, which had been marshalled into the sitting room, she was almost sorted. It was a good feeling to have got this far. Sarah often found that while her hands were busy, her mind could work away at any prob-lems worrying her. As a GP, she had often enjoyed a eureka moment with a diagnosis while sorting the laundry or tackling a mountain of washing-up. Today, she'd had her thorniest problem ever to deal with – the body in the beach hut. But despite her best efforts, nothing was any clearer – except the thought that all this was easier for the police. She'd even seen the two constables, Dumbarton and Deeside, plodding down the high street on her way back from the Beach Café, calling in at all the shops. She wished she knew what they had gleaned.

Her thoughts turned restlessly to Charles Diggory. Could he be guilty? He'd seemed the most shocked of Merstairs' residents by far, at the initial news. Apart, that was, from Daphne, who'd run up and down the beach screaming. But Sarah, much though she loved Daphne, felt that that was something her friend could probably do if the Jolly Roger ran out of her favourite Dubonnet.

The beach hut had changed hands with dizzying frequency in the last few months. First Francesca Diggory, then Charles, now Daphne. Was it normal for there to be such a red-hot trade in what was basically a shed, albeit with an amazing view of the Kent coast? It seemed like a game of pass the parcel. Daphne, Sarah was sure, had just blundered into the mix at the wrong moment.

But perhaps that wasn't the case? Everyone in Merstairs seemed to have a view on her friend. Had someone counted on Daphne being the kind of person who never quite got round to sorting her life out? In fact, if Sarah hadn't moved here, and if Daphne hadn't kindly offered her storage space, it could have been months, or even years, before the awful discovery had been made.

Now that the corpse was out in the open, as it were, there seemed to be an array of people who could be involved. At least the *Merstairs Marketeer* clue had helped eliminate the Tai Chi group. Gus had been put in the hut either on or just after 12th February, the body hadn't been moved, and then had been found around six weeks later. Tai Chi had been on pause throughout that period.

Who else might Gus have fallen out with? Though it was a stretch for Sarah to see the Scouts themselves stashing a body, it wasn't hard to picture sleazy Bill Turbot doing something untoward. And there must be others in the frame – hut-owners

Charles and his nearly-ex-wife for starters. She remembered that silk scarf she'd seen. Mavis had confirmed it was Francesca Diggory's, and neither she nor Charles had found it odd. But the mayor of Merstairs could still be involved... couldn't she?

It was like an almighty tangle in a skein of wool, and struggling with it was spoiling Sarah's lovely cup of tea. The evening light coming in through the kitchen window, as well as a sudden rumble from her stomach, reminded her that the very large slice of cake she had tucked into had been a few hours ago. It was dinner time.

Sarah stuck her head into the fridge hopefully, but there was nothing that could be magicked into a delicious, quick supper. Hamish was fine, she would never run out of his favourite dog's dinner. He was now chewing contentedly on his rubber bone in his little basket, a very happy pooch indeed. But they'd have to pop out. She gathered up a light jacket, her bag and Hamish's lead, locked the door, and then paused on the path down to the road. Should she just see whether Daphne was around? Her friend might fancy a stroll into town and a dinner on the seafront. She went through the gate – which no longer squeaked, she'd oiled it earlier – and she and Hamish picked their way up Daphne's path.

The lights were on in the cottage, but once they'd skirted Daphne's collection of garden gnomes and were on the step, contemplating the vibrant purple door, Sarah was slightly regretting her impulse. 'What do you think, boy?' she asked Hamish.

The dog put his head on one side and whined gently, but before Sarah had even rung the bell, the door was flung open.

'Aha, thought I heard someone loitering!' said Daphne, arms open wide. Once Sarah had been well and truly hugged, Hamish was submitted to a vigorous petting. 'Come on in, you two. We're just about to have something to eat.'

Sarah, who'd just realised from the sight of a Zimmer frame, handbag and coat in the hall that Daphne had company, immediately demurred. 'Oh, I don't want to butt in...'

'Nonsense, nonsense, it's high time you met Patricia anyway.' Daphne swept Sarah onwards towards her kitchen.

The layout of Daphne's house was identical to Sarah's, but it was as though the place had been in the middle of an explosion in a soft furnishings factory. Every surface was awash with colours and merrily clashing patterns. The result was a feast for the senses, or a prelude to a migraine – depending on your personal taste. Sarah, who was used to it to some extent, tended to block a lot of it out.

Hamish didn't know quite what to sniff first, but was assailed by a good whiff of eau de Mephisto while thinking it over. Instantly he was bristling, keen to get his own back after being bested in the Tarot shop yesterday.

Sarah picked him up, deciding discretion was the better part of valour, and Hamish woofed to show his total disapproval. But as he was now tucked under Sarah's arm, he was at the ideal height to be greeted by Daphne's guest.

'Who's a gorgeous boy, aren't you? Aren't you?' crooned a little old lady, of about eighty if Sarah was any judge. She had quite a bent back and was the victim, Sarah deduced, of osteoporosis and worn cartilage in the joints. It was a relief when she sat back down. Sarah drew her own chair up to the kitchen table, which was heaped with a profusion of dog-eared books and old biros. In amongst the mess were two bowls containing bright purple soup.

'We were just about to have some of my famous borscht,' Daphne said, ladling out a serving for Sarah and cutting her a doorstep of crusty bread.

Sarah took up her spoon. 'Mmm, this looks...'

'Very purple,' Daphne broke in, her shoulders shaking. 'Well, you know it's always been my favourite colour. And Patricia here loves beetroot, too.'

'Call me Pat,' said the old lady buttering her bread thickly. 'Pat by name, Pat by nature, I say,' she added with a wink.

Sarah raised her eyebrows. 'And where do you know each other from?'

Daphne took a slurp of soup and dabbed her lips with her orange linen napkin. 'We help out with the Scouts, don't we, Pat?'

'Oh, really? You didn't say,' Sarah said, surprised. She felt Daphne should have mentioned this – after all, it could help establishing who'd done what in the hut.

'I go every week. Not sure when you last went, Daph,' said Pat.

Aha, thought Sarah. So it was like Daphne's other enthusiasms, a custom more honoured in the breach than the observance. 'You're there all the time, then?' she said to Pat, an idea forming in her mind.

'Mm,' said Pat. 'Well, who wouldn't want to be around that hunk of beefcake?'

'Um, who's that?' Sarah asked, taking a spoonful of soup.

'Bill Turbot, of course,' said Pat. 'Don't tell me you haven't seen him about the place, with those short shorts... He's always on the beach in them, all weathers, taking his morning constitutional in full uniform. A right tease, he is.'

Sarah virtually spat out her soup. She reached for a napkin and then took a sip of water. 'Good gracious,' was all she said.

'Course, we don't meet when the kiddies have school holidays, but the rest of the time Bill's there, leading us all. What a man,' Pat said in admiring tones.

'School holidays? When would the half term be?' Sarah asked quickly.

'Oh, I remember, it was the week of Valentine's Day. The twelfth to the sixteenth of February. I was disappointed because it would have been a perfect time for Bill to make his move,' Pat said with another huge wink.

Sarah found Pat's evident crush on Bill rather disturbing –
but she couldn't help feeling a jolt of adrenaline at the idea
that there'd been no Scouts meetings during the crucial
window when the *Merstairs Marketeer* had to have been
placed in the trunk – with Gus Trubshaw squeezed in on top.
That meant the Scouts were off the hook. But Bill Turbot
would still have had the hut key, even if the troop wasn't
meeting...

'You've gone very quiet, love,' said Pat. 'Soup going down all
right, is it?'

'What? Oh, er, yes. Delicious,' said Sarah, realising she was
being rude. 'I'm looking for retirement activities, maybe I
should help you two out with the Scouts?' she suggested, though
in reality it was the last thing she'd be signing up for.

'Nah, you're all right dear, not sure we want the competition, do we, Daph,' said Pat, nudging Daphne so hard with one
bony elbow that she almost fell off her seat.

Daphne shot to her feet. 'Now, anyone for more soup? And
eat up your bread, do. It's from the Beach Café. Hannah is a
fantastic baker,' she said, pushing the loaf towards her guests.

'Merstairs is going to ruin my waistline,' said Sarah ruefully.
She'd thought fish and chips would be her nemesis, but it
turned out absolutely everything was delicious, including the
golden yellow butter she was spreading on her bread.

'Oh, chasing around after murderers will keep the pounds
off, I expect,' said Daphne jokily.

'Interested in all that business at the pub, are you?' said Pat
with a gleam in her eye. 'That Gus, always horsing around.
Took it too far, sometimes. Like when he barred my Bill.'

'Wait. You mean he banned Bill Turbot from the Jolly
Roger?' Sarah's ears pricked up; could this be a motive?

'Yes, in the New Year. Jealous of Bill's way with the ladies,
he was,' said Pat.

Sarah decided this was hardly likely. Gus had been very

happy with Trevor. But perhaps he'd been protecting his customers.

'Looks like the last laugh's on Gus, though,' Pat carried on, adding a ferocious, and rather unfeeling, cackle.

'Poor man,' Sarah ventured.

'Oh, you're all the same, you younger generation,' said Pat dismissively. 'Lily-livered, the lot of you. Scared of reality. Of death.'

'In that case,' said Sarah, flipping through the photos on her phone, 'I wonder what you make of this.' She tentatively pushed the picture of Gus in the trunk towards Pat. The old woman snatched it up, eager to see what the fuss was about. 'Who do you think would want to do that to him? Quite a punishment for barring someone from his pub,' Sarah said. 'Do you think it was Bill?'

Unfortunately, Pat wasn't quite as tough as she made out. She took one look and started to splutter. Daphne rushed to pat her on the back, while Sarah fetched a glass of water. Then Daphne saw what was on Sarah's phone.

'Good heavens, Sarah, why on earth would you be showing Pat that?'

Sarah looked down at the picture. 'I just wanted to know if it jogged any thoughts.'

'Poor Pat, that's all she needs.' Daphne hovered over the old lady, still thumping her back.

'Daphne, you'll bruise her, and you might even dislocate something,' Sarah said. 'You can't really choke on soup, it's not solid enough. Pat, how are you feeling?'

'Not as good as before you got here,' Pat said succinctly.

Sarah sighed. 'I'm very sorry. I just thought you might have some ideas about what happened to Gus. If you do, then that would be incredibly helpful.'

'And what are you, the police?' said Pat, turning her face, still red and very cross, to Sarah.

'I don't know why you would take a photo like that in the first place,' said Daphne.

'He was poking his nose in where it didn't belong, was Gus,' said Pat hoarsely. 'Just like you are, now. Wouldn't you say so, Daph?'

Daphne sat down heavily and started twisting her napkin in her hands. 'To tell you the truth, Sarah, I'm beginning to wonder if all this is a good idea. Mari has already told us to drop it. What good can it really do, ferreting around?'

Sarah looked at her friend in surprise. 'But you've got more reason than anyone to find out what happened to Gus. After all, someone dumped him in your hut. Someone wanted you to take the blame.'

'But everyone knows I'd never hurt a soul. And they respect my work with the Beyond...' Daphne said fiercely. 'Oh dear, soup gone down the wrong way again, Pat?'

Pat covered up a snort by pretending to blow her nose. 'Here, take these, love,' she said to Daphne, passing her the empty bowls. Sarah couldn't help staring. Pat's hands had the tell-tale swelling around the joints that betokened arthritis. But they looked large and capable. Strong enough to stuff a dead body into a trunk?

'To go back to Gus...' she said, somewhat tentatively. 'You knew him well, Pat. He was a joker, he had a temper. Anything else?'

'Oh, he was a nice enough youngster, despite what he put my Bill through,' said Pat, though the man in Sarah's photograph had to be well over sixty. 'Fell on hard times at the end, though.'

'Why was that?' Sarah asked.

'Usual story, round here. Got on the wrong side of the powers that be, I reckon.'

'Oh, you mean that business with the brewery, and the other pub, the Ship and Billet, is it?'

'The Ship and Anchor,' Daphne rushed in. 'Terrible lot, they are. Incomers, you know.'

'Oh, how long have they been here?' asked Sarah, now a Merstairs veteran of a few days.

'About twenty-five years, I suppose,' said Pat, and Daphne nodded, topping up everyone's glasses.

Sarah digested that thoughtfully. She'd already started feeling quite a fixture – but now it seemed it would probably be at least half a century before any locals shared the sentiment.

'That wasn't really the trouble, though. It was when Gus tried to squeeze the brewery,' said Pat, shaking her head. 'He used to tell us regulars about it. Wanted to knock money off the price of the kegs he bought. Them corporate bigwigs weren't having it, were they? Even said he'd have to get his beer else-where. But that weren't his biggest problem.'

'Wasn't it?' asked Sarah. She only had the haziest idea of how pubs worked. She knew some were 'free houses', which meant they weren't affiliated to a brewery. The Jolly Roger seemed to be a tied pub, from what Pat was saying, meaning it got all its beer from a particular brewer. Maybe she needed to have a word with them, whoever they were?

Meanwhile, Pat was shaking her head meaningfully. 'Oooh no. No, no. That weren't what did for Gus. You mark my words.'

'Well, then,' said Sarah, wondering if she was finally getting somewhere. 'What on earth was it?'

Now Pat looked around, and lowered her voice. It was somewhat ridiculous, as they were sitting in Daphne's kitchen, with Hamish the only other potential witness. And he was hardly going to talk. But Daphne and Sarah leant in obligingly. When Pat did speak again, it was in a hoarse whisper.

'Ask the Crazy Golf gang.'

'Who on earth are they?' Sarah said.

Pat looked at her with a strange gleam in her eye. 'Only the roughest, toughest group in town. Desperados, some say. You don't want to mess with them, girlie. Believe me, some that do – well, put it this way, they don't hang around after to tell the tale,' she said. Then she leant back in her chair and gave an almighty, spine-tingling cackle.

TWENTY-ONE

The next morning saw Sarah shoving books onto bookshelves in her sitting room in a rather abstracted way, while thinking about the night before. Pat's bombshell about the Crazy Golf gang had shaken her a bit, especially as the old lady had got up and left immediately afterwards, as though the hounds of hell were after her. It had all been quite uncanny.

Sarah was also worried about Daphne. She had been cross with her about the photo business. She was a little ashamed of herself for showing it to the old lady – but at the time she'd felt justified. Daphne had actually known Gus Trubshaw, though. She must feel the full sadness of his loss in a way that Sarah didn't, as she'd never laid eyes on the man in life.

If Sarah was going to do what she was itching to get on with – find out more about the Crazy Golf gang – she could do with some company, she decided. Hamish, currently curled up in his basket and looking askance at her efforts to tidy the books away, was not big or scary enough to deter a hardened gang of potential criminals, if that's what this golf lot really were. Of course, Pat might just be deluded. But Sarah had heard from Pat and others that Gus was always banning people from his pub –

could he have done this with one of the gang members, perhaps? If so, could killing him have been revenge for that slight? She had so many questions – and all the answers might be at the course, which her map of Merstairs showed her was just a little further along the promenade from the Beach Café.

Sarah slotted another volume into the bookshelves, then she washed her dusty hands and addressed her dog. 'Well, come on then, Hamish boy. It's about time we gave you a walk. And if it involves picking up Daphne and then moseying to the crazy golf course, then so be it.'

Sarah had Hamish at the word 'walk', and he came bounding over to give her the reward she richly deserved.

'All right, boy, enough of that. Let's get your lead,' she said, fending off the little black ball of licks and picking up her handbag. As she locked the front door, she was hoping against hope that Daphne would be in, and that they could get over their difficulties of last night.

Things couldn't have turned out better. Sarah and Hamish were just strolling down their path when there was a deafening call of 'Coo-ee' from across the way. It was Daphne, resplendent in a red scarf and pink linen trousers, flapping in the breeze coming off the sea.

One of the loveliest things about Daphne was that she never held a grudge. Ancient spats at school, the occasional disagreement about parenting styles, even Sarah's misgivings about the whole Tarot business, and Daphne floated above them like a cloud on high. Today was no different. She greeted Sarah and Hamish like long-lost friends, not neighbours she'd had a bit of a tussle with the night before. But Sarah didn't want to let things lie, if Daphne was secretly harbouring any resentment.

'Are you OK now about me showing that photo to Pat?' she asked, coming right out with it.

'Well, I suppose I am, if you're OK about never showing it to me or anyone else again.'

At this, Sarah did have to think for a second. 'Well... I'll do my best. Unless it's absolutely essential for my investigation.'

'*Your* investigation, now is it?' said Daphne, her hairdo wobbling perilously. 'Wait until I tell Mari!'

Sarah turned to her. 'Well, that was probably the wrong word... I meant enquiry... Oh, I don't know what I meant,' she said, her shoulders sagging. Maybe she just wasn't cut out for all this?

Immediately, she was engulfed in one of Daphne's epic hugs. 'Don't be silly, Sarah. I won't say a word. I know you're just doing it because you like a puzzle... You always had your head in a crossword at school. And honestly, anything that keeps your mind off all the Peter business is just what you need right now.'

Sarah was glad Daphne wasn't going to inform on her to Mari. But she was a little stung too. Peter's death wasn't an inconvenient mess that she could brush over by doing a couple of sudokus. Grief was a complex thing, and people who ignored it or minimised its importance often found it coming back to bite them.

That wasn't to say she was keen to wallow, either, however much she'd loved Peter. But this was too much to say to Daphne. She was so well-meaning, and her own marriage to a total scoundrel had been more or less over before the ink dried on the certificate. So Sarah sank into the hug, and even patted Daphne a few times on the back, before gently disengaging herself.

'There's one thing I must admit I'm worried about,' Daphne said as they started walking again. 'I didn't tell you straight away that yes, I've occasionally helped out with the Scouts. But you don't really suspect me, do you?'

'Daphne, come on. How many years have we known each other? Wait, don't answer that! The point is, you may be many things, Daph, but you're not a killer.'

Daphne showed her relief with one of those huge laughs that shook her from her sandals – not slippers today, thank goodness – to her scarf. She took her friend's arm more firmly and they marched off along the costal path to Merstairs. The little town was almost shimmering in front of them today in the bright morning sun. 'Looks like it's going to be another lovely day in paradise. Where are we off to, then?'

'I was thinking... the crazy golf,' said Sarah blithely.

Daphne immediately dug her heels in, dragging Sarah to a stop. That left Hamish plunging on ahead and then whipping around in comical surprise. What on earth was his owner up to today, was his transparent thought. This wasn't going to get them nearer to the beach, where all the interesting smells were.

Sarah looked at the little dog in apology and then turned to Daphne. 'What's the problem?'

'You did hear what Pat said last night? About the... gang?'

'Yes. That's why I want to go and see the place. Don't you think it's an ideal spot to ask some questions?'

For once, Daphne was silenced. Then she pursed her lips, adjusted her hairdo, and finally said a very definite, 'No.'

'No?' repeated Sarah. 'Why ever not? We really need to get on and find out what's going on with all this... if Gus fell foul of the golfers for some reason. The way Pat was talking about them made them seem so sinister.'

They walked on a little, with Daphne staying quiet, then something struck Sarah. 'Haven't you heard about these golfers before now? You've lived in Merstairs forever,' she added, still a little stung by last night's revelation that she was apparently going to be classed as an interloper for a few decades to come.

'Yes, of course I've heard the rumours. But I've made a point of not getting involved. You know me, Sarah, I like to keep a low profile,' Daphne said, almost being propelled along now by the breeze catching her pink linen trousers. 'Besides, I'm sure they aren't the sort of people who believe in the Beyond. All the more reason for us not to be troubling them,' she said firmly. 'We should leave it all to the police.'

'To your Mariella, you mean?' Sarah said cunningly. If Daphne really thought the golfers were bad'uns, the last thing she'd want would be for her daughter to be lumbered with investigating them.

'Oh well, I suppose I was hoping those big constables would deal with them... I wouldn't want Mariella to get involved. Maybe you're right,' Daphne said in an uncharacteristically tentative voice. 'It probably won't do too much harm if we just pop round and see what's what.' With that, Daphne grabbed Sarah's arm again, but this time it felt as though she was doing it for reassurance.

They walked without talking for a while, passing Marlene's Plaice, Charles Diggory's antiques shop and the Jolly Roger bar. Sarah was already growing familiar with the sights and smells of Merstairs, the tangy ozone in the air and the cries of the gulls. It was another gorgeous spring day, the breeze ruffling daffodils in big tubs along the seafront. They really did look as though they were dancing, reminding Sarah of the Wordsworth poem she and Daphne had laboured to memorise at school all those years ago.

It was a day for new beginnings, for fresh resolutions – and for a moment Sarah was sorry that they were having to spend it digging into a rather unsavoury business. But passing the row of beach huts, including Daphne's dilapidated stripy number, reminded Sarah forcibly that only a few days ago it had harboured poor dead Gus Trubshaw. It was a horrible thought. Anyone who could stuff a body into a beach hut so near to innocent families taking their much-needed annual holidays had to be rooted out quickly, for the good of the community.

'Has Mariella heard anything about the inquest on Gus Trubshaw?' Sarah asked. The inquest was always an important stage in an investigation. Sarah had often had to give evidence at coroners' courts, reporting on her findings when a death might be suspicious.

'You know, she's not supposed to tell me anything.' Daphne squeezed Sarah's arm. 'But just entre nous,' she said, at her usual full volume, 'she's getting a bit fed up. The trouble is that the coroner is swamped. Merstairs does have quite a large *elderly* population, you know,' she said, in a way that made it clear she was not part of that group. 'Old dears dropping off their perches keep them very busy.'

'They ought to at least open and then adjourn the inquest, that will help the police move on with their investigation,' Sarah said. And then, she hoped, they could get a few more titbits of information from Mari.

'Tell me about it,' said Daphne, but her tone had that airiness that suggested she hadn't really considered the implications. She was only annoyed because her daughter was put out.

Sarah, realising with a sinking feeling she really was going to have to get on and make other arrangements for poor Peter's clothes, as the hut was likely to be out of bounds for some time, did sympathise with Daphne. She had a lot on her plate, what with the Tarot and Tealeaves shop and her many clubs and activities. And putting pressure on the police to hurry up with the crime scene would be difficult, in her position, as her daughter was amongst their number.

'Maybe I should take up your suggestion and ask Charles Diggory if he would, erm, have Peter's things,' Sarah said slowly.

'To sell, you mean? Oh, I think that would be very positive. Mind out now,' said Daphne, as they crossed over the road to the beach and walked the few steps down. Sarah immediately took off her sandals, but Daphne ploughed on, apparently unbothered by the clods of sand working their way into her shoes.

'Besides, that way, you can do loads more flirting with

Charles,' said Daphne over her shoulder as she plodded efficiently over the beach, which was still damp from the morning
tide.

'What? Flirting? I haven't been doing any flirting at all with
Charles,' said Sarah. Her voice was somewhat shrill – but she
put that down to the difficulties of walking over the wet sand.
Maybe it also explained her hot cheeks and generally flustered
air.

'Oh, whatever. You'll be the only one who hasn't, then,'
Daphne said cheerfully.

'How much further is this crazy golf place anyway?' Sarah
asked tersely.

'Yes, change the subject, that's a good idea,' said Daphne.
'It's just past the Beach Café. Want to go in and grab a tea first?'

Sarah noted Daphne's hopeful tone, and couldn't deny that
she too would like to put off the crazy golf encounter. Pat had
made it all sound so threatening, somehow. But it was a bit like
sticking plaster – better to rip it off quickly. Deal with the tricky
stuff straight away. That had always been Sarah's strategy, and
retirement – and a frisson of fear – weren't going to change
things now.

'Let's have a lovely tea afterwards,' she said firmly, over-
taking Daphne now and ploughing on through the sand, which
was furrowed with ripples from the vanished tide. Walking over
the lumps and bumps in her bare feet was giving her calf
muscles quite a workout.

Beyond the beach hut, the sands stretched out for a
distance, until they came to a little brick enclosure, right up
against the sea wall. It looked as though the tide never reached
this far, as the sand was warm and powdery and beautifully
white. Within the closed-off area was a nine-hole mini-golf
course, complete with a motley selection of famous and not so
famous landmarks – or rather, slightly wonky small-scale rendi-
tions of them.

Sarah could see the Taj Mahal, the Eiffel Tower, a Dutch windmill and Big Ben for starters, all with holes worked in at their bases. There was also a castle, with Cinderella escaping in her pumpkin coach, and a pyramid poking up into the blue Merstairs sky. But, although the models were charming, they were all a bit weather-beaten. The pyramid was a few blocks short, the windmill was missing a sail, and Cinderella's paint was so worn that she looked like she'd had a very hard night on the tiles. Considering most of the rest of Merstairs – with the exception of Daphne's beach hut and her shop – looked as though it got a fresh coat of Dulux every morning, the crazy golf course was decidedly down at heel.

And it was deserted. While the beach was busy, despite the early hour, and the café was doing a roaring trade as usual, not a single punter was playing crazy golf. There was no one in the little ticket booth either, so even if Daphne and Sarah had wanted to have a go, they wouldn't have known where to start. They stood looking at each other blankly, each willing the other to have a brainwave – which was stubbornly not appearing.

'Maybe the owners are on holiday?' Daphne ventured eventually.

'Right at the beginning of the season here?' Sarah shrugged. 'It seems like a funny time to be away.'

'OK, OK, don't have a go at me about it,' said Daphne grumpily. 'I'm just making helpful suggestions.'

Sarah, who rather took issue with the word 'helpful', wisely maintained her silence. Instead, she started having a closer look around the course.

'Are you searching for clues?' Daphne said excitedly, as usual her voice ringing out loud and clear.

All of a sudden, another voice chimed in, sounding not so much excited as infuriated. 'Clues to what, exactly?'

Sarah looked all around in a comic double-take, while even Daphne appeared baffled. Then, just as they were beginning to think the crazy golf course itself had somehow spoken, a small figure emerged from behind the pyramid.

It was a thin little old lady, tiny and as wizened as a dry leaf. She was directing a suspicious but clear-eyed gaze towards Sarah. 'You heard me, love. What clues? Not trying to pin it on us, are you?'

'Um, pin what, exactly?' asked Sarah, playing for time. She was pretty sure what the elephant in the room must be, if a gaudy orange and pink striped hut could be described that way.

'Like that, is it? Look, do you want tickets or not? I've got stuff to be getting on with.'

Immediately Sarah wondered what on earth the old lady had been doing behind the pyramid. Had she been hiding something? Playing a round of crazy golf would give them the perfect excuse to have a proper look. 'Two entries, please,' she said, proffering her bank card.

The woman sniffed, and shuffled over to the ticket office, going through the rigmarole of opening it up and establishing herself inside it before she would take the payment. Meanwhile, Daphne was shifting from foot to foot.

'Do we really have to do this?' she said in a perfectly audible stage whisper to Sarah. 'I really think we'd be better placed chatting at the café, for instance...'

'You can do that after, love,' said the grumpy woman, handing over two tickets to Sarah. 'After you've had *lots* of fun playing golf, that is.'

Was it just Sarah, or was there something in the old woman's tone that sounded distinctly ominous?

TWENTY-TWO

'All right then, Ma, get on with you and put the kettle on,' said a cheery voice as a beaming middle-aged woman breezed onto the crazy golf course. Immediately, the old woman retreated, with a mischievous smile at Sarah and Daphne over her shoulder.

'I hope you didn't listen to any of my mother's nonsense. She gets some funny ideas in her head these days,' said the woman, presenting them with a putter and a handful of neon-coloured golf balls each. 'The colour's so's you don't lose them, see? They stand out nicely, they do. Bit like your trews,' she added to Daphne, who preened a little and stroked the vibrant pink linen.

'So, you start over there by Cinderella, go round her castle, and then follow on up to the pyramid, off to the Eye-ful Tower and over to Amsterdam. You'll soon get the idea,' she said. 'Fancy a tea to take round with you?'

'Now you're talking,' said Daphne with one of her laughs, and a few minutes later they were teeing off at the castle, balancing their takeaway cups somewhat precariously on the turreted ramparts. Daphne took the first swing, only for her ball to fly right out of the crazy golf compound. She stomped off miserably to retrieve it from the beach, while Sarah and Hamish sat on top of Cinderella's sturdy pumpkin coach, which had been warmed nicely by the sun. Sarah closed her eyes and felt the rays beating down. If it hadn't been for the whole murder business, this would have been a very pleasant way of whiling away a morning. As it was, she had the nagging feeling that she should be cross-questioning the Crazy Golf gang, seeing if any of them were barred from the Jolly Roger by Gus – but she couldn't do that if they weren't around, could she? A shadow fell across her and she opened her eyes abruptly, but it was only Daphne, hot and sandy but clutching the bright pink ball in her hand.

'I suppose we'd better get on then,' her friend said, taking another swing at the ball – with exactly the same result. This time she threw her club down in disgust, before seeming to consider for a moment. 'Hamish, you wouldn't fetch that ball for me, would you?' Daphne asked, pointing hopefully into the distance.

Sarah was about to veto this idea, because if Hamish got that far away onto the beach, he might never bring himself back. But luckily Hamish was already wise to Daphne's ways, and was gazing at her, head on one side, as though he'd never heard the English language before. Daphne harumphed and went on her reluctant way, leaving Sarah to give Hamish's ears a quick stroke and whisper, 'Good boy,' to him.

When she looked up, she got rather a surprise. The crazy golf course had been deserted all this time, apart from the three of them. But now she spotted a cluster of figures sitting along the far edge of the boundary, closest to the sea wall. Although the sun was doing its best to mitigate the effects of the spring breeze, she suddenly felt a chill. Was this – could this be – the Crazy Golf gang at last?

At this distance, they looked pretty menacing – a group of

men who were all preternaturally silent and still, and seemed to be gazing in strange unison right at her.

Well, thought Sarah, swinging her golf club. She'd just have to see about that. 'Come on, then, Hamish,' she said as brightly as she could to the dog. 'Let's go and have a quick word with those people.'

From the way Hamish stayed sitting, she judged he was thinking better of her plan. But it was now or never. Daphne was bound to get back from her second search for her ball soon, and she wasn't always the most tactful presence to have by one's side during an interrogation. This was Sarah's chance to get a bit further on, and she wasn't going to let it slip by... even if she was a bit scared.

With a final swig of her tea for good luck, and clutching her golf club hard, Sarah got up from Cinderella's coach and made her way past the windmill, the Taj Mahal, the pyramid and a strange structure that could have been a large set of rotting dentures but was more likely to be an unsuccessful rendition of Stonehenge.

The closer she got to the little group sitting on the wall, the more she could see what a motley collection of men they were. All different shapes and sizes were catered for, but they seemed to have a uniform pinkish shade to their skin – not quite on a par with Daphne's trousers or the golf ball, but still a few shades darker than normal Anglo-Saxon pallor. Were they all full of red-hot fury, did they have blood pressure problems – or was it due to sitting on that wall, exposed to the Merstairs sun all day?

It didn't do to let the enemy see your weakness, so she did her best to consciously relax, loosening her grasp on the club and letting Hamish scamper across on his own to carry out his usual elaborate meet-and-greet routine. By the time she'd caught up with him, he was somewhat overdoing it – lying flat out on the sand, wriggling ecstatically, and having his tummy tickled by at least two people.

'Hello there,' she said, trying to sound as friendly as possible. The ticklers immediately withdrew, and she stiffened, wondering what was going to come next. Threats? Violence? But, instead of macho swagger and outright hostility, she found herself confronting six glum-looking, rather weedy chaps, all looking far more hangdog than Hamish caught stealing sausages. For a second she was confused, then relief washed over her. Perhaps this wasn't going to be as terrifying as she'd thought.

'Are you having some sort of a meeting? Mind if I join you?' she said. Without waiting for an answer she plonked herself on the wall at the end of the line. 'Nice to meet you all. I'm Sarah,' she said, stretching out a hand towards the nearest man.

He looked at it in consternation, before shaking it limply. It was one of the weakest handshakes Sarah had ever encountered, like pressing the fin of a dead fish.

'Um,' she said, trying to regroup. 'What are we all up to here? A discussion or something, is it?'

There was silence as the men all looked at each other, then eventually one spoke up. 'It's our session, yes.'

'Ooh, a session. Of what, I wonder?' said Sarah, injecting lots of bonhomie into her tone. Sometimes, with nervous patients, this fake cheeriness served to soothe their jitters. On other occasions, of course, it failed dismally. There was a second short silence and Sarah began to accept she was going to get no further. But then the man in the middle spoke up again.

'We're the Merstairs Men's Movement,' he said, with tentative but unmistakable pride.

'Oh,' said Sarah. 'Not the Craz oops, I see. You're a *men's group*.'

'Yes. We meet as often as we can. We find it... beneficial.' He sounded defensive, as though expecting Sarah to ban him immediately from attempting any such thing again.

She tried to sound as encouraging as she could. 'There's

nothing like getting together, is there? A problem shared is a problem halved, that's what I always say!'

'So few people understand,' said the same chap. He seemed to be the official spokesman. 'It's difficult, these days... there are so many strong, er, people, in Merstairs. So many feisty, powerful, um, folk. So we use the group to uplift each other, you know.'

It was true that, so far, Sarah had met a lot of quirky and forthright ladies – and only one man who looked capable of standing up for himself. For a second she remembered Charles Diggory's blue eyes, then shook the thought away.

'Your group sounds like a great idea,' she said enthusiastically. 'I'm Sarah,' she prompted, and as she'd hoped the leader then introduced himself.

'Dave. Dave Cartwright,' he said. 'And these are the boys.'

Sarah nodded to them. But the name Cartwright was ringing a bell. 'You're not related to Albie Cartwright, are you? He works at the Jolly Roger.'

Immediately Dave frowned. 'That's my son,' he said. 'Stepped in to help out when the owner disappeared, didn't he? Favour to his uncle Trev, my wife's brother. Always been close, they have.' He rubbed his hand across his face. 'Albie was such a good little boy. Been nothing but trouble, recently, though. Graffiti, first of all. Such an embarrassment,' Dave shook his head. 'He had to do community service for that. And that's not the worst of it.'

'It's not fair, what they've said about him, though,' piped up the chubby man on the end of the row. 'That new police girl, the redhead, she was casting all sorts of nasturtiums.'

Sarah pondered this for a moment. So Daphne's Mariella was suggesting Albie had been up to something illegal? 'How awful,' she said, manufacturing a concerned look. 'What did he – I mean, what did she *say* he'd done?'

'Drugs.' Dave shook his head. 'But my boy wouldn't stoop

that low. We haven't seen eye to eye for years but that's out of order.' He thumped his fist down on the wall and the rest of the men muttered their approval. 'I've got a good mind to prosecute her, blackening our good name like that.'

Sarah, meanwhile, thought back to her encounter with Albie and the way he'd hung around the group of young men. She'd even seen some sort of transaction take place. A pub was probably an ideal place to work if you were a small-time drug dealer. But there seemed little mileage in countering Dave's version of events. She decided to change the subject instead.

'At least he's got a steady job at the Jolly Roger.'

'Yeah. He's always loved his Uncle Trev. Trev used to help him with his stamp collection when he was small. Albie gets on much better with him than the rest of the family, truth be told. Fallen out with every single one of us over the years, that boy has. Even his mum. And he wasn't a big fan of Gus, neither.'

'Really?' Sarah said, storing the information away. 'Well, it's great that he's there for Trevor, it's such a difficult time for the poor man.' Then an idea struck her. 'Tell me, was Gus in your group?'

Just as she had got to this interesting point, with the leader of the group obviously trembling on the verge of saying something potentially fascinating, there was an almighty kerfuffle behind her and suddenly Daphne was upon them, spraying sand everywhere as she jumped onto the wall and set Hamish off in a volley of surprised barks.

The hiatus did give Sarah a bit of time to wonder why Daphne's friend Pat had led them to believe that the Crazy Golf gang was a sinister gathering of ne'er-do-wells. Far from being a criminal, Dave Cartwright seemed positively outraged at the idea of his son being labelled as a lawbreaker. Maybe it was all Pat's idea of a joke, perhaps she had some sort of bias against men's groups – or could it be some sort of revenge for being shown that picture of Gus? Sarah wouldn't put it past her.

'Look, found my ball,' Daphne boomed, waving it around in front of all and sundry. The men on the wall seemed to shrink into themselves. Daphne's glorious self-confidence was probably their worst nightmare.

'I was just asking whether Gus was in the men's group,' Sarah said, determined to keep things on track.

Dave Cartwright shook his head. Sarah thought that was all the answer she was going to get, but then he spoke again. 'Trevor joined. But Gus wasn't happy about it.'

'Really?' Sarah said. 'Did Gus, er, did he bar any of you from the pub?' The men just looked at her, as silent as half a dozen oysters sitting on the wall. She'd have to take that as a no. But could Gus's disapproval of Trevor joining the group have led to his murder?

'Maybe we should get back to our round,' said Daphne, already bored with the uncommunicative men.

'OK,' said Sarah, sensing she wouldn't get any more out of them now anyway. 'But I could leave Hamish here to have a little play, if that would be all right?' She felt rather sorry for the little group. Hamish always cheered her up, maybe he would work his magic on them.

There was some shy nodding at the idea. Sarah took Daphne's arm and, as they turned away, she could hear a big fuss being made of her little dog.

'What on earth was that about? Who is that bunch of weirdos?' Daphne said, craning round and scowling.

'That's the Crazy Golf gang we were warned about. Pat must have really enjoyed winding us up last night! She did have a rather odd look in her eye. Honestly. Can you believe it?' Sarah said, then she and Daphne both got the giggles as they started to play again. Sarah knew her own laughter was mostly relief, after a night worrying about the terrifying band of outlaws that had sounded like a Merstairs version of Hell's Angels. Instead, she'd met the kind of people who 'couldn't blow the skin off a rice pudding', in the words of her beloved late mother.

'You're not concentrating at all,' bellowed Daphne, who was now on the far side of the Taj Mahal, having achieved a triumphant hole in one at the pyramid. After her early wild shots, she really seemed to have got her eye in.

'Just... having a think. But you're right, I must focus,' said Sarah, taking a swipe at the ball but somehow still managing to miss it. This wouldn't do. She collected herself, stared hard at the ball, flexed the club in her hand – and shot it through the middle of the wobbly windmill until it landed with a satisfying thunk in the hole. That was more like it!

It was not for nothing that Sarah had managed a challenging career and brought up two children as well. Of course, she'd had Peter's unstinting support – and a network of carefully chosen nannies, childminders, schools and friends making sure that the many crises of family life were dealt with smoothly. Sarah knew she had a competitive streak. She always wanted to succeed if she could. That went all the way from crazy golf to this beach hut business. She wanted to see the matter solved, because it fitted her notions of justice for the poor victim – and because she enjoyed the satisfaction of working things out.

'That's more like it! That's the Sarah who trounced me every week at tennis,' Daphne said, without rancour, as Sarah rapidly putted her way through the remaining holes until they were neck and neck.

'Trust you to remember that,' said Sarah fondly, taking a swing she hoped would put her ahead, and on track to go first through the pièce de résistance of the course, a slightly tipsy rendition of the London Eye. But, as her ball bounced ahead towards its target, Hamish cocked his ears and barked excitedly. Clearly tiring of the men's group's attentions, he leapt forward and grabbed the ball in his mouth.

'Oh my goodness, I hope he hasn't hurt his teeth, that was going fast,' said Sarah, dashing to his side. But Hamish appeared to be none the worse for his feat, gripping the ball in jaws that seemed to be grinning widely. 'Drop,' said Sarah sternly, but all she got for her pains was a lot of excitable tail-wagging. To make matters even more infuriating, she could hear titters of laughter coming from the group sitting on the wall.

But then, as Daphne surged ahead to take her final hole, Sarah couldn't help seeing the humour of the situation. 'All right then, you win, Hamish,' she said, laughing and giving him a good pat, at which he immediately dropped the ball.

'Too late now, I've taken the championship,' crowed Daphne. 'First time that's happened since school.'

'All right, all right,' said Sarah good-naturedly. 'We might as well have an early lunch. It's on me,' she said. 'We can go to the Beach Café. Maybe Mavis will have a bit more information for us. And I wonder if the men's group will join us?'

She bumbled over the sand to ask the little huddle on the wall, but Dave seemed shocked at the idea, saying it would eat into their meeting time.

Sarah and Daphne gave in their clubs and balls at the ticket office, thanked the supervisor for a lovely game, and plodded through the soft sand to the Beach Café. There was no sign of the old lady who, thought Sarah, had actually been a lot more scary than the Crazy Golf gang.

Though maybe she was making a mistake, underestimating the men? Hadn't the notorious murderer Dr Crippen been a mild-mannered chap – who turned out to have buried his wife's body in his cellar?

TWENTY-THREE

Sarah spotted an empty table at the café and Daphne sat herself down with the happy sigh of one who had indulged in honest toil. As they were looking at the menu, Mavis came over with her notepad. 'Been down with the crazies, I see,' she remarked with a bit of a smirk.

'Oh yes, I suppose you can see from here,' said Sarah, looking over and spotting the tiny figures of the men still sitting on their wall, seemingly in the middle of earnest discussion. 'But they're hardly crazy, are they? They were rather nice, I thought.'

Mavis snorted. 'Didn't spend that much time with them, then, did you? Did they tell you about their plans for total segregation?'

'Segregation of what?' said Daphne, looking up from the menu and frowning.

'Men and women. They want to set up men's groups all over the region, for everything – choirs, sports, hobbies – you name it.'

Sarah couldn't help but laugh. 'Maybe the best thing would

be for them to try it. There might not be too much take-up –
most men quite like the company of the opposite sex.'

'You could be right. But still, I don't hold with them putting
silly ideas in folks' heads,' said Mavis more darkly.

'I've heard Gus Trubshaw wasn't in their group, but Trevor
was, is that right?' Sarah asked.

'Not for long. Gus wouldn't have it. He was a character –
but you couldn't cross him,' said Mavis. 'Now, what can I be
getting you today, ladies?'

'I'll just have one of your superfood salads,' said Daphne,
with the pursed lips of the deeply virtuous. 'With a side order of
chips, ooh and a large serving of your coleslaw... and you could
bring me some mayonnaise to go with that, too. And a large
Coke.'

'Diet Coke, is that?' said Mavis, scribbling furiously on
her pad.

'Of course not,' Daphne shot back. 'Those additives. No,
give me good old-fashioned plain Coke every time,' she said,
sitting back as though she'd headed off a major dietary disaster.

Mavis bit her lip and noted it all down diligently. 'Now, for
you?' she turned to Sarah.

'I'll have the mushroom omelette, please. And a side salad.
And you know what, I'll have the chips too.' She smiled as she
put the menu back on the table.

'Very good, ladies. With you in a couple of ticks.' Mavis
bustled off to put their order in.

'I could get rather used to this,' said Sarah, fishing in her bag
for her sunglasses and popping them on the bridge of her nose.
The sun was high in the sky now and, while it wasn't as warm as
yesterday, the weather was fresh and breezy, clouds scurrying
across the blue sky and whipping up the waves. After a
moment's thought, she loosened the straps on her sandals and
dug her toes into the sand. Bliss.

'This is the life,' agreed Daphne. She had her eyes shut, and her face tilted to the sun. Sarah decided to enjoy the moment, too. After checking Hamish was gainfully employed with his tennis ball under the table, she closed her own eyes, enjoying the feel of the sun caressing her lids.

Just then, the warmth abruptly stopped. Sarah snapped her eyes open, to see that a dark shape had come between her and the sun. For a second, it felt like her night terrors over the Crazy Golf gang again as the figure loomed closer. She shrank back in her seat.

Then a familiar voice said heartily, 'What's up, Sarah? You've gone white as a sheet. Everything OK?' It was the drawling tones of Charles Diggory.

'Oh, um, Charles. Didn't recognise you at first. The sun was in my eyes,' said Sarah hurriedly.

Charles looked at her quizzically. 'You two having a bit of a siesta? Odd place to choose, the middle of the Beach Café,' he said.

Daphne opened her eyes and sat up a bit. 'Just waiting for our lunch. Want to join us?'

Immediately Sarah sent her a quelling look, but it was too late. Charles was finding himself a chair and settling down at their table.

'Your food probably won't arrive at the same time as ours,' Sarah pointed out, then wondered why she was being so unfriendly. She rather liked Charles – or had done, until she'd met his wife. But all that was none of her business. No, it was really his involvement in beach hut ownership that troubled her, she decided. 'But it's nice of you to join us,' she added somewhat belatedly.

'Is it?' Charles raised his eyebrows. 'Well, it's a treat for me, that's for sure. I was having a very slow morning in the shop.'

From what she'd seen the other day, that didn't surprise Sarah one bit.

'Oh, that reminds me,' said Daphne. 'Sarah needs to talk to you about selling her husband's clothes.'

'Your husband's clothes?' Charles whipped round to Sarah.

'My *late* husband,' she clarified. 'But dealing with all that might be a bit premature... and in any case, we've got a lot on our plates at the moment.'

'Well, with what's going on in the beach hut, you won't be able to leave everything there for a bit. And you don't want it all cluttering the place up at home,' Daphne pointed out.

Inwardly Sarah smarted at the thought of poor Peter's things being considered 'clutter'.

Rationally, she knew she didn't need those boxes and had to let them go. But at the same time, they were all she had left of her beloved, and she couldn't help resenting his possessions being dismissed as junk to be dumped as quickly as possible.

Not for the first time, she felt grief rise up in her as a wave of irrational anger – partly against blameless Peter, who'd of course not wanted to die at all, but more especially against the ill fortune which had decreed this should happen.

And a little bit of Sarah's annoyance was reserved for Daphne who, she felt, really shouldn't have raised all this in front of a virtual stranger. She directed another cross look at her friend, but it was water off a particularly well-oiled duck's back.

'So that's settled then,' said Daphne, cheerfully oblivious, while Charles smiled at Sarah with sardonic amusement. She couldn't help it, she just couldn't sit there a second longer.

'I'm just going to...' she said. Hamish leapt to his feet too, but Daphne grabbed his lead.

'The loos are just round the back, Sarah,' she said, loudly and helpfully. 'Now, Charles, what are you going to order?'

TWENTY-FOUR

By the time Sarah returned, her uncharacteristic temper flare soothed by a few minutes of calm reflection and some of the deep breathing she'd often counselled her patients to try, their food had arrived. Her mushroom omelette looked delicious, and the kitchen had rustled up Charles's cheese and ham toastie in double-quick time so that he could eat with them. She sat back down, feeling a bit silly, and they all busied themselves with knives, forks and paper napkins.

Hamish, relieved to see his mistress restored to good spirits, but resigned to the fact that she was unlikely to drop him any treats, sidled up to Daphne as the likeliest soft touch. But he'd reckoned without her appetite. No one was getting between Daphne and her lunch today. Hamish settled himself on his paws and went to sleep instead.

'You know, I ought to be jolly cross with you for selling me that hut full of tat,' said Daphne, pointing a chip at Charles.

Charles put his hands up. 'Mea culpa. I know it's caused you endless trouble. But you do realise I didn't have the least idea what was in the blasted shack.'

'So, your wife passed it on to you. Do you think she knew?' Daphne asked.

'Ex... well, *estranged* wife, anyway,' said Charles ruefully, with a quick glance at Sarah. 'I mean, I rather hope not. Because obviously that would have quite a few implications. Francesca may be many things, but a murderess she is not,' he added with an air of finality.

'Well, they all say that, don't they?' Daphne said breezily, scooping up a large forkful of coleslaw.

'Do they?' Charles shrugged a little. 'I wouldn't know. I really have very little idea about murderers myself.'

'As far as you know,' said Sarah darkly, cutting a neat corner off her omelette.

'I must say, it's all a bit much,' said Daphne. 'I was telling Sarah when she arrived that there's no crime in Merstairs. And now this!'

'Perhaps Sarah brought it with her, from the big city,' said Charles lightly, his ice blue eyes holding hers in a way she found very disconcerting.

'I've hardly had time to infect the place, even if I'd wanted to,' she said. 'I've been here less than a week. And this is no joking matter. This is going to cast suspicion over so many people. Your wife... sorry, *estranged* wife, the scoutmaster man – not to mention Daphne.'

'Oh, no one thinks I did it,' Daphne insisted blithely. 'Well, not any more.'

Sarah wasn't so sure. It had certainly helped, when they'd been questioned, that Daphne was Mariella's mum. Twee-dledum and Tweedledee hadn't seemed aware of this before (despite the fairly large clues of hair colour and surname), but surely DI Blake wouldn't just let Daphne off because of who she was? It was probably better for her friend not to worry, though. And when Sarah found the culprit – as soon as she possibly could – Daphne's name would be officially clear.

'Anyway,' Daphne carried on. 'Don't forget the Merstairs Mermaids. We set off every day from just about where my hut is,' she mumbled, already deep in another chip.

'The Mermaids?' echoed Sarah. It was the first she'd heard of yet another of Daphne's tally of hobbies.

'I'm not sure they ever did store their kit in the hut, not while Francesca and I owned it. So maybe that gets them out of the frame?' Charles chipped in.

Daphne turned to Sarah. 'Phew. There's nothing like swimming in the sea. Although – is it really good for you, Sarah? I'd hate to be doing it for nothing,' she guffawed.

'Any exercise can be beneficial. As to the many claims made for sea bathing... they're hard to prove. But of course I'm all in favour of people giving it a try,' said Sarah, trying to do the subject justice.

Charles sat up a little. 'So, you're a... health professional?'

Sarah nodded. 'Yes, I'm a GP. Retired now.'

'Aha. You kept that quiet. Well, you will be an asset to the place, I'm sure,' he added with a little bow.

'Oh, Sarah never likes to tell people, in case they start showing her their rashes,' Daphne chortled.

Sarah smiled, but unfortunately, Daphne was quite right. There was nothing destined to get people banging on about their ailments – whether trivial or toe-curling – like the news that there was a doctor about the place. Sarah had often stood frozen to the spot at parties while people insisted on dragging her through the most gruesome symptoms.

'Well, I promise not to bring up my acid reflux, as it were,' Charles smiled broadly. 'Especially not at lunch. How is your omelette?'

Sarah, who'd just taken a big bite, had to chew frantically before she could reply. 'Delicious, thank you. I was just wondering, while we're talking about the hut... Francesca also seems to have stored her own things there.'

'Oh, I don't think so,' said Charles dismissively.

'What about the scarf I saw? I mentioned it to you and Mavis, remember?'

'Well, it was her hut... so leaving her things there doesn't mean she had anything to do with Gus's death. Obviously.'

'Hmm,' said Sarah.

'She might have been looking for something and then mislaid it. Maybe she was getting the ski equipment, for instance. She takes the grandchildren every year,' he elaborated.

'Oh, how lovely,' said Daphne. 'For Christmas?'

'No,' said Charles. 'We, er she, prefers the February half term. Bit less busy in Courchevel.'

'So she would have been away... all that week?'

'Two weeks, in fact. We, er she, always goes then. Great snow.'

'You went too, did you?' Daphne asked innocently, while Charles turned a shade of brick red.

'Well, hard for her to handle the grandkids on their own, you know. Just helping out,' he said, playing with his knife and refusing to meet anyone's eyes.

Sarah inwardly digested this news. It sounded as though both Francesca and Charles were out of the frame for murder. She should have been glad – she was certainly whittling down her list of suspects. But she wasn't at all sure elation was the emotion she was feeling. Charles had been most insistent that his marriage was over – yet it really didn't look that way from where she was sitting.

'Penny for them,' said Daphne, who'd finally worked her way round to her superfood salad, and was picking through it as daintily as any model.

'Oh, just thinking how lovely it is here,' Sarah said quickly. 'Apart from the murder, of course. The sooner we clear that up, the sooner all the unpleasantness will be over,' she added.

'Still fancying yourself as a sleuth, are you?' said Charles, finally looking her in the eye.

'Not at all,' Sarah said. It wasn't entirely truthful – but then it seemed Charles hadn't been honest with her either. 'I just know that Mariella, Daphne's daughter, you know, is over-stretched... anything I can do on a practical level might be useful.'

'But Sarah, don't you realise?' Charles started, then tailed off. 'Well, perhaps it's not for me to say.'

'No, go on.'

'It's just, well... it could be very dangerous, what you're doing. There's someone around here who has a secret they really don't want told. Don't you think you're putting yourself in harm's way?'

Sarah felt a chill, despite the gathering warmth of the day. She'd been treating this whole Merstairs mystery like a diag-nostic puzzle. But Charles was right. The stakes were a lot higher.

'Oh, Hamish will protect me,' she said lightly, partly to diffuse her own sudden tension. Under the table, Hamish raised one sleepy eye, gave a single, rather unenthusiastic bark, then lapsed back into slumber. They all laughed – but Sarah felt as though someone had walked over her grave. Once Daphne had returned her attention to her plate, Charles gave Sarah a long, serious look. She avoided his eyes, but, at the same time, she was thinking hard.

What would Peter say, if he could see what she was doing? She knew immediately, as though hearing his voice. *Are you serious, Sarah? Do you always have to sort the whole world out?* But then he'd add, *Well, if that's what you want to do, of course you should.*

For a second, her eyes misted over. Peter wasn't around any more to give her that unconditional support. But he'd always had faith in her judgement and her instinct to help others. He'd want her to continue. She took a breath and looked up. Charles was still staring at her, but with a slight smile now. Daphne had relented and was sneaking one of her last chips to Hamish, who seemed to be liking her better by the second. And Sarah? Well, she was resolved. Whatever the personal cost, she was in this deep. She intended to continue, right to the very end – whatever that might mean.

Though, as she thought later, if she'd known what was about to happen the next morning, she might not have been so keen to solve the Merstairs mystery at all.

TWENTY-FIVE

Sarah slept badly, realising halfway through the night that, if Charles and Francesca Diggory were no longer suspects, as they'd been on a cozy holiday together during the crucial time when the newspaper (and Gus) found their way into the trunk in February, then Bill Turbot was probably now the most likely suspect.

She'd heard from multiple sources that Bill had been banned from the Jolly Roger by Gus, whose sense of humour disguised a hair-trigger temper. Bill was the type of man whose swagger and predatory ways with the ladies hid a fragile sense of self-esteem. She'd seen this for herself when he'd made a beeline for her in the pub, and then swerved away at a moment's notice and gone to sulk in a corner when knocked off course. He would, surely, have been furious that Gus had publicly humiliated him by throwing him out of his favourite bar. Revenge could easily have been the next logical step.

There was also the fact that so many of Sarah's suspects had now fallen by the wayside. The Mermaids were out, as they hadn't used the hut during the period in question. The Tai Chi group had been having a break. The Crazy Gang were not crazy at all in person.

No, there was only one outstanding candidate for the job of Merstairs murderer – and it was Bill Turbot.

Having come to this conclusion in the early hours, Sarah couldn't get back to sleep. Her next problem was what to do about her hunch. Eventually, she decided she would tackle the scoutmaster in the Jolly Roger, as he seemed to spend large portions of his day there. She'd take her phone, ask him some pertinent questions, record the answers and play it all back for Mariella.

Then she wondered if she should just confide her suspicions directly to Mariella instead. Would Mariella take her seriously, though? She'd told her mother she didn't want amateurs meddling – and Sarah had nothing more than a hunch to go on.

No, her best bet was to confront Bill, and to do that, she had to wait for official opening time at the pub. But, by the time she'd come to this conclusion, Sarah was wide awake.

At 6 a.m., after tossing and turning for what felt like hours, she gave up the attempt to go back to sleep. There was nothing for it but to get up and out. Hopefully a good long walk would help clear her mind, get ready for the ordeal ahead – and give her time to concoct some clever questions.

* * *

Twenty minutes later, a hastily dressed Sarah and a rather surprised Hamish were toiling up the coastal road to the beach. Dawn had already broken but the sky was still streaked with fingers of pink and orange, and there were wisps of cloud hanging in the sky. The sea was as restless as Sarah was, as the breeze ruffled through her hair and wafted away the certainties of the night. Was it really going to be a good idea to confront Turbot? She remembered what Charles Diggory had said only yesterday about killers. Even in the crowded pub, could the scoutmaster somehow get the better of her? She shivered in her warm cardigan.

'Oh well, boy,' she said to Hamish as they skirted the long row of beach huts. 'We don't really have any choice, do we? Bill Turbot is just about the only person left on our list, so we must talk to him if we can. We'll go home now, and find him at the Jolly Roger later.'

Sarah was just turning back, enjoying a last look at the glorious reflection of the streaky sky and passing clouds in the pools of seawater left by the tide, when she came to a sudden halt. She'd caught sight of something sticking out beyond the last beach hut in the row, not far from Daphne's stripy monstrosity.

It looked like – but surely couldn't be – a foot.

TWENTY-SIX

Sarah edged carefully round the beach hut, clutching Hamish's lead tightly. Her heart was beating fast, and she was preternaturally aware of the sudden silence all around her. Even the gulls wheeling above them seemed to have stopped screeching.

The blood was pounding in her ears as she finally got to the front of the hut, and took in the full horror of the sight before her.

A man was lying flat out on the beach, not far from the lapping waves. His arms and legs were spread and he was in full Scouts uniform. His stomach rose up in a solid mound, making him look absurdly as though he had just eaten a giant Easter egg.

It could only be one person. Bill Turbot.

She shook her head in disbelief, and then ran forward. There might still be something she could do. His spindly legs, below his khaki shorts, looked curiously vulnerable. For a second she was worried about him catching his death of cold – but as she approached it was clear it was far too late for that.

Now that she was within spitting distance of the man, she could clearly see the cause of death. Around his neck was the traditional Scout neckerchief. Its ends had been fed through a knotted ring of leather – a woggle. Sarah remembered making a feeble joke about them in the Jolly Roger the other day. But this wasn't funny at all. The neckerchief had been pulled tight. Much, much too tight for poor old Bill Turbot, whose scarlet face, staring eyes and lolling tongue all proclaimed he had died from strangulation.

Sarah stepped back. Bill Turbot was not a pretty sight. But then, she reasoned, he hadn't really been in life, either. And death so rarely brought out people's best side. She got out her phone and rang 999 – but she killed the call as she saw a figure approaching at speed, with familiar red hair standing out proudly against the grey morning skies. It was Mariella, looking extremely sombre.

'So, you already know about Bill Turbot?' Sarah said.

'I do,' said Mariella, her face shuttered. 'The question is, what on earth are you doing here, Aunty Sarah?'

'Hamish wanted an early walk,' Sarah said, feeling as though she'd somehow been caught red-handed. 'I was just ringing the police when I saw you.'

Mariella looked at her sternly for a moment longer, then smiled. 'Don't worry, we were alerted by a dog-walker – someone up even earlier than you. He's being questioned over there.'

Sarah looked where Mariella was pointing, and spotted a man with a large Labrador talking to DI Blake. Phew, she felt as though she'd been let off the hook. 'I suppose you'll have already called the pathologist,' she said.

Mariella nodded. 'Dr Burns can't make it today, so it's Dr Strutton, but she's been delayed.'

'What a shame. It's so important to get on with the examination, isn't it?' Sarah fixed her gaze on the corpse. 'Still, at least there's not much doubt about the cause of death.'

Mariella seemed to wrestle with herself for a moment. But

in the end curiosity won out. 'I really shouldn't be asking you this… and well, you shouldn't even be here. But since you are – any ideas about a timeframe?'

'Well, I won't touch the body, of course,' she said before Mariella could even mention this massive no-no. 'But judging by the look of him, I really don't think he's been there long.'

'Would he have been killed right on the spot, would you say?' said Mariella, stepping closer to the corpse and gesturing to Sarah to join her, forgetting her earlier animosity in a way that reminded Sarah strongly of her friend. Daphne's emotions flowed strongly but fast, and the temper of a moment could be blown away in seconds if a more pressing impulse came along.

Sarah took a good look, from a distance of a couple of feet. She squatted down – ignoring her creaking knees – and scrutinised the man's complexion and extremities as carefully as she could, before venturing an opinion.

'It's difficult to tell without moving the body – which obviously I'm not going to do – but from what I can see, it looks like he was killed here. If I could touch him, I could determine whether rigor mortis has set in or not. But without doing that, I can see there's no lividity around the underside of his neck or legs, which is one of the first places we'd be able to spot it – as you'll know, the blood starts to pool in the tissues after death, sinking downwards thanks to gravity. A sort of distinctive marbled pattern gradually begins to develop in the lowest areas. There's none of that, suggesting death was recent and in situ. Also, and this isn't a medical view but a practical one, you can see that the sand and pebbles in the area have been disturbed, as though there's been a violent altercation of some kind.'

Sarah straightened herself up, rubbing her kneecaps unobtrusively, and pointed to the markings etched on Merstairs beach. It looked almost as though Bill Turbot had been trying to make a 'snow angel' shape in the sand – but it had rather more sinister implications.

'I think while he was being strangled, he was flailing around with his arms and legs, a bit like a beetle on its back. You might want to wonder why a grown man would be doing that, instead of trying more actively to fight off his attacker. To me, it's as though he might have been asleep on the beach, and then he half-woke and started to struggle, and as you see was quickly overcome. But why on earth would anyone sleep out on the beach? Especially on a morning like this.'

The breeze coming off the sea was distinctly chilly now. Even Hamish was looking rather mopey, his fur being blown this way and that in a fashion he clearly wasn't enjoying.

'That's very interesting, what you've said.' Mariella spoke carefully. Sarah knew the girl's views on amateurs poking around in serious cases. But if she managed to get a jump on her colleagues, that could only help her professional progress – and maybe help her move from trainee to plainclothes detective.

'Does it make sense to you? I wonder what on earth he was doing down here so early anyway,' Sarah mused.

'Maybe he was opening up the Mermaids' beach hut, getting stuff out for the day.' Mariella shrugged.

'But he wasn't a swimmer, was he?' Somehow, the thought of that sausage-like man bobbing around in the waves with the nice ladies of Merstairs was not appealing.

'Oh no. But since Mum bought her beach hut, the Scouts have moved their stuff in with the Mermaids' kit, a couple of huts along. It made sense, really.' Mariella grew silent and looked out to sea. Although her hair had been sensibly tied back, a few vivid strands had worked loose and were flapping against her face and neck and she brushed them away with an irritable gesture. Sarah's own cap of blonde hair was flying this way and that. The wind was really getting up.

Just then a woman with a harassed air and a large medical bag arrived.

'That's the pathologist,' Mariella murmured to Sarah, as the

SOCO team arrived to erect a white crime scene tent over the mortal remains of Bill Turbot.

Dr Strutton nodded briefly in Sarah's direction, somehow able to tell she was a fellow medic without being told. Sarah understood – she often had the same instinctive reactions herself. And she couldn't help noticing that this recognition, slight though it was, impressed Mariella much more than any heavy-handed attempts to 'help' would have done.

Now the waves slapping the shore were gunmetal grey, and the sky suddenly looked threatening. Merstairs, in this weather, was no longer the holiday playground that Sarah had grown to love so quickly. On a day like today, on this windswept beach, it was a different place entirely. And now that a second murder had been done, it suddenly seemed the most godforsaken spot she had ever been to.

TWENTY-SEVEN

Sarah sat with Daphne in the Jolly Roger bar a short while later, sipping an emergency cup of tea rustled up by Trevor. If anyone had told Sarah a week ago that she'd be on good enough terms with a pub landlord to be allowed in before official opening time, she would have been astonished. And as for being embroiled in not one but two murder cases, well – that would have stretched credulity all the way from London to Merstairs and back. But this seemed to be her lot, now. So much for the quiet retirement Peter had set his heart on.

'You must have got the shock of your life, Sarah,' said Daphne sympathetically. 'I dropped everything when I got your call. I was just deworming Mephisto, but it can wait.'

Sarah closed her eyes. Somehow that image was almost on a par with her sighting of Bill Turbot – but not quite. When she opened them, she spotted something.

'Surely that's your dressing gown, Daphne?' She looked down and, sure enough, her friend was wearing a fleecy number, teamed with her slippers again.

'Well I was in a rush! Pat stayed the night last night – she was round again and we got chatting and didn't get to bed till the early hours. I've left her with the cat. Anyway, what I'm wearing doesn't matter, not when you think about poor Bill Turbot! He wasn't a very nice man, but that's no excuse at all,' said Daphne, shaking her head, earrings and headscarf in disapproval. 'At any rate, I'm glad it's Pamela Strutton doing the post-mortem. I doubt she'll be asking Mariella for coffees every two minutes like Dr Burns. Mari says she's a safe pair of hands.'

'I wish we knew more about what was going on with the enquiry,' sighed Sarah. She was glad to hear that Daphne had Pat as an alibi for Bill Turbot's murder – though her friend seemed blissfully unaware that she needed one.

'Well, I've heard all the regulars here are going to be questioned again, as well as Trevor, Albie and all the Scouts' parents,' Daphne said. 'They might even haul us in again, too! What fun.'

For a second, Sarah smiled at the thought of Dumbarton having to interview Daphne again, then she grew serious. 'The awful thing is, I convinced myself last night that it had to be Bill Turbot who'd killed Gus. He was my prime suspect, after Charles turned out to be away with Francesca,' said Sarah ruefully.

'So you're back at square one?' Daphne asked and Sarah nodded sadly. 'Oh look,' Daphne added, peering out of the part of the bar's window that wasn't obscured by fake fishing nets. 'Those two constables have just shown up, they're talking to Mari and DI Blake. And there's Dr Strutton too.'

Blake marched away importantly and Sarah watched the way Mariella tried to offer her insights to the uniformed constables. Neither got out their notebooks and their body language was not encouraging. In fact, they turned their burly shoulders away from her and crowded her out of the scene. The pathologist must have spotted her bright red hair, though, and consequently stepped forward to have a brief chat with the girl. Sarah was pleased on Mariella's behalf. Daphne had a good brain concealed under that scarf of hers, and Sarah remembered that her daughter had also consistently got top marks at school and uni. She was sure it wouldn't be long before Mariella achieved her dream of joining the CID – with her help, if possible – though it was always going to be tricky to juggle her job with her family commitments. At least her husband, John, seemed dependable.

It wasn't long before a mortuary van turned up, and Bill Turbot's remains were carried away with as much dignity as could be contrived on the lumpy, bumpy beach. As it was still early, there were very few holidaymakers around to have their mornings wrecked by thoughts of sudden death. Sarah lifted her mug to her lips.

'Well I, for one, needed a good cuppa,' said Daphne, taking a far heartier swig. 'Gosh, the things we've seen this week. Just think, the last time we were in here, Bill Turbot was propping up the bar, without a care in the world. He was right over there, wasn't he?'

Daphne pointed over to the far side of the pub and Sarah suddenly remembered. She'd been sure Turbot was going to approach her, with a distinctly predatory look on his shiny face. Then he'd turned tail, and shot off to the other end of the room. He'd sat there nursing his drink until she'd left. What had happened to make him change course so radically?

Sarah absently tapped her saucer with her spoon as she tried to remember the sequence of events. Daphne broke in. 'You're driving me mad with that clinking. My nerves are shredded anyway, with what's happened,' she announced with a theatrical shiver.

'It's probably all a lot worse for Bill Turbot,' said Sarah drily. 'What about his family? Who does he have at home?'

'Well, his wife's long gone. She divorced him years ago. Or he divorced her. Depends who you listen to,' said Daphne.

This news didn't entirely surprise Sarah. 'Does his ex still live around here?'

'Well, obviously she does,' said Daphne, goggling at her friend as though she'd finally taken leave of her senses. 'You know that.'

'Do I?' Sarah raised her eyebrows. 'You mean I've met her?'

'Of course, silly,' said Daphne, raising her mug to her lips again.

'Well, come on,' said Sarah, tiring of the suspense. 'Who on earth is the ex-Mrs Bill Turbot? I haven't got the foggiest idea.'

'It's Hannah Betts, of course,' said Daphne.

Sarah, who'd just taken a sip from her own tea, was mortified when it went down the wrong way. She coughed and spluttered, and tears ran down her face, as Daphne unceremoniously thumped her on the back.

When she'd got her breath back, and Hamish had stopped barking protectively, Sarah said, 'You know, it really doesn't do any good to hit someone like that. A glass of water is the best remedy. But remind me to show you how to do the Heimlich manoeuvre if someone really is choking.' Sarah mopped her face with a tissue. Hannah Betts from the Beach Café and Bill Turbot. Well, wonders would never cease.

'Can I get you anything else, ladies?' said Trevor Bains, appearing by their table. 'You know you're not really supposed to be in here, it was just with the news... since I happened to be standing in the doorway...'

'Yes, yes, we know, Trev. And we're so grateful. I know you've been having a time of it with the police. Did they ask you about the newspaper? The *Merstairs Marketeer*?'

Trevor just rubbed a tired hand over his sore eyes. 'Did they ever. No idea what they were on about.'

'Thanks again for the teas. A quiet moment was just what we needed to get over the shock,' said Daphne, while Sarah thought ruefully her coughing fit had hardly been quiet.

'Well, I should really be asking you to leave now,' said Trevor apologetically. 'I've got the brewery rep coming in a minute, and you know what that's like.'

'Oh, nightmare,' said Daphne sympathetically. 'Still having that trouble with them? And the Ship and Anchor?'

Trevor rolled his eyes. 'Always. They never give up. Did you see their blackboard today? "You don't need to walk the gangplank to get a drink here – come aboard the Ship". I ask you!' He polished their table furiously. Although he'd said he was keen for them to leave, Sarah got the feeling he wanted to talk. She decided it was now or never.

'Um, I met someone from the Merstairs Men's Movement yesterday, and they said you were in the group?'

'Aye. Not for long, but they're a good bunch of lads,' Trevor said.

'Gus wasn't so keen, though, is that right?' Sarah asked.

Trevor straightened up. 'You don't look like the nosy type, but ye are, aren't ye?' he said, but in a good-natured way. 'Aye, Gus didn't go a bundle on things like that. He just had a wee word with me and I was fine with it,' he said.

'You didn't... resent him telling you what you could and couldn't do?' Sarah's eyebrows were raised.

Trevor stared at her for a moment. 'You're not suggesting that would be a reason... for doing something terrible?' There was no disguising his shock.

'Absolutely not!' said Sarah, who had been wondering this exact thing. 'Not for a moment.'

'Um, any news on the situation with Gus's funeral?' Daphne asked quickly.

Immediately, Trevor's face lost its angry look as the misery of the situation rose up again.

'Oh, no. The police... We don't even know when they'll release him back to me...' He rubbed a hand across his face again. 'I've been told it could take weeks.'

Sarah felt for him. She thought he seemed even sadder today than he'd been on Wednesday. But then, grief was like that. Some days were bearable, others were full of little stabs of pain. Then there were those that were plain agony.

Just then, Hamish woke up with a yap of a bark. 'I suppose that's our cue to leave. Sounds like this boy wants to stretch his legs,' said Sarah.

'Well, see you ladies later, then,' Trevor said wistfully.

'He's finding it hard to come to terms with things, don't you think?' Sarah said as they stood outside on the doorstep, taking in gulps of the fresh briny air. The weather had calmed down, the wind dropping, and the sun was peeping through dark-edged clouds that were moving rapidly away to other, less fortunate, parts of the coast. 'Shall we give Hamish a little run around on the beach?' she added casually as they crossed over the road.

'You just want to have another look at the scene of the crime,' accused Daphne. 'Honestly, it's not going to do any good for your aura, getting involved in all this.'

'I don't suppose my aura was great anyway,' said Sarah lightly, unclipping Hamish's lead as they got onto the beach. As she'd thought, he took a second to orientate himself, and then set off right for the flapping yellow and black police tape not far from the row of huts.

'That's where you're wrong, your aura has always been a lovely green.'

Sarah raised her eyebrows at Daphne. 'What on earth does that mean? That I'm unripe, or something?'

Daphne shook her head at her friend's lack of insight into the mystical world. 'It's the colour of healing.'

'Don't tell me, let me guess. Your aura is...' Sarah pretended to shut her eyes and ponder. 'Red, purple and pink.'

Daphne came to a sudden halt. 'But that's uncanny, however did you know?'

Sarah smiled wryly. 'Just dumb luck.' They were also exactly the colours Daphne had on today. 'Come on, let's see where Hamish has got to.'

'You know full well he'll have run to where poor old Bill was found,' Daphne grumbled, throwing off her slippers. 'Oh, the sand is cold today,' she said.

They both strode out across the beach. Daphne was right, it was still rather chilly but, despite this, there were now a fair number of families on the sand, some close to the huts. Sarah supposed the news of the second murder hadn't got out yet. Surely if it had, they'd be giving the place a wide berth.

She wondered what the consequences of all this would be for little Merstairs. As they walked along, she couldn't help shooting out suspicious glances as they passed the little knots of holidaymakers – all innocent, no doubt, and going cheerfully about their business, setting up windbreaks, getting out the buckets and spades for a hard day's digging. Did any of them know more than they should about Gus Trubshaw, and now Bill Turbot? What on earth was going on in Merstairs, and how was Sarah going to get to the bottom of it?

'Can you think of anyone – anyone at all – who'd have it in for both Gus and Bill Turbot?' Sarah asked Daphne.

'You're assuming it's all connected,' her friend said, shoving her scarf a bit further up on her forehead. 'But it could just be random. Some weirdo who's just been passing through... and decided to bump a couple of people off on his way out of town.'

Sarah almost rolled her eyes, but just managed to stop herself. 'But Daphne, Gus Trubshaw was killed weeks ago. And Bill died in the early hours today.'

'See! How can they possibly be connected, then? It must be *two* random weirdos, in that case,' said Daphne with an air of great relief.

Sarah shrugged, astonished her friend found the idea of more than one psychopath in the area reassuring. But Daphne was looking for any crumb of comfort. Just then, Hamish bounced up to her, with the air of a dog that's accomplished a very good deed. Instantly, Sarah was suspicious, and scanned the area for any picnics short of a sandwich. It wasn't an enormous surprise when what looked like a rat on springs bounced over to them a few moments later. It was Tinkerbell, Charles Diggory's minuscule pooch. This must be what Hamish had been so smug about, as Tinkerbell, instead of shunning the Scottie as she always had before, this time pranced over to him and gave him what almost looked like a kiss on the nose. Hamish immediately set to, diligently sniffing the tiny creature's rear end. Sarah averted her gaze. Sometimes being a dog owner was mortifying.

She combed the horizon instead. Surely if Tinkerbell was on the loose, Charles Diggory wouldn't be far behind? Her hand went up involuntarily to her hair, but she brought it down again. She ought to know by now that being out on the sands at Merstairs was totally incompatible with looking groomed. And, ahem, who cared, anyway?

But just then, she caught sight of a familiar figure. It was not Charles Diggory, though, but Francesca, clad in her trademark tweeds, which as usual contrasted oddly with the surrounding holidaymakers' minimal beach attire. Sarah's own serviceable cotton three-quarter-length trousers and simple top, and even Daphne's scarf, gown and slippers combo, looked much more appropriate by comparison.

'Quick, duck,' Daphne whispered urgently to Sarah, but it was too late. Francesca had spotted them.

TWENTY-EIGHT

'Ahoy there,' Francesca Diggory yelled across the beach. Daphne, who'd already started to crouch down, drew herself up to her full height slowly and giggled, as Francesca marched as best she could over the uneven terrain, clods of sand flying off her green Hunter wellies.

'Ah, you again, Sally, and it's Daffy, isn't it?' said Francesca, with a withering glance at the pair as she got within easier shouting distance.

'That's Sarah and Daph-*ne*,' said Sarah, very clearly, as her friend seemed to have temporarily lost her voice in annoyance.

'Yes. Exactly.' Francesca shrugged dismissively. 'Now, I've got a bone to pick with the pair of you...'

It was a threatening beginning, accompanied as it was by a fierce look from Francesca's bitter brown eyes. Sarah had always previously associated that shade with lovely, sweet, gently warming things, like chocolate and treacle, but Francesca's stare was the colour of the hardest toffee going – the sort that would yank out your fillings in a trice, and probably crack a molar or two for good measure. She was also wearing a silk scarf knotted under her chin again, in that odd Princess Anne style, and her mouth was one long straight letterbox of disapproval.

Sarah decided a bit of sympathy was most likely to win the day. 'Great to see you, Francesca. Though you must be so busy with this awful business...'

'Business? What business?' sniffed Francesca, eyes swivelling all over the beach as though the answer was likely to pop out at her.

Sarah lowered her voice. 'I meant with the, um, murders...'

At this, Daphne broke in. 'Or *unexplained deaths*, I prefer to say. I've been telling Sarah it's probably all the work of an isolated madman or two,' she continued in conversational tones, as though this far improved things.

Francesca sniffed again and ignored Daphne completely. 'I fail to see what I have to do with this... unfortunate situation. I just wanted to warn you. Again. I've heard various, ah, rumours about your little romantic lunches and so on. Charles may appear charming... but he's not what he seems.'

Here, Francesca actually tapped the side of her nose, like someone from a 1940s gangster film. Sarah looked at her, rather stunned. It was disconcerting to know that someone had seen fit to inform Francesca she'd had lunch with Charles yesterday – with Daphne in tow, for goodness' sake. What did she think Sarah was going to get up to, in public, with a third party at the table? Francesca obviously thought she was a hardened Jezebel from the big city, which was downright laughable.

And why on earth was the woman wasting so much energy telling people to back off, in the middle of an apparent killing spree in Merstairs? That was surely much more serious than any domestic matter. Anyway, were Francesca and Charles separated or not? They were as good as divorced, from what he said – but then they'd been on that recent holiday together...

Sarah suddenly realised this might be her chance to get to the bottom of all that. She swallowed, and said in the airiest tone she could manage, 'Charles said you both took the grand-children skiing at half term. Must have been quite like old times,' she couldn't help adding.

'Hardly. Charles could only stay a few days before he had to rush home,' said Francesca, with a discontented twist of her mouth.

TWENTY-NINE

Sarah's jaw sagged. Bang went Charles's alibi for Gus's murder! If he was around shortly after 12th February, he could easily have lined the trunk with the *Merstairs Marketeer* and stashed Gus's corpse on top of it. Dr Burns had said the body had lain there undisturbed for six weeks – but a few days more or less than that timespan was perfectly possible. 'Why did Charles have to leave?' she asked.

'I don't think that's any of your business, is it?' Francesca said crossly. 'But I suppose if you must know, there was a burglary at his shop.'

Sarah stored the information away. A break-in at the antiques emporium sounded like a thin excuse. If the shop had been hers, she would have been thrilled if robbers had made off with the lot. Charles loved it – but had he lied in order to escape from Francesca and the holiday? Or so that he could nip back home and bump off Gus?

In terms of her investigation, it was quite a breakthrough. Why, then, did she feel so agitated at the thought that Charles was suddenly back in the running? And, more to the point, why had he let her think he had been out of the country at the time of the killing?

No wonder Francesca still seemed to feel territorial, if they had been away together so recently, even if it had ended badly. Sarah couldn't help feeling that Charles had been disingenuous about many things. She was just opening her mouth to explain that she and Charles had been chaperoned at their 'illicit' lunch, when Daphne leapt into the fray.

'Did I hear you say Charles was charming, Francesca? Yes, that's exactly the word for him, all right! I was saying to Sarah, she could do worse if she wants a bit of a fling. I mean, why not? He's got all his hair, and that's saying something round here.'

Francesca goggled at Daphne, her face growing as puce as the floral motifs on today's silk scarf. There was a pause, during which both Sarah and Daphne watched Francesca with interest. She was clearly running through a whole list of expletives in her mind, then dismissing them with great reluctance as unmayorly. 'Well *really*,' she ground out eventually, the words hissing out like air escaping from a particularly bad-tempered balloon. With that, she turned on her heel and left. Or she would have done, if she hadn't tripped over her own dog.

Tinkerbell, tired of the flirtation with Hamish – he was so obviously her slave, *very* little challenge there – had been looking up at her mistress, tiny tail wagging away, when Francesca had attempted to stomp off. Seconds later, there was an unseemly tangle of tiny canine limbs and much larger welly boots, and Francesca was lying full length on the sand.

'Oh goodness,' said Sarah. She wasn't worried about broken bones, as Francesca had had a soft landing on the beach. But Tinkerbell was underneath the woman, judging by the high-pitched whines. That could be quite serious for such a tiny dog. 'Help me, Daphne.'

Between the two of them, they hoisted the mayor back up, and even started brushing the sand from her tweeds. But

Francesca, winded for a moment, recovered quickly and fought off their aid. 'I can manage, *thank* you,' she said, flinging herself away from the women, picking up the quivering Chihuahua – who luckily seemed none the worse for the adventure – and stomping off down the beach.

Daphne was hard pressed to contain her laughter until Francesca was out of earshot, and even Sarah, despite her new concerns about Charles, caught the giggling bug just as she always had at school. She suggested they regain their equilibrium over cups of strong tea at the Beach Café, as it was only a step away. They found a table and Mavis bustled over immediately to serve them, confiding that Hannah was being questioned by the police about Bill Turbot.

That was enough to stifle their giggles for a while – until, in fact, a familiar figure hove into view. It was Charles Diggory. For Daphne, he was so closely allied with the cause of all their hilarity that it set her off again. But Sarah was feeling more complicated emotions. Charles had wilfully misled her over the skiing business and had a lot of questions to answer. She looked up at the tall man with the blue, blue eyes while Daphne tried to disguise a snort of laughter as a sneeze. He swept off his hat in a courtly gesture.

'Is this seat taken?'

THIRTY

'Do join us,' Daphne said to Charles Diggory before Sarah could gather her thoughts. 'We were just wondering... You know, Sarah has seen so much, in her years as a doctor. Pathological jealousy – do you know much about that?' she asked, disappearing into her tissue again with her eyes twinkling.

Sarah shot Daphne a *do-shut-up* look and jumped in before Charles could ask her friend what on earth she meant. 'The thing is...' she said slowly. 'We were just hearing a little more about your skiing holiday. We bumped into Francesca.'

'Ah? Ah. I see,' Charles said, and the look he gave Sarah was a little hunted. 'I suppose she mentioned the fact that I... left a little early.'

'She did,' Sarah said drily. 'She also said there had been a break-in at the shop?'

'Strange, because as a fellow shopkeeper, I never heard anything about that,' said Daphne.

'Um, well, ladies,' said Charles, shrugging his lean shoulders, 'I'm sorry about my little subterfuge. The thing is... Francesca had asked me to join her to help out with Calista and Max – the grandchildren, you know. But it turned out what she actually wanted was, um. Well, she had some hopes of, er, rekindling things. I felt it was better to make an excuse and bow out than endure a situation which could have been embarrassing for us both.'

By the end of this explanation, both Charles and Sarah were a little pink, and had their eyes firmly fixed on the sea in front of them. Daphne looked from one to the other with interest. Then she spoke.

'Well, that's great news, Charles.'

'It is?' said Charles, still a little flustered.

'There is a problem, though,' said Sarah, meeting Charles's gaze somewhat reluctantly.

'Oh? What's that?' Charles said.

'Well, that means you're still a possibility for the first murder.'

'The *first* murder?' Charles frowned. 'Wait, you mean... there's been another?'

'Bill Turbot. Haven't you heard?'

Charles looked thunderstruck. 'Oh my Lord! Are you serious?' Both Sarah and Daphne nodded that they certainly were. Charles shook his head, his face pale. 'I suppose that's what all the kerfuffle on the beach this morning was. How appalling,' he said sombrely. 'What a terrible loss.'

'Did you like him?' Sarah asked in surprise.

'Couldn't bear the man. But he was useful, running the Scouts. It's difficult for kids in a place like this... a lot of hanging around in the off-season months. You're seeing Merstairs now at its best,' Charles said, crossing his long legs and recovering his poise as he warmed to the theme. 'The golden sands, the sun, the sea. It's all so inviting. But in winter, the place can be pretty grey. And the winds. Well, it was rather cool this morning, wasn't it, before the sun got up. Daphne, tell Sarah what it's like.'

'No fear,' said Daphne quickly. 'Don't want to put her off.'

'I suppose organisations like the Scouts do keep children busy...' Sarah said slowly. But she was suddenly wondering what Charles had been doing up so early – early enough to have realised it had been a very cold morning. Had he, perhaps, been on the beach?

'Exactly. The devil makes work for idle hands, so they say,' said Charles. 'We'll definitely miss old Turbot as the nights draw in.'

'Surely someone else will volunteer to fill his shoes? He can't be the only person capable of running an organisation.'

Charles raised his eyebrows at Sarah. 'Are you pitching your application? Because I can put in a word with the powers that be.'

Sarah, assuming he meant the mayor, carefully avoided Daphne's eyes in case her friend started laughing again.

'Um, no, not really. I haven't even got my boxes unpacked after my move,' said Sarah, fudging the truth a little. In fact, she had the cottage sorted out pretty much to her liking – but even when every single thing was in its rightful place, she still wouldn't be remotely tempted to become the new scoutmaster. 'You'd seem like the obvious choice to me.'

Charles smiled in surprise. 'You think so? But sadly I'm much too busy with the shop,' he said, with an elegant shrug.

A shop that no one went into, Sarah thought to herself – even to burgle. He'd more or less admitted the theft story was just a ruse to get away from Francesca. Why was it that Charles was so determined to pretend the antiques business was all-consuming? But they were getting off the topic she wanted to examine.

'Did Bill Turbot have any enemies, would you say?'

'You know, you sound more and more like a policewoman. Perhaps you should volunteer to help out there, instead of with the Scouts.' Charles said it lightly, but was there an edge to his voice? Sarah wondered.

'Oh, I don't think they're looking for someone like me,' she batted back. 'Besides, I don't know the first thing about Merstairs. That's why I keep having to ask people for information. You were saying, about Bill Turbot?'

'I'm not sure I was.' Charles's blue eyes regarded her steadily. 'But for what it's worth, I wasn't his biggest fan.'

'Oh?' Sarah said, trying to keep her voice casual. At last, she might be getting somewhere. Then Daphne broke in.

'Look over there! Isn't that Marlene, Bill's sister?'

Sarah craned her neck. There was a woman walking back from the direction of the beach huts, her face, even from this distance, looking distinctly wan. It was the lady from the little restaurant, Marlene's Plaice, where she'd had her fish and chip supper the other night. 'Is she Bill's sister?'

'Poor love. Her vibrations are really off today.' Daphne craned forward, her scarf slipping over one eye.

'Well, that's not surprising. Her brother's just been murdered,' murmured Sarah.

'Do stop saying murder,' Daphne repeated very loudly. 'Can't we just leave it at "found dead"? It's too dreadfully upsetting. And you're so matter-of-fact about it. I'd have thought, after everything that happened with Peter, you'd be a bit more careful.'

'What happened with Peter?' Charles said, sitting forward suddenly, and putting both hands on the table.

'Nothing,' both Sarah and Daphne chorused as one. 'Oh, there's Mariella again. Looks like she's questioning people on the beach,' Sarah said.

'Huh. I suppose you want to go and join her, see what you can find out. With no thought for my turmoil,' said Daphne, pressing a hand to her head.

'I wasn't aware that you had a high degree of turmoil,' said Sarah quickly. 'But in any case, I'm very happy to sit here with you and enjoy my tea.'

This wasn't strictly true. Sarah watched, fascinated, as Mariella carried on stopping people and making notes of their comments. She wasn't sure if she was imagining it, but it seemed that there was a lot more police activity today – which was not perhaps surprising. The more murders, the more bobbies on the beat, she supposed. Charles, seeing her interest, smiled.

'Well, ladies, what are you up to today? Sounds like you need a distraction to take your minds off... all this,' he said.

'There is one thing I'd be very interested to do,' Sarah told him. She turned to her friend. 'If you have time, Daphne?'

'Well, I have a busy day booked at Tarot and Tealeaves,' Daphne said defensively. When both her companions widened their eyes at this, she conceded. 'But I suppose I could cancel my appointments. For you, Sarah. Not that any rendezvous with the Beyond should be treated lightly, you understand.'

'Oh, we understand,' said Charles, with a sidelong look at Sarah. 'Now, where is it that you'd like to go, Sarah?'

Sarah realised that Charles had somehow got in on this invitation. But, as he was now a suspect for not just one but two murders, it might be a good idea for her to keep a close eye on him. 'Well, um, I've... er, always wanted to see how a brewery works.'

THIRTY-ONE

'A brewery?' Charles looked at Sarah in complete astonishment.

'Since when have you even drunk beer?' Daphne was more forthright.

'Well, I've seen the Merstairs Monk beer taps in the pub, and they look so attractive, I just wondered...'

'Oh, I see,' said Daphne in disapproving tones. 'You want to find out if the brewery did Gus Trubshaw in, because he was trying to chisel them on the price of their barrels. And then, after going to the brewery, what's the betting you'll be begging us to go to the Ship?'

Sarah gave Daphne an uncharacteristically pleading look. 'I just want to satisfy myself about a few little points. Then my mind will be at rest. And it will help you, in case anyone still thinks you might have a connection to... everything that's going on. Through the hut. *Your* hut,' she said, turning her attention to Charles.

'All right. Well, as Sarah has made plain again, both of us have a reason to want to disentangle our names and reputations from this matter,' said Charles. 'I vote we do what she says today, and then hopefully, by tomorrow, we can hold our heads up high in Merstairs, without a stain on our characters.'

Yes, thought Sarah. Either that, or one of you could be behind bars. And I know which my money's on.

Accordingly, the little trio – or quartet, if you counted Hamish, which as far as he was concerned was a given – trailed back to the cottages and hopped into Sarah's car. They didn't even stop for a restorative cup of tea, as Daphne suggested, since Sarah pointed out that they had only just had one.

With Hamish pressing his little face against the window, and Charles in the front passenger seat next to Sarah, on account of his undeniably long legs, they set off. There was only a little good-natured bickering from Daphne and Charles on directions, and within twenty minutes Sarah's Volvo was gliding to a halt in the car park outside a gleaming metal factory building. It was as far from the saintly picture of a monk on the pub taps as you could get.

'Is beer really made in this tin can of a place? No wonder I never feel like drinking it,' said Sarah.

'Oh, but it's so hygienic,' said Daphne vaguely, dropping used tissues everywhere as they walked up to the reception desk. Behind it was a girl with a bright smile who, to Sarah's eyes, looked just about old enough to be starting secondary school.

'May I help you?' the receptionist enquired, her eyebrows just touching her fringe and implying, without need of another syllable being uttered, that she had never seen such a motley crew in her pristine building before. 'And I am afraid dogs are not allowed in the brewery. Cute though he is.'

Hamish gave his best head-on-one side beseeching look, but it was to no avail. Just as Sarah thought she'd have to step outside with him, and miss her chance at getting any further in the investigation, Daphne very nobly offered to do the honours.

'Thanks, Daphne. We'll be as quick as we can,' she said,

pressing her friend's arm and giving Hamish a please-be-a-good-boy pat.

Once Hamish and Daphne had padded out, Sarah and Charles looked at the receptionist expectantly.

'I'm afraid I still don't know what it is you want,' the girl said with a smile that was brighter now the unwanted canine was off the premises.

'Ah.' Charles was suddenly at his most suave. 'We heard that you did tours of the premises, for, erm, true afficionados of your brew.'

The girl looked from Sarah to Charles and back again. 'And that's what you two are, is it? Big beer fans?'

'Huge. *Huge* beer fans,' said Sarah, trying to look as though her dream was nothing less than a peek at the inner workings of this ghastly factory.

'Well, normally you'd have to book months in advance... but as it happens there is a tour going on at the moment, and we've had a couple of no-shows. It's for public houses that are considering swapping to our brands, but I suppose as you are such enthusiasts...'

'Oh we really are,' Sarah said, nodding her head fervently. She hoped the girl wouldn't test her on anything to do with beer as Sarah couldn't have told her a single fact, except that the stuff was made from some grain or other. Hops? Not wheat, definitely. Maybe barley... but there was no time to fret about the recipe. The receptionist had summoned a man who emerged from a side room, all smiles, and led them off to a sort of changing room.

'Little late, but no worries, we'll catch up in no time,' he said cheerfully. 'Now, just slip on these shoe covers, overalls and hair protectors and we'll be off.'

Once Sarah and Charles were unrecognisable in glorified shower caps and lab coats, they trailed behind their guide and were soon deep in the body of the shiny space-age building, in a large hall, almost as big as those cavernous hangars at the end of a Bond film where 007 shoots droves of minions before saving the hapless damsel and, of course, the world. Charles shot Sarah a smile that suggested he was thoroughly enjoying the whole experience, while Sarah, worried they were about to be unmasked at any second as imposters, tried her best to look inconspicuous. Soon they were ushered to join a little knot of similarly attired people clustered around one of the huge metal containers that dominated the space. A man at the front was droning on about fermenting times, yeast addition and hop varieties – ah, so it *was* hops, thought Sarah.

Despite herself, she found she was becoming intrigued by what the man was saying – she'd always had a passion for finding out how things worked. But she was well aware that this wasn't getting them any further in their quest for knowledge about poor old Gus Trubshaw. She was just wondering whether it might be possible to sidle away and try and find someone who might know about pricing policy, when a voice spoke at her side.

'He does go on a bit, doesn't he?'

She turned to see the speaker. He was a middle-aged man, kitted out in the same garb she was wearing, but he had a way about him that she instantly found attractive. It was the sort of amused confidence and self-possession that Peter had projected. It was more appealing, at any rate, than Charles's current slack-jawed marvelling at everything in this place. She peeped over at him, and saw from his glazed expression that he was still rapt. Inwardly she tutted.

'Do you know the man speaking?' she asked the newcomer.

'Well, you could say that.' The man winked at her.

Sarah thought for a moment. Either he was overegging things, or he was some kind of bigwig at the brewery, who enjoyed being incognito in a crowd like this. If it was the latter, then it would definitely be worth picking his brain. She leant over and, thinking herself very forward, put a hand on his arm. 'You know the way this place is run, I imagine.'

The man gave her a shrewd, appraising look, and seemed to like what he saw. 'You're not the type that usually joins brewery tours,' he said.

'I could say the same of you,' she replied.

The man smiled. 'Well, suppose we peel off and I give you a bit of a special viewing,' he said. 'They're just going to look at the lautering room now, you know, where the mash tun is used. They always show this boiling room first as the kettles are so dramatic,' he said.

'Absolutely,' said Sarah, wondering what on earth he was on about.

'Shh!' said Charles, his brow furrowed with concentration as the speaker got to the end of his spiel and encouraged the group to follow him.

This time, the man grabbed Sarah's arm, and as people started to follow obediently behind the speaker, he guided Sarah to the side. They sheltered behind one of the giant containers until the last footsteps had died away. Then Sarah looked around. They were now completely alone, in the vast warehouse-like space, with only the muted hisses and rumblings of the strange metal containers for company.

Suddenly she wondered what on earth she had been thinking of. The man beside her was a complete stranger, and worse, she couldn't even really be sure he worked for the brewery or would be any help to her. Meanwhile, what she did know was that two people had recently met unpleasant deaths in Merstairs, with a possible connection to this place. And, on top of that, Charles now had no idea where she was and probably wouldn't even think to look until every step of the brewing process had been explained to him in minute detail.

She was just beginning to feel the start of a cold sweat,

which she knew was a symptom of her fight-or-flight response kicking in, when the man beside her gave a soft laugh.

'Alone at last, eh?'

She turned to him, schooling herself to show no signs of her growing alarm. 'Yes. Yes, you could say that.'

'So... what are you really after? You don't want a job here or something, do you? Mind you, you don't look quite like our usual prospective employees,' he said, giving her a quick once-over.

'Everyone looks a bit of a ninny in this get-up, I imagine,' she said feistily, and was glad to feel her irrational fears ebbing away. There were probably people within shouting distance if this man did turn nasty, and what was he going to do, anyway? Throw her into one of these boiling vats? Oops, thought Sarah. Don't go there. *Not* helpful. 'So, I admit, I didn't come here to find out about brewing. There've been some... odd goings-on in Merstairs recently. I dare say you've heard about them.'

The man leant back a little and instantly Sarah felt more comfortable. Perhaps his unnecessarily close proximity before had been setting off her internal alarm systems.

'Oh I see, are you some kind of true crime nut?' he asked.

'Would anyone ever say yes to a question like that?' Sarah replied in reasonable tones. 'I'm going to give it a no, anyway. I know true crime is really popular nowadays but it's not something I've ever felt drawn to... until I found a body. A body I think you might know?'

Now the man was leaning closer to her again, and Sarah felt her unease welling up, even as she got a whiff of his expensive cologne.

'If you're talking about Gus Trubshaw, then all I can say is that he got what was coming to him,' the man said. 'He was always chiselling away at our margins, insisting we lower our prices to be in the most popular bar in Merstairs. But, as I told him at our last meeting, there's more than one pub in town. We have no objection to dealing with the Ship. Anyway, was I glad when he seemed to disappear a few weeks ago, and take all his conniving ways with him? Yes, I was. But that doesn't mean that what happened to him was my doing, even if he was selling cheaper beer on the sly.'

Despite her physical unease, Sarah felt a prickle of excitement. At last, she was getting somewhere. The brewery knew all about Gus's death – the connection had been proved. And if he had been substituting their beer for a downmarket alternative, they had a legitimate reason to be angry with him.

Just then, there was the sound of the heavy door at the end of the room being flung open, and footsteps came running towards them. 'Mr Grimes, Mr Grimes!' A breathless youth came bombing round the side of the vat. 'Ah, there you are, sir. Thank goodness.'

'What is it?' asked Sarah's companion irritably.

'You're needed in the control room, sir,' panted the boy. 'The hops...'

Grimes didn't wait to be told twice. He hurried off after his assistant, turning only once to glare at Sarah.

Sarah, relieved to be left alone again in the cavernous room, wondered where on earth she ought to go now, to catch up with Charles and the tour. She didn't want to accidentally find herself tangling with the hops or, indeed, encountering Mr Grimes again. She looked at the doors at the end of the room, wondering which the tour had disappeared through initially. But she didn't have long to ponder, as one opened and the group straggled back in, complete with the speaker and Charles.

Sarah wove her way round the large tanks and popped up again at Charles's elbow. He looked round, somewhat owlishly, and said, 'Ah, there you are. Thought I'd lost you somewhere there for a minute.' It was as though he'd been breathing in so deeply he was intoxicated by the fug of beer fumes.

Sarah shook her head slightly and was glad when the

speaker announced that this concluded their tour, saying that if they'd like to proceed to the gift shop and refreshment area, they could continue to explore the wonderful world of Merstairs Monk beers. Charles started to wander off joyfully in the direction of the shop, but Sarah managed to waylay him with a reminder that poor Daphne had been outside all this time, with Hamish. They needed to get back to the car.

* * *

It was hard to tell who was most disgruntled about their long wait, Hamish or Daphne. Both appeared to be in high dudgeon, standing by the boot of the car but looking in opposite directions. Daphne had her arms folded across her ample bosom in an uncharacteristically militant manner, and if Hamish had been able to do the same with his little fluffy legs, he would have done. But as soon as they saw Sarah and Charles coming, both perked up immeasurably.

'Well, you took your time,' said Daphne, with a wounded look at her friend.

'Yes, I'm so sorry,' Sarah said, bending down to give Hamish the thorough petting that he deserved after being such a good boy, such an excellent boy. She fumbled in her handbag and brought out a dog treat and an old but still edible Twix bar, and handed them out to two very grateful recipients. Daphne apparently didn't notice for a second that she was getting the same treatment as a small dog – or maybe she just didn't mind.

'Well, you two have been incredibly patient,' Sarah went on. 'Thank you so much for looking after each other.' This was one of her well-worn tactics when her daughters had been small. Give the child plenty of praise for a quality that they have demonstrably not shown, and everyone feels a whole lot better. Both Daphne and Hamish started to look smug instead of deeply cross.

'Now then, let's hop back in the car and I'll tell you what I've discovered,' Sarah said with a smile.

'Yes, you'll never believe the number of processes the mash goes through before it gets delivered to the pub...' Charles started.

'Well, not that,' said Sarah patiently. 'I did manage to have a word with one of the brewery top brass, and he said Gus could have been substituting Merstairs Monk beer for something cheaper and, I imagine, pocketing the difference. That's a motive, if you like! Daphne, could you google who the head of Merstairs Monk is while I drive?'

'That doesn't sound like Gus,' said Daphne, getting out her phone and pressing a few buttons. 'I'm sure he was honest. And as for Trevor, he'd never do that.' A moment later she was waving a mugshot in front of Sarah's face, blotting out the road ahead. Luckily there was a farm truck in front of them, so they were only going a few miles an hour. Sarah glanced at it for scarcely a second. It was enough.

'That's him! Stephen Grimes. He's the man I was talking to. Well, that's brilliant. I think we're making some progress at last.'

'Wait, what did he say exactly?' Daphne put her hands on both of the front seats and tried to insert her head as far as it would go between them, so she was almost level with Sarah and Charles. Hamish, who'd previously been perfectly happy looking out of the window, tried to get in on the act with a few choice barks. Confronted with Hamish's noise and Daphne's scarf flopping onto her shoulder, Sarah hushed them both.

'Come on, you two. I'm trying to drive. Sit back and I'll explain.'

But, once Sarah had gone through the full substance of her conversation with the brewery chief, and had triumphantly concluded, 'So you see, there is a link!' there was a marked silence in the car, not the stream of congratulations she had expected.

'Well? What's wrong? Don't you see this proves the brewery and Gus were at daggers drawn?'

'It might prove that,' said Charles in his characteristic drawl. 'If it were actually true. I bet it was this Grimes man's idea of a joke. But it also wouldn't really have mattered to Merstairs Monk Beer at all.'

'Why not? The man seemed absolutely furious about it all.'

'Maybe he was cross. But as he said to you, there was a remedy right in front of him all the time. Go to the Ship instead. Gus didn't have a leg to stand on if the brewery decided to play hardball. They could just take their product away and go to someone more amenable – or trustworthy.'

'And anyway,' said Daphne thoughtfully. 'They haven't, have they?'

'Haven't what?' said Sarah, frowning now as she negotiated the narrow country lanes – and fought down her disappointment at the way her breakthrough was being dismissed.

'They haven't gone elsewhere,' Daphne spelled it out. 'The Jolly Roger is still serving Merstairs Monk beer, at the right price. So, however aggressive Gus was trying to be, and whether he was cheating or not – and I really don't think he was – they sorted it all out at some point and now the deal is continuing – presumably at the price the brewery always wanted.'

'Now that Gus is out of the way. Now he's been murdered,' Sarah said. 'Don't you see? That gives them a motive to get rid of him.'

'Yes, but Sarah,' Charles said in infuriatingly reasonable tones. 'If the brewery killed every landlord who was trying to negotiate a price cut, there'd be no pubs left in England. I just think you're...'

'What? What do you think I am?' Sarah said crossly, and Hamish started to bark again, hearing the annoyance in her voice.

'Well, Hamish has just put it rather well,' said Charles suavely. 'You're barking up the wrong tree.'

There was a pause, then Daphne started to giggle. It took a few moments, but Sarah couldn't help herself. She had to join in too. So the little car puttered back to Merstairs, its inhabitants shaking with the kind of irresistible mirth that had got Daphne and Sarah into endless trouble at school – and with the mystery of Gus Trubshaw and Bill Turbot's grisly deaths no closer at all to being solved.

THIRTY-TWO

Sarah flung back her bedroom curtains, admiring the pattern of intertwined roses and ribbons and the jingle of the brass curtain rings, but enjoying the view from the window even more. Spring was just glorious in Merstairs, and the sea outside was at its playful best, a deep blue with just a sprinkling of white horses, the wind less blustery than yesterday.

It felt as though the world had turned over a new leaf, and Sarah hoped that applied to the mystery surrounding Gus Trubshaw and Bill Turbot, too. She was still fiercely disappointed that the trip to the brewery hadn't yielded richer rewards. But a watertight case wasn't built in a day. She pushed her feet into her slippers and wrapped her dressing gown around her, almost tripping over little Hamish as she turned to go down the flight of stairs.

'You really will be the death of me one day, boy,' she tutted, as she grasped the handrail firmly. She'd dispatched enough patients to A&E with twisted ankles and broken arms to know that pets, as well as lowering blood pressure and keeping people active, could also do some serious inadvertent damage to their owners.

A sudden thumping on the front door did nothing to calm her pulse rate. She rushed down the last few steps and opened the door a crack, with Hamish bristling by her side.

It was Daphne, her face wreathed in seraphic smiles. 'You'll never guess what's happened,' she said, bustling in and all but pushing Sarah aside as she strode into the kitchen and filled the kettle.

'Help yourself, do,' said Sarah drily, wondering when she was going to be able to enjoy being a lady of leisure. She'd had visions of rising at 10 a.m. in her retirement and taking perfumed baths before being ready to meet her public, something that definitely wasn't happening so far in Merstairs. But she'd also been deeply worried about being bored and lonely, and she had to admit that the place, and Daphne, were anything but dull. 'Go on, put me out of my misery. What's the news?'

'Mari just rang me. The police are about to make an arrest!'

Sarah was about to say she was sure Mariella shouldn't be divulging that sort of information. But she stopped herself in the nick of time. For one thing, it was absolutely useless saying such things to Daphne. And it was hugely in Sarah's interests to know what the police were up to.

'Who on earth are they going to pick up?' Despite herself, Sarah felt a stab of what she recognised, rather shamefacedly, had to be disappointment. It was her competitive spirit again, she supposed, but she would have very much liked to get there before the boys in blue – and girls, she thought hastily, thinking of Mariella's contribution. But oh well. At least it was a mystery solved, and a very dangerous person off the streets of Merstairs. That was more important than her ever-present need to get to any given solution first.

'It's only the mayor!' said Daphne, her face flushed with excitement.

Immediately Sarah leapt into action. 'But that's absolutely ridiculous. It can't possibly have been Francesca Diggory.' She thumped her mug down on the table, and for once ignored the hot liquid sloshing everywhere. 'Wait there, I'm going to get changed.'

* * *

Five short minutes later, and Hamish found himself being yanked along by his mistress at top speed along the coastal road. He loved a walk as much as the next dog, but this pace was a bit much.

Sometimes, before they'd left the big city, Sarah had been very sluggish, almost as if she had a broken paw, moping about the place like a bloodhound with an extra-long face. He supposed it was all to do with his master being put in a box at the place with the bad singing, and never coming back.

She'd perked up a good deal since getting to the sea, and her new friend was quite generous with chips. But she did also own that awful cat that it was now his life's mission to eat, and eat quickly.

All this very fast walking was taking him further and further away from the ginger beast, who'd been lurking in his back garden again, taunting him by licking his second-favourite tennis ball. He looked around wistfully for a moment.

Sarah turned as Hamish dragged slightly on the lead. 'All right, boy? Not too fast for you?'

Hamish speeded up gallantly. He'd be back to get his revenge later, and then that ugly great lump of fur better watch out.

'It's almost as though he understands every word I say,' Sarah marvelled.

'This pace might be fine for him, but it's definitely too much for me, Sarah,' panted Daphne crossly. 'What on earth are we doing, anyway? Where are you rushing off to? Nothing much is going to be open now, anyway, if you're thinking of places for breakfast.'

'Food is the last thing on my mind,' Sarah said, picking up the pace a little more.

'Oh,' said Daphne, disappointment showing in the droop of her scarf. 'Well, I might need a little something pretty soon, just to keep me going...'

'Any updates from Mari, since her earlier message?' Sarah said over her shoulder.

'Sarah, I'm going too fast to look. If you want me to get my phone out, you're going to have to stop for a minute.'

Reluctantly, Sarah slowed down while Daphne did some theatrical wheezing and then searched in her bag for her mobile. While she was waiting, Sarah scanned the horizon, hoping to see that flash of red hair that had alerted her yesterday to Mariella being on the scene. Nothing doing. Drat it.

She'd been gambling on the police having arrested Francesca Diggory near the Mermaids' beach hut, but what if they'd actually chosen to intercept the mayor at her own home? Sarah still didn't know where that was, and didn't imagine Charles's nearly-ex would be issuing her a gilt-edged invitation any time soon.

Maybe she should concentrate on Charles Diggory instead? But it was unlikely he'd be in his shop yet. It wasn't as though there was a pressing demand for curios or gentlemen's outfits at any time of day, as far as Sarah could discern, but this early it was doubly unlikely. The Jolly Roger, the other place where he might hang out, had its doors firmly shut. After all the excitement (that probably wasn't the right word, but Sarah couldn't think of another) surrounding the discovery of poor Bill Turbot's body yesterday, the pub probably didn't want to get a reputation for flouting licensing laws when there were police about.

'Rats,' said Daphne. 'Can't find my phone. But there's no

police cars anywhere – they can't have arrested Francesca yet. So, how do you know she didn't do it, anyway?'

'She was away on holiday, remember, for the whole of the vital period – she went on the twelfth of February, when the *Merstairs Marketeer* came out, and wasn't back until two weeks later. And Gus had been dead for a minimum of six weeks when we found him, with the newspaper under him undisturbed.'

Daphne held up a hand as if to ward off the information, but Sarah hadn't finished yet. 'Also, with Bill Turbot, there was a disturbance at the scene, showing he fought back. And that woggle was pulled devilishly tight. Francesca just wouldn't have had the strength to subdue a grown man, then strangle him. She's got quite skinny wrists and is shorter than either of us.'

'Oh,' said Daphne, blenching.

'Well, you did ask,' said Sarah bracingly.

'OK then,' said a chastened Daphne. 'So, where are we off to now?'

'Good question,' Sarah said honestly. 'I thought the police would be on the beach. I'm a bit stumped to be honest. Wait, do you think Charles knows?'

Daphne squared her hairdo and wrapped today's cerise pashmina around her shoulders more securely. 'Dunno. Only one way to find out.' With that, she strode off down the little parade of shops.

'What do you mean? He must live near Francesca, doesn't he?'

Daphne had come to a halt in front of the antiques emporium, which had its sign turned to 'closed'. 'No, he lives above his shop. I thought you knew that?'

With that, Daphne started rapping on the smaller wooden door next to the glass shop entrance. As Sarah knew to her cost, this was a horrible way to get a wake-up call. But, when Charles eventually opened the door a crack and peered out at them, she thought he was looking a lot better than she had after her own early morning encounter with Daphne.

Daphne bustled past him in her inimitable way, and shot straight up the stairs, followed by an enthusiastic Hamish. This was a new place – his favourite type of human habitation – and besides, there was a strong smell of bacon.

Sarah and Charles were left looking at each other awkwardly. At least Charles was actually dressed, which was more than Sarah had been when Daphne had pounced on her this morning. True, his hair was standing up in tufts, making him look less debonair than usual, but his manners were impeccable as ever.

'Well, I seem to be receiving visitors for breakfast so, after you, dear lady,' he said, gesturing for her to follow her companions.

When she arrived at the top of the flight of stairs, she was pleasantly surprised. The whole floor was open-plan, with large windows facing out onto the beautiful sea. The floors, walls and ceilings were white, setting off an eclectic collection of modern art. There was a pair of large modular sofas in dove grey cord with a long, low coffee table in between, covered with the type of arty books Sarah had often assumed interior designers bought by the yard. These were being read, though, as there were bookmarks sticking out of some of them and one had even been left splayed over the arm of a chair.

'Come and sit down,' Charles said, beckoning her to a scrubbed pine table with mismatched chairs around it. Daphne had already got comfortable – but at least she hadn't done her usual trick and popped the kettle on. Sarah saw this as a sign she was on her best behaviour. Hamish was in the small kitchen area, nose twitching as he stared longingly upwards at the frying pan on the hob. A low flame flickered and the aroma and sizzle of browning bacon had Sarah's stomach rumbling.

Then she remembered, with a stab of unease, that they were

there for a reason. And it wasn't to mooch a free breakfast off Charles, but to tell him that his semi-ex-wife, or whatever the situation was, would shortly be arrested. She cleared her throat.

'Something on your mind?' Charles said brightly, looking up from the cafetiere he'd just filled with coffee grounds.

'Um no. That smells delicious,' said Sarah weakly.

THIRTY-THREE

Once they were all settled with mugs of coffee and large bacon butties, and Daphne had doused her roll to her satisfaction with every condiment going from ketchup to brown sauce, via mayonnaise and back again, Sarah cleared her throat.

'Charles, I think I should just say—' she started, when Daphne drowned her out.

'Sarah just wants to say a very big thank you from us all, for taking a bunch of waifs and strays in off the street.' Daphne hoisted her mug in a salute and Sarah joined in a little mutedly.

What on earth was Daphne playing at? She'd told her that Mariella was about to swoop on Francesca Diggory. Didn't Charles deserve to know that? It didn't seem right to keep him in the dark. But, as she met her friend's eyes, she saw a martial light there that only appeared in dire emergencies – the last time, if memory served her, had been when the meanest school prefect, Lavender Carshaw, had nearly caught them filching biscuits from the kitchens in the dead of night. Sarah had been about to step on the wonky floorboard outside the refectory and Daphne had stopped her with this very same glare.

Then there was a ring at the doorbell. Sarah almost

jumped out of her skin. There was something about the tone which made her immediately suspect it was the police. So extreme was her reaction that Hamish looked up for a second from his dedicated snuffling around the scene of a dropped bit of bacon, and Daphne frowned at her again over the rim of her mug.

'I wonder who that can be?' Charles said mildly, putting down his cup and sauntering over to the huge windows looking out onto the parade. 'Ah,' he said, with a pointed glance over at the women.

'Oh yes, Charles, didn't I mention the police? Mari said they were going to make an arrest. I could have sworn she said Francesca, but now I'm *almost* beginning to think she might have meant...' said Daphne, sounding very flustered.

Charles rubbed a hand over his eyes, then squared his shoulders and made his way down the stairs. At the door, they heard him welcome the newcomers and Sarah heard the measured plod of three sets of feet trudging back up to them. It was with no surprise that she greeted PCs Dumbarton and Deeside.

'Ladies,' the stouter of the two men said. 'Funny how you keep on cropping up.'

'Hahaha, yes so funny,' trilled Daphne unconvincingly. 'As it happens, we were just going,' she added, scooping up the remains of her bacon bap and cramming it in her handbag. Sarah looked on, wincing at the bacteria that must be lurking in the cavernous innards of that receptacle. And she very much wanted to stay put, too. Who knew what interesting titbits they might hear?

'OK, Sarah, come on then,' said Daphne, standing up and brushing a lapful of crumbs onto Charles's pristine flooring, much to Hamish's delight.

Sarah took a sip from her coffee, and another bite from her roll, and tried to look as though she was bustling while actually moving as slowly as possible. Charles, surveying her with raised eyebrows, finally turned to the policemen.

'I don't mind if these ladies stay,' he said.

'I don't think so, sir,' said Deeside firmly. 'If you'll just be on your way, now, madam and, erm, madam,' he said, turning aside from the route to the stairs.

'Oh, of course,' said Sarah brightly, as though she hadn't been dawdling at all. 'And Charles, do, um, give us a call later if we can help with anything,' she added.

Sarah and Daphne then clumped down the stairs, with an unwilling Hamish squirming under Sarah's arm. The problem with having no carpeting, Sarah mused, was that although it was a terribly modern, clean look – excellent if you had pets or lots of fabulous art and wanted your place to look like a trendy gallery – it did make every footstep very audible. When they finally reached the hallway, Sarah stopped Daphne with her hand on the doorknob. She put her fingers to her lips and gestured upwards towards the flat meaningfully. Upstairs, all was promisingly quiet... they must be about to start the interview, thought Sarah, and she'd be able to hear every word from here. Just then, one of the constables poked his head over the bannisters and eyed them beadily.

'Having trouble with the lock there, ladies?'

'Oops, no, I mean, yes, but I've got it now,' said Daphne, opening the door at last.

Outside on the step, with the door closed, she whipped round to confront her friend. 'Well? What on earth was all that about?'

'Come on, Daphne. Didn't you want to hear what those policemen were going to say to Charles?'

'Oh, he'll tell us himself in a minute. They can't seriously suspect him. What motive could he have?'

'He had the opportunity, unlike Francesca who was abroad. He had the physical strength. And yesterday he admitted he didn't like the man. *And* he was out on the beach in the early morning.'

'Well, when you put it like that... But hardly anyone liked Bill. Half of Merstairs could be in jail, frankly,' Daphne said.

'Could Charles have done it to protect Francesca?'

'From what? Bill would never have made a pass at her, she's too scary. And why on earth would Charles want to protect her anyway? He doesn't even like her enough to finish a holiday with her,' said Daphne.

Sarah didn't agree – she was sure Charles would be chivalrous enough to stick up for his former wife whatever the state of their relationship. But she still felt relief washing over her at Daphne's words. 'Well, if Charles *didn't* do it, I suppose Francesca could have paid someone else to kill both Gus and Bill. I don't think she'd think twice about it. She must have staff coming out of her ears.'

'I think one of Hannah Bett's daughters does her cleaning, actually...' said Daphne.

'Well there you are! And Hannah Betts was Bill Turbot's ex-wife.'

'Ye-es,' said Daphne slowly. 'But why would Francesca kill Bill? And Hannah doesn't have any connection to Gus. She hardly even goes to the Jolly Roger, she's always too busy with the Beach Café.'

'Maybe she killed him as he was competition for her custom?' Sarah said, searching for ideas.

'I mean, hardly. The Beach Café is tea and snacks, while the Jolly Roger, well it's a pub. It's busiest in the evening, when the café is closed.'

'None of this gets us any closer to why they want to question Charles. It has to be something to do with Francesca. There can't be any such thing as a coincidence in a murder investigation.'

'Oh well, even if they are questioning him, he'll be fine,

don't you worry about him,' said Daphne, patting Sarah's
shoulder.

'Me? I'm not worried,' Sarah squeaked, cheeks pink. She
shouldn't have worn this cotton jumper today, it was just that
little bit too thick for the weather, which was perking up with
every minute that passed.

'Good. Because I'm getting a strong message from the
Beyond that all will be well with Charles,' Daphne intoned.

Just then, the door to the flat opened, and Charles emerged,
flanked by the two constables. He had his arms out straight in
front of him. Sarah wondered why he was walking so
awkwardly. Then she saw. There were handcuffs on his wrists.

THIRTY-FOUR

Both Daphne and Sarah watched in horror as Charles stumbled past them. Even Hamish let out a little whine, at seeing his new hero, the bacon cook, being led firmly away. The squad car was double-parked on the pavement outside Marlene's Plaice, a couple of shops down from Charles's antiques store. One PC opened the rear door while the other put a hand – quite roughly, in Sarah's view – on Charles's hair and pushed him into the back seat, just the way they did with violent detainees in the cops-and-robbers TV shows that Sarah secretly adored.

'Why do they do that thing with people's heads?' Daphne murmured, fascinated, at Sarah's side.

'I've often wondered,' said Sarah. 'I think it's to stop the culprit banging their head on the car and then suing the police – but that's not the important thing!'

'No, it isn't,' said Daphne, but her voice was a bit dreamy. Sarah hoped she wasn't going to pull any clairvoyant nonsense and say the spirits had told her this would happen. If they had, why had they only just announced everything was going to be fine, and why had her chin been on the floor, like Sarah's, only a few seconds ago?

Then Charles spoke, his voice sounding husky and unused, as though he'd already been incarcerated for days. 'Ladies! Can you please call someone for me? It's—' he said, just before they slammed the door on him.

'Yes, yes, of course! Byeee,' said Daphne, waving to him as though he was off on a delightful trip.

Sarah opened her mouth but no words came out. She didn't know when she had last been so shocked – which was a bit ridiculous really, as Charles had been her prime suspect on and off ever since they'd found Gus. But somehow it still seemed completely wrong that he was being carted off like this.

The car drew out into the road, still pretty clear of traffic as it was early yet, and soon it was just a speck in the distance, which both women watched intently until it disappeared.

With a sigh, Daphne pulled away. 'Well, that's that, then,' she said, shifting her handbag until it was more securely on her shoulder and preparing to walk off.

'Hang on a second, we've got to call whoever Charles wanted us to ring,' Sarah reminded her. 'Did you get what he said? I couldn't quite hear.'

'Nope,' said Daphne. 'I thought you heard. Oh no!' she added, suddenly distraught. 'This is terrible. His last request, and we don't know what it was.'

'Well, let's not panic,' Sarah said, though her heart was racing. 'What do people usually want in a situation like this?'

'A cigarette? Special meal? A priest?'

'Come on, Daph! They're not going to shoot him,' Sarah said, more confidently than she felt. 'This is Merstairs. He probably just wants us to call his next of kin...'

'That'll be Francesca,' said Daphne.

'Or a lawyer! I bet that was it,' said Sarah quickly. 'Do you know who that would be?'

'Not a clue,' Daphne confessed cheerfully. 'Do you?'

'Well of course not! I've only been here two minutes,' said

Sarah. She couldn't help it, her tone was grumpy. Daphne had made Charles a promise, which she apparently had no intention of fulfilling. That sort of thing didn't go down well with Sarah. 'I suppose we'll just have to find one. Or maybe...'

'What's that?' asked Daphne.

'Well, assuming Francesca hasn't been arrested too... You did originally think Mariella was off to get her first thing this morning. But if she's still at liberty, as it were, she might know who Charles uses.'

'Yes. I suppose they must have had someone who dealt with the divorce,' said Daphne, sounding as though all that was now perfectly sorted out.

Sarah snorted. 'But they're not divorced, are they? Who knows if they've even done a proper separation agreement. Anyway, that's none of my business,' she added quickly. 'I just think Francesca is probably our best bet.'

'Well, that's lucky, I suppose, because I do have *her* number. I need it for when I store the Tai Chi equipment,' Daphne said, with that virtuous air she adopted when talking of all her various hobbies.

Sarah glanced at her. She already had her suspicions about Daphne's wild swimming with the Mermaids. And she was pretty sure she did precious little Tai Chi either. But that wasn't relevant now. 'Great,' she said. 'Well, let's give her a ring.'

'OK, but seeing Charles hauled away like that was such a shock, I really need to sit down,' said Daphne plaintively.

Sarah patted Daphne's arm. Her friend did look quite upset. 'Of course. Where's the nearest café? Well, I suppose we're right outside Marlene's. If she's open, we could grab a tea here and you could make the call.'

'Oh, that would be so much better,' said Daphne, plonking herself down immediately at one of Marlene's twiddly metal tables. Hamish stationed himself by her feet, seemingly just as fed up as she was with the events of the morning.

Sarah surveyed them both for a second, and then pushed on the door to the restaurant. To her surprise, it opened. Inside, the place was spick and span, with a regiment of tables, each perfectly dressed with violet cloths, sparkling glasses, dainty napkins and pristine menus. There was no one in sight but some noises off in the kitchen area sounded promising.

'Excuse me?' she said as she walked towards the source of the sounds. There was a short silence, and then a woman bustled out. It was Marlene.

'Can aye help you?' Marlene asked, her mauve apron toning with the lilac walls and violet tablecloths. She was obviously almost as much of a fan of purple as Daphne was. Her eyes, however, were pink, and Sarah suddenly remembered that she was the late Bill Turbot's sister.

'I'm sorry to trouble you, especially given... um, everything. I was so sorry to hear about your brother,' she added.

'Thank you,' said Marlene quietly, raising a lavender hanky to her brimming eyes.

'I just wondered whether you were open yet?' Sarah went on. 'You see, we've, um, just also had rather a shock, and my friend and I could do with a cup of tea.'

'Oh? Oh, in that case...' Marlene, who had seemed to be on the verge of insisting she was closed, softened in the face of adversity, perhaps because her own family was going through such a calamity at the moment. 'Aye dare say aye could rustle up a pot of tea. Outside, if you have your little dog with you again.'

'You have a good memory,' said Sarah, surprised. 'Outside would be great.'

'Aye never forget a face. In this business, it pays,' said Marlene sagely. 'You're with that Daphne, are you?' she added with the slightest suspicion of a sniff.

'I am. Thank you so much, we really appreciate it.'

Marlene seemed mollified at this and permitted herself a

small smile. 'Go and make yourselves comfortable, then,' she said kindly.

Sarah forbore to say that Daphne had already installed herself. Instead, she thanked the woman again and went back outside.

'Any luck?' she asked, taking a seat. Daphne and Hamish looked very comfy, both gazing out at the waves over the road with similar faraway expressions on their faces.

'Luck? With what?' Daphne said dreamily.

'With ringing Francesca,' said Sarah a little sharply. How on earth could Daphne have forgotten?

'Oh! Oh, I knew there was something...' Daphne said, rooting in her capacious handbag.

After waiting with what passed for patience for a few minutes, while all sorts of ill-assorted objects appeared and disappeared from the depths of the great big purple bag – including the bacon butty – Sarah couldn't help but say, 'Well?'

Daphne looked up, shamefaced, and replaced the bag on her knee, where Hamish gave it a rapturous sniff. 'I'm sorry, Sarah, I've just remembered! I've left my phone at home. I spoke to Mari before leaving the house and then I must have forgotten all about it.'

'Drat! How are we going to ring Francesca now? I don't have her number.'

'That's simple, we'll ring the town hall. They'll have it.'

'Yes, but will they give it to us?' Sarah fretted. She got her own phone out, and googled Merstairs town hall. As she'd thought, no one picked up – it was still early. But at the end of a long, rambling recorded message there was a reminder that if the matter was urgent, callers should contact the police. Of course! They should just ring Mariella. She must know what was going on. There would be a duty solicitor that Charles could use temporarily at the police station, and Mariella could get the number of his preferred legal representative and either she or they could call them.

Sarah was just explaining her train of thought to Daphne when Marlene arrived with a fancy mauve tray complete with matching teapot, teacups and saucers, milk jug, sugar bowl and strainer, with a dainty piece of lemon lying in its own special bowl. She set it down with a bit of a clatter – it must weigh a ton, Sarah thought. Then she started fussing around handing out the cups.

'Well, ladies, so you've had a bit of a to-do this morning, have you?' Marlene said, still puffy around the eyelids but seeming eager to be distracted from her woes. She held the mauve teapot aloft. 'Who's for tea?'

Sarah gave her a nod and a slightly tight-lipped smile, but Daphne immediately burst into speech. 'Oh, Marlene, you wouldn't believe it! You must have seen the police car earlier. You're only a couple of doors down from Charles.'

'Charles, was it?' Marlene said, pausing in pouring the tea into Sarah's cup. Something about her expression made Sarah sure she was making a series of rapid calculations in her head. 'Arrested, was he?' she said, finishing off the cup and now holding the tiny milk jug. 'Milk?'

'Just a dash,' said Sarah, hoping Daphne wouldn't give anything else away. But the floodgates had opened, and Daphne was thrilled to have an audience after her dramatic morning.

'It's so terrible,' she said, shaking her head and putting a hand to her cheek. 'That poor, poor man. To think of him, all alone, and in peril.'

'In peril, is he?' Marlene held up the sugar tongs. 'One or two, dearie?'

'Oh, I think three, don't you, Sarah? For the shock.'

Sarah, who privately thought Daphne was exploiting the situation for all it was worth, gave the tiniest of nods. It was

possible, though, that Marlene might let some useful information slip, even while she was trying to extract it from them.

'Do you know why the police might be wanting to question
Charles?' Sarah asked her, cursing herself a little for her lack of
subtlety. Still, if they wanted to help the poor man, the sooner
they got to the nub of the matter the better.

'Aye'd imagine it'd be about that business with the brewery,
wouldn't it be?' Marlene said absently. 'Questioned by the
police, you say? Taken off in a police car?'

'Yes,' said Daphne. 'I thought you said you'd seen him being
driven away?'

'Not exactly...' said Marlene. 'But it makes sense, doesn't it?'

Sarah sat up. 'What was the business with the brewery?'
None of this was getting them any closer to finding Charles's
lawyer, or even ringing Mariella to get her on the case – but it
was intriguing, nevertheless. They'd been at the brewery headquarters yesterday for hours, and not once had Charles
mentioned any particular issues he had with the firm.

'Oh, he did kick up a fuss with Gus, he did, about the way
the brewery lorries parked outside his shop, delivering casks to
the Jolly Roger. Not that it made the slightest difference to his
trade, really,' said Marlene. 'Well, who wants to buy all that
nasty dirty old stuff in his shop, when you can get lovely new
things that are so *tasteful*,' she added, looking at her mauve tea
set fondly.

'Mm, absolutely,' murmured Sarah, eyeing the lurid teapot
sideways. 'But what exactly did Charles do?'

'Oh, it was silly really,' said Marlene, warming to her remi-
niscence. 'He started small, you know, just putting up a sign
outside his shop saying no parking. Well, that wasn't enforce-
able. The lorries are so big, they take up quite a bit of the road
when they stop to unload. Aye don't think they wanted to be in
his way, but the streets are narrow here. It's part of our quaint
olde worlde charm,' Marlene said firmly.

'So did he just give up?'

Marlene gave a trill of laughter. 'Oh you don't know our Charles, does she, Daphne? Charles doesn't give up. Next he started putting out those traffic cones on the pavement. Well, of course they just moved them, took them two seconds. And then he got out the big guns.'

'Oh really? In what way?'

'The town hall bunch,' said Marlene darkly. 'You know. That lot. Well, he's got an in with the mayor, hasn't he? Of course, they couldn't do a thing. But it did mean he was at daggers drawn with poor old Gus.'

'Was he? Really?' Sarah took a sip of her tea. 'Mm, this is delicious,' she said, but she was a little distracted. And, to be honest, pretty worried. They'd come here and sat down to try and help Charles – but it looked like Marlene had finally provided a motive for him to bump off pub landlord Gus Trubshaw.

THIRTY-FIVE

It didn't take many more sips of tea for Sarah to come to the conclusion that the whole idea was absurd. Would anyone really kill a fellow human being over something as trivial as a lorry parking outside their shop? But then, if the lorries could be blamed for blighting one's livelihood... Though Sarah secretly rather agreed with Marlene on the contents of Charles's shop.

Thankfully, a series of distant bumps and crashes signalled a crisis of some sort in Marlene's kitchen, and she left them to it, obviously with a tinge of regret that she hadn't drained every last drop of gossip from this promising cup. As soon as she bustled off, Sarah turned to Daphne.

'We must ring Mariella straight away! Poor Charles, he's been in police custody for ages now and we've done nothing at all to help him.'

'Well don't look at me, you know my phone's at home.' Daphne shrugged.

Sarah pointed to her own mobile on the table. 'So tell me the number, please, and I'll call her.'

Daphne looked at her, open-mouthed. 'I don't know Mari's

work phone off by heart. Don't tell me you know everyone's numbers these days either, I won't believe you.'

Sarah sat back, feeling a little stymied. Daphne was absolutely right. Mobile numbers were so long, she barely even pretended to try and memorise them. Apart from Peter's, of course. She knew that off by heart. But there was no use ringing it any more.

'So what on earth do we do? We made Charles a promise.'

Daphne waved a hand. 'Oh, he won't expect us to do anything really,' she said confidently.

But Sarah couldn't let it rest. If her last words to a friend, when she was being dragged off in handcuffs by the police, were, 'Please call somebody-or-other,' she'd feel very let down if they didn't. 'I'm sorry, I just can't leave it at that.'

Daphne, draining her cup, got to her feet decisively. 'All right then, let's go home and I'll ring Mari from there. We can look up all the solicitors in Merstairs, too. One of them must deal with the Diggorys.'

'Great idea, Daphne,' said Sarah, feeling galvanised all of a sudden. She popped her head round the door of the restaurant and quickly paid Marlene. Luckily, the woman was quite distracted and didn't ask anything else about Charles. There was an extremely ominous hissing sound coming from the kitchen. 'Maybe the espresso machine's on the blink again,' she said, grimacing.

Sarah and Daphne walked quickly back to their cottages, with Hamish surging on ahead importantly, as though he understood the air of urgency and endorsed it with all of his doggy being. He was quite a Charles fan – and even more so after this morning's butties. Had he fully understood that it was Tinkerbell's owner they were trying to save, he would have run every step of the way. As it was, they arrived breathless and slightly dishevelled in next to no time. Thankfully Daphne found the keys to her cottage on the first try and they were soon brushing past the array of umbrellas, walking sticks, benches, wellingtons and hats in the hall to get to the kitchen.

There were still signs of the purple soup-making from a couple of nights ago, Sarah noted with dismay. A large purple-splattered pan was on the hob and there was a pile of dishes in the sink. Normally, she would just have rolled up her sleeves and got stuck into the washing-up, but today poor Charles had to take priority.

'OK, so where exactly is your phone, Daphne?' Sarah asked, as Daphne put her bag down on the overflowing table and kindly filled up a bowl with water for Hamish, who licked her hand in appreciation when she put it down on the floor for him.

'Oh, goodness, now you're asking,' said Daphne, putting her hand to her forehead and shutting her eyes. Sarah hoped she wasn't going to start communing with any spirits about it.

'I'm sure it was somewhere round here...' Daphne turned round, shedding an earring as she went.

Sarah sighed. 'Let's be systematic about this. What were you doing when you spoke to Mari?'

'Oh, that's easy. I was in here, doing the washing-up... or was I putting the dishes away... or feeding the cat? No, wait, I was putting the wash on...'

'All right,' said Sarah quickly. 'We might get further if you just start looking by the sink, and I'll search the rest of the room.' She hurried to the table and started leafing through the great piles of electricity bills, pizza delivery leaflets, local news-papers and books strewn everywhere.

'I could have been upstairs, I suppose,' said Daphne, still standing in the middle of the room and no nearer to searching anything. 'Or possibly outside, because I had to get Mephisto in this morning, I promised the milkman I wouldn't let him out until after the delivery...'

Once Sarah had checked the phone wasn't on any of the chairs, she skirted round Daphne and started to look near the cooker and sink. No sign, though she found a pair of socks – mercifully clean – and a string of beads in the washing-up rack.

'Think, Daphne! It's really important,' she exhorted her friend, while scanning the cookery books on the windowsill. She couldn't have put it in one of those, could she? But stranger things had happened...

Just when she was beginning to feel Daphne's phone would never be seen again, she lifted the lid of the big teapot propping up the books on the sill. Inside was a large shiny phone.

'Oh my goodness, Daphne, it's in here! You could have poured boiling water on it,' Sarah exclaimed.

'Well, hardly, that's where I always keep it, nice and safe,' said Daphne, taking the phone and calling Mariella.

Sarah subsided onto a chair and met Hamish's eyes. *People*, he seemed to be saying, and his mistress wholeheartedly agreed.

Mariella's line was engaged, so Sarah started googling solicitors in Merstairs. There were a surprising number, for a place that Daphne always insisted was so law-abiding. Which on earth was Charles's firm, though? She scanned the list of names. There were so many, she'd have to take a stab at random. Which would it be, Glasier Noble? Maybe Smith, Smith and Smith? No, that sounded too pedestrian. Could it be Trumpington-Stanley-Harcourt? Realising she had to start somewhere, and conscious of how much time had gone by since Charles had been arrested, Sarah quickly dialled the Trumpington number as it sounded the poshest.

'Trumpington, how may I help you?' fluted a young girl in impeccably cut-glass tones.

Sarah explained she was looking for whoever dealt with Charles Diggory, and if it wasn't their firm, would they possibly know who it was? There was a short silence, then Sarah heard the girl press a button, clearly thinking she had muted the call. Then her voice rang out in a much less cultivated accent, 'Oi, Stan, do you know who does for that Diggory geezer?'

'Charles, you mean? Poor blighter, I think Francesca's had all his dosh, hasn't she? No point doing any work for him,' said a smug-sounding man.

'Yeah, but someone must be handling his stuff, innit? Boyce, weren't it?'

There was a pause, then the man answered. 'More fool them. But you're right, Trudy. Who wants to know, anyway?'

The girl pressed another button, probably to 'unmute' the call and get Sarah's name, but she actually cut her off. Just as well, as Sarah hadn't fancied explaining why she needed the information. 'The firm is called Boyce,' she said, turning excitedly to Daphne.

'Boyce? Gosh, I wouldn't have thought...' said Daphne.

Sarah hastily found their website, and then saw what her friend meant. It had a decidedly low-rent look about it, a tone set by the lurid banner running across the top of the landing page: *No win, no fee injury claims – tripped over a pothole? Hurt at work? Call us now!*

'Hmm,' said Sarah. 'They look like ambulance chasers... I wonder what Charles is thinking of?'

'Well, beggars can't be choosers, I suppose,' said Daphne, sipping her tea.

Something about that phrase made Sarah think. Her mind drifted to Charles's antique shop, and his rail of carefully curated suits. The fact that the place was perpetually empty began to strike her as poignant, rather than absurd. Poor Charles, waiting throughout each long day for a sale, ready to charm and beguile the very few people who ventured in – and the even tinier number who really wanted to make a purchase. And those suits, so well-pressed, speaking of a leisured past, where pale linens and exquisitely cut jackets had been de rigueur. She didn't know why it hadn't struck her before, but they were all pretty much the same size, tailored carefully for a rangy, long-limbed frame. They would all look great on a patrician-looking man of a certain age... They were *his* suits. He was penniless, but doing everything he could, right down to selling his own clothes and possessions, to hold his head up and keep his lifestyle going.

Then Sarah also remembered Charles's lavish hand with the drinks in the Jolly Roger, and even the bacon they'd eaten this morning. It had been of the finest quality, wrapped in greaseproof paper from Merstairs' one good butcher, not in a plastic supermarket pack. If Charles was so poor that he needed to flog the clothes off his back, wouldn't he be wise to be more economical with his food and drink?

But Sarah bit her lip here. It was all very well for her to moralise about what people should or should not do with their own money. Life would be pretty bleak if you couldn't enjoy a treat now and then. Perhaps Charles only splashed out on a rasher of good bacon once in a blue moon – and they'd come round this morning and scoffed it all.

'Sarah? Sarah, are you going to ring Boyce, or do you want me to?'

'Just dialling,' said Sarah, looking up into Daphne's large brown eyes.

'Great. I'll make a fresh pot of tea,' said her friend, bustling over to the sink. Hamish, moving restlessly under the table, clearly wondered if this was a signal indicating a snack was incoming. He bustled over to join Daphne and help with the tea preparations, while Sarah took a breath and made the call.

This time, the girl on the end of the phone was chirpy and unashamedly local, no pretence at all. 'Boyce, what can we do you for?'

'Oh, um, hello,' said Sarah. 'I was just wondering, could I possibly speak to, um, the person who deals with Charles Diggory?'

There was silence on the other end of the phone for a beat. 'What've you heard about Charles?' asked the girl. Then there was the sound of a scuffle, as though the phone was being wrenched away from her. Another voice came on. 'Boyce, how may I help you?' This time the speaker was a man, and his accent was a lot smoother – though not quite as mellifluous as the lawyer at Trumpington.

'Oh, well, this is a bit tricky, but we were with Charles Diggory earlier and, ahem, he's had a spot of bother...'

'If by that you mean his arrest by Merstairs' finest, then don't worry, we're already on the case,' said the man, sounding highly amused. 'May I ask what your interest in the matter is?'

'Actually, Charles asked us to phone you... well, we couldn't quite hear what he was saying, but we think it was that. Anyway, do you know what he's actually been arrested for?' Sarah asked. 'And when might we expect him to be, er, let out?'

'I'm afraid I cannot discuss my client's case with you. Unless, of course, you are Mrs Diggory?'

'Oh, no. No, I'm not,' said Sarah hurriedly.

'Thought so,' said the man, now sounding insufferably self-satisfied. 'I will wish you a good morning, then.' With that, the call was disconnected.

Daphne put a fresh cup of tea at Sarah's elbow and the pair stared at each other, disconsolate. Though Sarah had often considered the possibility that Charles was involved in the appearance of Gus Trubshaw in the beach hut, she realised she had only toyed with the notion in the way you might tinker with a tricky crossword clue. She had never once really believed he could have put those long and elegant hands of his around Gus's neck and squeezed hard enough to stifle the life out of him – or drugged him either. Nor, surely, could he have pulled Bill Turbot's woggle tight. Cold-blooded killing just didn't seem Charles's style. He had the dandified air of the gifted amateur, the gentleman who drifted into things as an amusement, but was never entirely serious about anything.

Was all that just a façade? Was it possible that Charles was so broke that he would actually consider killing Gus? But how on earth could he gain financially from that? Unless it was, as Marlene had suggested, something to do with his parking war with the pub landlord. Surely he couldn't really think the shop would thrive if only the brewery vans never obstructed his shop doorway? But people would do a lot, to maintain their way of life. Someone who wasn't willing to compromise on bacon might well have their priorities skewed about many other things – like life, death and morality.

'I know Charles is a regular at the Jolly Roger, and he's said he really liked Gus. But they did have that argument about access to his shop...' Sarah said tentatively.

'You're wondering if that went really sour? And whether Charles might have done away with Gus, to get him to stop?' Daphne said, her eyes round with disbelief.

'Well,' said Sarah, a little shamefaced. 'Anything's worth considering. It's not like we've got a lot of other great theories to choose from. And maybe Charles is so hard up he can't afford to lose even a single sale.'

'He's broke all right,' said Daphne slowly. 'But that doesn't make him a murderer. And what about Bill? Why would he kill him? In any case, I thought we were all friends. We had a lovely day out yesterday at the brewery.'

Sarah raised her eyebrows. As far as she was concerned, that had been a fact-finding mission designed to further their investigation. But yes, it had also been fun – in between the hair-raising moments with Mr Grimes – she couldn't deny it. 'I mean, I hardly know Charles really,' she said.

Daphne snorted. 'Tell that to Francesca. She's funny about Charles. They didn't get on at all, and split up ages ago. But why aren't they divorced yet?'

Sarah assumed this was a rhetorical question, as she had no answers to provide. 'Oh, none of this is getting us any further with helping Charles get out of jail. Perhaps you should just ring Mariella again and see what's going on at her end, if the lawyer won't tell us anything?'

'She hates it when I poke my nose in,' said Daphne, but she took up her phone cheerfully enough, redialled and put it on speakerphone.

'Mum, I've got a lot on, I'll ring you later,' came Mariella's harassed tones.

'Hi love, just wondering why your lot dragged Charles off this morning,' said Daphne chirpily.

Sarah could hear Mariella's heavy sigh clearly. There was a scrabbling sound as Mariella took the call somewhere more discreet. 'Listen, I'm only telling you this because he'll tell you himself. We were acting on a tip-off.'

Daphne gasped. 'Who tipped you off? Was it about the parking? Just nod your head if it was,' she said excitedly.

'Mum, we're not on a video call. I'll see you later,' said Mariella, and put the phone down.

'You heard her,' Daphne said to Sarah. 'It *was* about the brewery vans outside his shop. Well, thank heavens. They'll soon realise that wasn't serious,' she said with a big smile.

Sarah wasn't quite sure how on earth Daphne thought she'd got confirmation from Mariella, but she was more worried about something else. 'Listen, seriously, if Charles didn't do it, who do you think did?'

'Well, I did think the Crazy Golf boys were going to be our killers. But that was a washout, they're such a bunch of weeds,' said Daphne disconsolately.

Sarah, who didn't disagree but wouldn't have put it quite like that, frowned and thought. 'Who have we got left, then? The staff of the Jolly Roger, I suppose – in case it was some sort of workplace rivalry. Then regulars. I really thought Bill Turbot was the prime suspect, but, well, not any more. The brewery people, but they surely wouldn't stoop to that. Maybe someone at the Ship? But no matter which way you look at it, no matter what the police might say, Charles is still on that list. He drank in the Jolly Roger all the time, he knew Gus and Bill, he owned the beach hut...'

'But why would Charles do such a thing?' said Daphne plaintively. 'Why would you think he could be a cold-blooded killer?'

'Yes, why?' came a familiar drawling voice from just outside the kitchen. Both Sarah and Daphne whipped round, to see Charles Diggory lounging in the doorway, a thin smile on his face.

THIRTY-SIX

'Daphne!' said Sarah. 'You really shouldn't leave your front door open, not when there's a...'

'A murderer on the loose?' said Charles, his smile sardonic.

'Oh, haha, not *you* of course,' said Daphne loudly, as Sarah blushed. 'I did think I'd shut it, but the latch can't have gone down properly,' she said, furrowing her brow.

'It was swinging open when I got here,' said Charles. 'I'd love a cup of tea.'

Immediately, both Daphne and Sarah jumped up guiltily.

'You must be exhausted, after your terrible morning. How were the police? Were they nice to you? No, of course they weren't, how silly of me. We rang your lawyers, anyway,' Sarah babbled, trying to make amends while they bustled about making the tea.

'It's all right,' said Charles wearily as they all sat down. 'I don't blame you for suspecting me. I'd suspect me too, in your shoes. The thing is, though, well, it's like this. I didn't do it.'

Sarah bit her lip, but Daphne spoke up. 'That's all very well, Charles dear, but you see the thing is – that's exactly what a murderer would say.'

The words were brutal enough, but there was something about Daphne's delivery, and the droll way she was holding a violently knitted yellow and green tea cosy in one hand, and one of her beloved garden gnomes in the other, that suddenly made Sarah see the funny side. She started to giggle and, having started, couldn't stop. After a few seconds, Charles joined in too, and soon they were all laughing helplessly, sitting round the table heaped high with old newspapers, crumb-smeared plates and mugs.

It was quite a few minutes before Charles mopped his eyes with a perfectly laundered linen handkerchief. 'Ah, I needed that,' he said, putting the hanky away – but not before Sarah had spotted the monogram. She remembered seeing it briefly on Wednesday in the Jolly Roger pub, but then it had been upside down and she hadn't been able to quite make sense of the initials. Today she realised it was a large, curly F D. No prizes now for guessing who it belonged to. Immediately, her own laughter died away. Only Daphne was left chortling now, her shoulders shaking while Hamish looked on at the little group in fascination. Humans were a very strange breed, he decided, as he rested his head once more on his folded paws.

'No, seriously, though, Charles. They haven't charged you with anything, have they?' Sarah asked.

'Course not,' said Charles robustly. 'Nothing they could stick on me.'

'But in that case...' Sarah started, then tailed off.

'No, go on. Say it,' Charles urged her, turning his piercing blue eyes her way.

'Well, why handcuff you and all that? If they had nothing on you. Why not question you in your own home? Why drag you down to the station?'

'Yes,' Daphne piped up. 'It looked like you wouldn't be coming out for the next twenty years.'

'And now everyone in Merstairs will think that too,' said

Charles ruefully. Suddenly things didn't seem at all funny any more. But Sarah was still waiting for an explanation. Charles sighed. 'The thing is, the police were pointed in my direction. By someone who is, let's say, not a well-wisher.'

'But who is it? Do you know?' Daphne's eyebrows were perfect half-moons of puzzled enquiry.

'Three guesses,' said Charles with a wry twist to his mouth.

'Not... Francesca?' Daphne ventured.

Charles nodded once, then looked away. It was clearly a painful betrayal.

'But why would she do that? Surely it's not in her interests... For one thing, she'd have to do all the pick-ups at your grand-children's school,' said Sarah.

'It seems she'd consider that a very worthy exchange for putting me behind bars.' Charles shook his head.

'Is it just the woman scorned thing? Or is there more to it?'

'Sarah!' said Daphne, sounding scandalised. 'You can't ask all these questions. Poor Charles. Although, it's ages since you and Francesca split up. What's her beef?'

'Exactly my point,' Sarah said, a little defensively. 'I wasn't trying to be intrusive,' she added apologetically to Charles.

'Don't worry about it,' he said with a wave of his hand. 'After today, my life is going to be pretty much common knowledge. Francesca was fed up with me for years, and treated me like something on the sole of her shoe. But when I was the one to finally bite the bullet and leave, that didn't suit her at all. She felt humiliated, I think, which I do understand. But I was really left with no choice. I honestly didn't think she'd even notice my absence, as we were living such separate lives.' Here, Charles sighed.

Sarah couldn't help sympathising. Although she and Peter had had such a happy marriage, working in the surgery had brought her into contact with many who hadn't been nearly so lucky in their choice of life partner. It must be very hard to limp on from day to day with someone who was unhappy, or who made you feel that way.

'But what happened today? How on earth did she persuade the police to arrest you?'

Charles smiled grimly. 'Oh, it was over that blasted beach hut. Wish I'd never laid eyes on the thing. I took it off her hands in the hope that it would make her less angry with me. But of course appeasement never really works. Her resentment is the perfect renewable energy. If only we could use it to power Merstairs. None of us would ever need to pay a penny in electricity bills again.'

'Oh, right. We thought it might have been the parking row you had with Gus. But I still don't see how owning the hut would make the police think you were a murderer?' Sarah shrugged her shoulders.

'She fudged the dates a bit. She found out – goodness knows how, but the woman has her sources – that the police believe Gus died six weeks ago. I bought the hut from her a month ago, and then immediately sold it on to this dear lady,' Charles said, indicating Daphne, who preened a little. 'But Francesca said I bought it from her back in early February. I don't know how she thought that was going to hold any water, as Michael Benchley the estate agent has all the papers and it's written down in black and white, the dates of exchange and completion, the eye-watering price I paid, the whole lot. But it was enough to give me a very unpleasant morning in the cells. That's one–love to Francesca, I think.'

'You're not going to retaliate, are you?' Sarah asked anxiously.

Charles gave a dry chuckle. 'No, no. I've learnt my lesson there. I shall just accept that everyone in Merstairs now thinks I had a hand in Gus's death – and maybe even Bill's. Apparently Francesca also told the police I was out on the beach early enough in the morning to be the killer. Little did they know she'd actually arranged for me to walk our dog then.'

Sarah blinked. Well, that explained why he'd been up so early. 'Are you sure she's motivated by spite? On the few occasions I've seen her, she still seems to be very fond of you,' Sarah ventured.

'Ha! Hardly,' said Charles.

'Ah, but love and hate can be so close,' said Daphne portentously. 'My spirit guide, Pongo, is always making that point.'

Sarah looked at Daphne in alarm. This was the first she'd heard of a spirit guide. It seemed like an escalation of the Beyond. And the name Pongo was frankly ridiculous. Her eyes met Charles's and both goggled slightly.

'Well, anyway,' said Sarah. 'Now that you're safely out of jail, Charles, I think it's clearer than ever what we need to do.'

Now it was Charles and Daphne's turn to exchange a smile. 'So what's that, then?' Daphne asked. 'Or let me guess. We have to solve this murder, as quickly as possible, to get Charles off the hook.'

'Exactly,' said Sarah. 'I'm glad we're all on the same page at last.'

There was a short silence, as the trio all took sips of slightly cold tea, and each privately thought it was a very good job they were sane – unlike the other two.

THIRTY-SEVEN

Later, Sarah was never quite sure who had come up with the idea. She just knew it wasn't her, because it was frankly silly. First, they found themselves in the Jolly Roger because Daphne said Charles needed a little something. Looking at them both, as they sat in Charles's usual horseshoe-shaped banquette, dodging the dangling sea urchins and lobsters caught in poor Trevor's 'artistic' faux netting, she thought once again of how much her life had changed in the short week she'd been in Merstairs.

She spotted Trevor behind the bar as usual, chatting with the regulars, with no sign now of the red eyes of a couple of days ago. 'Do you think it's odd, that the pub hasn't been shut at all, out of respect?' Sarah asked her companions quietly.

Charles merely shrugged. 'I suppose the conventions could have been observed... but then, Trevor is going to need every penny to keep this place going. The Ship is always nipping away at his business.'

'Ugh, the Ship,' said Daphne.

'What is it with the Ship?' Sarah asked.

'Pub quizzes! Gastro meals! Fancy décor.' Daphne tossed

her head contemptuously, inadvertently tangling her scarf in a lobster's claws.

As she freed herself, Charles carried on. 'Don't forget, they get in the cheapest beers...'

'But, even though you were so interested in the beer-making process, you don't really drink beer anyway, do you? Whenever I've been in here, you've been on the double brandies.'

'That's because whenever you're around, I've always had a dreadful shock,' said Charles, with a gleam in his eye.

Sarah decided to let that one go. 'Anyway, what's wrong with quizzes and nice food? It all sounds very good to me.'

'When you put it like that...' Daphne looked as though she was wavering. 'But we owe it to the memory of Gus to stay faithful to the Roger,' she said more stoutly.

'OK, I suppose,' said Sarah. 'Well, let's get on with it, then.'

Both Daphne and Charles looked at her rather nervously. They had all agreed to their plan of action, but now it came down to it, both seemed extremely reluctant to move. Charles peered into the depths of his glass, now as dry as the Sahara Desert. 'Perhaps... one for the road?'

Daphne nodded enthusiastically enough to dislodge her scarf, but Sarah was firm.

'Hamish needs to get out and stretch his legs,' she said. Charles and Daphne both peered suspiciously under the table, but the little dog leapt obligingly to his feet at his mistress's words, and was now doing a good impression of needing fresh air desperately.

'OK, then,' said Daphne, in the same sort of tone she had used as a schoolgirl years ago, when Sarah forced her to finish a fiendish piece of trigonometry homework.

They waved to Trevor, who broke off an animated conversation with some newcomers to respond in kind, with a melancholy downturn of his lips as he met Sarah's eye. She supposed that was the way it was, if you were in the hospitality business. The show, or the pub, must go on.

Once they were all outside, Sarah wrapped her cardigan more securely round herself and held tightly to Hamish's lead. The wind had got up again. 'At least I'll never be bored with the weather in Merstairs. It seems to change every time I go outside,' she said, smiling at the others. Both had rather pensive expressions. 'Look, nobody wants to take this next step. But I really think we need to. For the sake of the investigation.'

'The investigation! That makes it so official. Whereas Mari keeps saying we're only meddling...'

'Daphne! When have you ever stopped doing anything because your daughter told you to?' Sarah asked her in scandalised tones. 'And as for you, Charles. Don't you want to get all this settled? Once and for all?'

Charles looked at his highly polished shoes. Despite living in a seaside town for all these years, he still dressed as though he was on his way to a posh garden party. Not for him the shorts and sandals – sometimes with socks! – that other Merstairs residents relaxed into. Sarah couldn't help acknowledging that the more formal look suited him.

'I suppose you've got a point, Sarah, but I really think, well... Perhaps I'd be better off doing it alone?' he mumbled.

'Ah, yes, but would you do it? Or would you just let the situation rumble on?' As ever, Sarah was practical and no-nonsense. Yet there was a little part of her that was dying of curiosity too. And a suspicion, that had started out no bigger than a speck on the horizon, had now grown so big that it rivalled the fluffy banks of clouds building up out at sea, right in front of them. 'No point dithering about this for a moment longer. Let's just get on, and get it done,' she said, smiling as brightly as she could at her two reluctant companions.

'OK then. Better hop in my car, I suppose,' said Charles, striding down the street.

Daphne caught Sarah's arm as they turned to follow him. 'Are we really sure this is such a good idea?' she whispered into Sarah's ear.

'Well – not entirely. And part of me thinks no one will even open the door to us when we get there. But on the other hand, I'm dying to get a bit further on with all this, aren't you? Anyway, do we have a better plan?' Sarah hissed back. Daphne just looked at her and shrugged, then they both started jogging to keep up with Charles as he sped off down the street.

THIRTY-EIGHT

It wasn't a long drive in Charles's dashing red vintage Citroën to Paddock Hill, a village just outside Merstairs. But for Sarah it couldn't be over fast enough, as the tension in the car soon became unbearable.

Charles's knuckles were white as he grasped the steering wheel, and he was surely taking every corner at unnecessarily breakneck speed. The pretty green hedgerows and fields of fluffy lambs flashed by terrifyingly fast. She was in the front, and Daphne was lurching around on the back seat. At least Hamish was secure, in Tinkerbell's crate in the boot.

Sarah hoped Hamish wasn't going to be carsick, he'd never really travelled at this velocity before. But, just as the little dog started to whine, they went round a blind bend and were immediately in a narrow lane, gravel flying everywhere. Charles finally slowed down as a charming house in mellow butter-coloured stone emerged at the end of a long drive, edged on both sides with towering rhododendron bushes, heavy with buds. The drive looped in a circle in front of the house. It was a Georgian manor, its imposing front door flanked by two huge urns, out of which grew tumbling hydrangea bushes. It was classically beautiful but, Sarah thought, somehow still a little cold. It suited its one lady owner perfectly.

As they started to get out, Hamish barking in excitement and running around in little circles, Francesca Diggory herself appeared at the front door, with Tinkerbell the Chihuahua in her arms. Both had identical expressions of haughty disdain on their well-bred faces.

'Ah, Francesca,' Charles said, trying his best at bonhomie. 'Great to see you! Just thought we'd pop in to... well, you know.'

Francesca stared at him frostily. 'You see, Charles, that's the thing. I don't know. I have no idea at all why you have chosen to invade my privacy this afternoon with your *friends*.'

Daphne and Sarah looked at each other. 'Hmm, bit of a domestic,' said Daphne in one of her loud whispers.

Sarah picked up Hamish, who was showing unfortunate signs of desperation to be reacquainted with his lady love. 'Thanks so much for seeing us, Francesca,' she said in a measured voice, which she hoped would take some of the strain out of the situation. She had sometimes found that a firm tone could soothe even the most nervous patient.

'Oh, do I have a choice?' Francesca replied icily.

Sarah reflected that, with especially difficult cases, firmness didn't work. What a shame she wasn't still in her surgery, with a full range of tranquillisers to hand. She banished that thought immediately, though. She'd never misuse drugs just to get her way. It was against all she'd stood for throughout her career and contrary to the Hippocratic oath she'd taken – even if very, very tempting sometimes. She looked quickly towards Charles, wondering what on earth had ever possessed him to marry this woman. But maybe she had been nicer, years before. Or perhaps she'd just hidden her true nature better back then.

'We'd love to come in, just for a moment or two.' Charles was at his most persuasive, and Francesca softened visibly. Sarah realised with a stab in the vicinity of her heart that this poor woman might just be in pain, and projecting it back at the man who had caused it.

But then, a second later, she knew Francesca was just horrible. 'You can come in, I suppose,' the woman bit out. 'But that mutt has to be tied up outside. I'm not having its filthy paws on my carpets.' Francesca glared at little Hamish, who put his head on one side and panted adorably at her, as though she'd just given him the best compliment he'd ever heard.

Sarah smarted at the injustice. Hamish was walking on the same surfaces as Tinkerbell – if his paws were dirty, then so must hers be. But maybe that was why Francesca constantly toted her dog under her arm, like a little snarling handbag, Sarah thought crossly.

As the others trooped in, Sarah looped Hamish's lead around one of the hydrangea pots and fed him a couple of his special snacks to keep him going. She gave him a last pat, and left him looking confused. He'd been counting on some quality time with Tinkerbell.

'See you in a bit, boy,' Sarah said as brightly as she could. Inwardly, she was seething. Whether Francesca Diggory knew it or not, she had just made an enemy.

THIRTY-NINE

Sarah stalked inside the house, resolved to hate everything about the place. But that lasted all of ten seconds.

She stood in the beautiful hallway and wheeled about, unable to stop herself from admiring the oil paintings on the walls, the exquisite antique rugs on the floor, even the bowl of highly scented lilies on the central marquetry table. Suddenly aware of Francesca's knowing glance, she willed herself not to show how impressed she was.

Francesca turned on her heel with a sniff, and walked into a room off the hall, the little group following her. It turned out to be a large drawing room decorated in a cool shade of green, with chintz sofas on either side of an ornate marble fireplace. Huge windows looked out onto immaculate lawns outside, with a trellis of white roses surmounting a terraced area. Once again, Sarah was pierced with envy. She loved her bijou cottage – but it was all she and Peter had to show for a lifetime of work. She found herself wondering how on earth Francesca's ancestors had accumulated such wealth. There must have been more than a few murders done over the centuries, she was willing to bet.

That made this afternoon's questioning seem less of an impertinence, and more of a vital public duty.

'Sit down,' barked Francesca. It was an order rather than an invitation.

Wordlessly, Daphne and Sarah took their seats opposite the lady of the house, while Charles slunk onto the sofa beside her. Outside, Sarah heard Hamish make his feelings known about the situation. Why wasn't he in there, with his lady love? Tinkerbell, meanwhile, perched on Francesca's knee, fixing Sarah and Daphne with a slightly deranged bug-eyed stare that was almost as intimidating as her mistress's glare.

It was hard to believe that this must have been Charles's home, as well as Francesca's, until fairly recently. There was no sign of a masculine presence in this exquisite room. There was a collection of elaborately framed photographs arranged on a baby grand piano and a pair of beautifully inlaid bookcases flanked the long windows, stocked with matched sets of leather-bound volumes. Sarah was willing to bet big money they had never been opened, much less read. Everywhere there were porcelain plates and ornaments, in arrangements that would have looked fussy if the room had not been so large, and the china of such fine quality.

Perhaps there were other rooms in the house that better reflected Charles's personality – or maybe this décor was an example of the discord between the former spouses that had led to their split. Charles's rather cool warehouse-style apartment, with its white walls and modern art, could not have been more of a contrast with Francesca's stunning Georgian doll's house of a home.

Charles coughed nervously on the sofa. He had had a hard day, but even so Sarah felt she was not seeing him in his best light. He appeared so diminished at the side of his ex-wife, who was currently crackling with ferocious levels of spite and anger that she was visibly struggling to contain.

'Well, Francesca, you must be a little surprised to see me,' Charles began with deceptive mildness.

For a few seconds, it looked as though Francesca was going to ignore him entirely. Then she seemed to shake herself and finally addressed him. 'Could you go and see about some tea?'

Charles shook his head. 'I don't think that's really my place, do you? Mrs Chivers might be quite surprised to see me in the kitchen after all this time. Mrs Chivers is our – my er, wife's – housekeeper,' he said to Sarah and Daphne.

Both ladies nodded, as though that was the sort of information they were here for. But, beneath an unruffled façade, Sarah was becoming increasingly impatient. Luckily, Charles spoke up again.

'I suppose I was just wondering, Francesca, why you chose to "dob me in" to the authorities, as I believe people say?'

'Really, Charles, I do wish you wouldn't use awful slang words. It just sounds ridiculous coming from you.'

Sarah, who couldn't quite disagree with Francesca on this, still felt she had to intervene. 'It would be really interesting to know, Francesca, why you felt the need to get Charles arrested?'

At once, Francesca turned her basilisk gaze on Sarah, and assessed her in a way that reminded her forcibly of the awful headmistress of the school she and Daphne had gone to. But Sarah wasn't a wobbly eleven-year-old any more, away from home for the first time. 'It just seems an odd thing for a family member, of whatever type, to do.'

'How dare you criticise me?' Francesca snarled, then turned on the sofa so that she had her back to Sarah. She addressed Charles frostily. 'Is this the sort of thing you do these days? Talk in some sort of silly patois, and bring people to my house to insult me?'

Charles shrugged and, instead of looking cowed, Sarah was glad to see the light of battle come into his eye. 'Is it the sort of thing *you* do, try and get me carted off to prison? Really, Frankie, I expected better of you.'

At the use of this nickname, Francesca shot to her feet. 'I suppose I'll just have to organise the tea myself,' she said. But as she rushed out, with a protesting Tinkerbell in her arms, Sarah was pretty sure she saw the glitter of unshed tears in her eyes. Whatever was going on between the Diggorys, it was far from over – on Francesca's side at least.

'Well, that hasn't got us very far, has it?' said Daphne in matter-of-fact tones. She delved into a cut-glass bowl of pot pourri on the coffee table between the sofas, picked up a piece and, to Sarah's horror, popped it into her mouth. The expression on Daphne's face as she realised her mistake was priceless, and she was just retrieving the soggy petal and replacing it in the bowl when Francesca bustled back in. To avoid laughing, Sarah dropped her gaze to the carefully curated collection of highly polished silver keepsakes on the coffee table. Then her eye caught on something.

'I've just remembered, I have an appointment in five minutes,' said Francesca, all signs of her tearful moment effaced – apart from the tissue clutched in one hand. 'So I'm going to have to ask you all to leave,' she added. Tinkerbell was now nowhere to be seen. Sarah hoped she wasn't outside, tormenting poor Hamish.

'I say, Francesca, that's not really on,' said Charles mildly. 'We do need to ask you some questions...'

'Which I have no intention of answering,' snapped Francesca. 'Who on earth do you think you are, the Merstairs police? Though goodness knows, they're so short-staffed at the moment, they've had to take on all sorts,' she said, with a pointed look at Daphne.

Sarah shot out a warning hand and laid it on Daphne's arm, just as her friend was about to let rip. Easy-going Daphne would brook many things, but criticism of her nearest and dearest was not acceptable. And in this case, Sarah thought, it was totally unwarranted. Mariella seemed to be doing a great job, in difficult circumstances.

Now Sarah got to her feet, to the surprise of Charles and Daphne. 'Well, I agree with Francesca, it's probably time we got going. We don't want to outstay our welcome, do we?' She turned to Daphne and made *hurry up* motions with her hand. 'Besides, I'm sure there'll be other opportunities for us all to have, um, a little chat,' she continued.

'Not if I have anything to do with it,' snapped Francesca, holding the door open with one hand while clutching her tissue to her breast with the other, like the heroine of some Victorian melodrama.

Sarah held her head high as she walked past, encouraging Daphne to do the same. Charles shambled along last, evidently a little confused that they had so willingly accepted this unceremonious dismissal. As they marched through the hall and out of the front door, he said nothing. But as soon as they were back in the car, with an ecstatic Hamish, he let rip.

'What on earth was the point of that, if we didn't really ask Francesca a single question? We're still none the wiser about why she gave me up to the police like that,' he said crossly.

'Oh, come on, Charles. It's quite obvious,' said Sarah dismissively.

'Obvious? I don't think so!' he stormed.

'Well, to spell it out for you, she's still very keen on you and is hurting badly, so she'd like to make you suffer. Is that clear enough?' Sarah said succinctly. Daphne giggled, but killed it when Sarah turned to look at her.

In the front, Charles said nothing, but gripped the wheel a bit more tightly. Sometimes, the truth was rather uncomfortable, Sarah mused. But he had asked, hadn't he?

'Anyway, didn't either of you two notice the biggest clue we've found so far? Right under our noses?'

As Sarah had thought, at this both her companions started talking at once, and Hamish got in on the act with a few choice barks. When order was restored, and it was more than abundantly clear that neither Charles nor Daphne knew what she was on about, Sarah decided to enlighten them.

'On that coffee table, between the sofas. What did you see?'

'Just that bowl of really horrible snacks,' said Daphne, with a moue of disgust at the memory. 'Honestly, you'd think Francesca could afford better. Oh, and a few knick-knacks.'

'The knick-knacks – can you be more specific?' Sarah raised her eyebrows.

'Well, there was a jumble of stuff in the silver bowl – that's where I used to empty out my pockets every night when, ah...' Charles tailed off, though it was hard to determine whether this was in regret or relief that he had escaped that habit, and all the others he'd shared with Francesca.

'Was there anything in the mix that caught your eye?' Sarah prompted, by this stage pretty sure she was going to have to come out and tell them.

'Oh, you're so keen to show off your cleverness, just spit it out,' said Daphne crossly, jangling her bracelets.

'All right then,' said Sarah, and she knew her voice was a tiny bit smug. 'Well, I just happened to see, in that silver dish...'

'Get on with it, do,' said Daphne, rolling her eyes.

'OK, well. It was a woggle.'

'A what? You mean...' Charles's eyes flicked to her, ignoring the road ahead.

'Watch where you're going,' Sarah chided. 'Yes, a woggle.'

'So our minds are supposed to boggle? Did you like my rhyme?' Daphne said, her shoulders shaking – before the penny dropped. 'Oh, a *woggle*,' she said, horrified. 'Like poor old Bill Turbot...'

'Yes, exactly. Like the one we saw pulled so tight round Bill Turbot's neck that he couldn't breathe.'

'Well, you don't have to rub it in,' said Daphne. 'Oh my God, do you realise what this means?'

Sarah looked at Daphne blankly.

'It only means you were wrong, Sarah, and horrible Francesca *is* the murderer after all,' Daphne shouted.

Suddenly, there was a screech from the car's tyres, and Charles fought to stop the car zig-zagging across the road. Time started to play tricks; the hedgerow hurtled towards them while the car seemed to be moving in slow motion. Really, thought Sarah, is this how it's going to end? We're about to catch a murderer – but now we're getting killed ourselves. That's an irony for you.

And then everything went black.

FORTY

It could have been five minutes later, or it could have been an hour. Sarah opened her eyes warily, conscious of an acute pain in her wrist. Hamish, thankfully, was fine in the boot, although he was shivering and his eyes were as wide as saucers.

Charles, at her side, had not got off so lightly. He was slumped against the steering wheel, and seemed to be unconscious. Silly man must have forgotten to put his seatbelt on when they left Francesca's. In the back, there was a moaning, which could only have come from Daphne. Good, thought Sarah. Any noise was a positive sign in a case like this. She craned her neck carefully, wary about whiplash, but managed to see that Daphne was in one piece, and conscious, if shaken. She unclipped her own belt and got out of the car tentatively.

They had landed up in a ditch. She let Hamish out of the boot, and then walked round to Charles's side of the car.

Once she'd pulled Charles's door open, she saw a trickle of blood on his forehead where he lay over the wheel. His arm was slumped over it and she quickly took his pulse. It seemed strong. Nothing much to worry about, then – apart from the chilling fact that he was unconscious.

'Daphne, have you got your phone?'

'What? What?' Daphne said, completely disorientated. Sarah sighed and went back round to her own side of the car again. She checked her friend quickly, ascertained she was basically doing fine, then got out her own handbag. Soon she was through to the emergency services and explaining succinctly what had happened. Going over it helped to clarify things in her mind. There had been nothing, no obstacle, no oncoming vehicle, that had caused Charles to lose control. It had been as though the car itself had suddenly failed to respond. Either that, or he had been so disconcerted at the idea of his wife, ex or otherwise, strangling the scoutmaster that he had driven straight into a ditch.

What could have happened, between their journey to Francesca's place, when the car had been fine, to their departure, when it had suddenly gone off the road?

There had been those few minutes when Francesca was out organising the tea. Was that long enough for her to have tinkered with the mechanism? Would she even have known what to do? Or was it more likely that Charles had lost concentration? Sarah's head was pounding by now, and she wasn't sure whether it was the aftermath of the crash or all the awful ideas swirling around her head. She leant against the side of the car, praying the emergency services would reach them soon. The more time that ticked by with Charles out of it, the more serious his injury was looking. Wearily, she walked round to his side again, and checked his vital signs. They were all still steady, but he was worryingly motionless.

Daphne, in the back, was now fighting to get her seatbelt off. Sarah opened her door and helped her stagger out of the car. 'What on earth happened? Do you know, Sarah?'

'I haven't a clue. One minute we were driving along, the next – smash!' Sarah shook her head, and immediately wished she hadn't as the pounding worsened.

'I suppose it was my fault. Go on, say it. I should have kept my big mouth shut,' Daphne said, her mouth sagging downwards for once as she drooped against the side of the car, her legs clearly still weak.

'I'd never say that. Don't upset yourself. Here, sit down by the verge. The grass should be nice and soft. Just put your head between your knees if you feel faint,' Sarah said, one hand on her friend's back. 'Listen, I think I can hear something! Someone's coming.'

It was the first sign of life on the road since they'd crashed. This countryside lark was all very well, thought Sarah, and no one appreciated the peace and quiet more than she did, normally. But on a day like today it was very inconvenient. Hopefully, this was going to be their salvation. It was coming from the same direction as Francesca's house, though, whereas the emergency services would be driving along the coast road, from the hospital round the bay, wouldn't they?

Sure enough, a car came into view – but it wasn't sporting the distinctive dayglo yellow livery of a police vehicle or a blessed ambulance. It was a navy blue boxy little runaround. Sarah's heart sank, but she stepped out into the road anyway and waved her arms over her head, shouting, 'Stop! Stop,' as loudly as she could.

'Watch you don't get run over. We don't need any more accidents,' said Daphne in shrill tones.

It seemed to be working, though. The driver was slowing down. A minute later, the car had parked tidily behind Charles's Citroën, which was at a rakish angle. The door flew open and a man got out, peering behind thick glasses.

'Trevor! Trevor from the pub,' Sarah babbled, a little incoherently.

Trevor Bains dashed over. 'What on earth is going on? Are you OK?'

'No we're not, can't you see?' said Daphne rather crossly,

from where she was nursing her sore leg on the grass verge. 'We've had a prang. And Charles is in a really bad way.'

'Well, we don't know that just yet,' said Sarah evenly, trying to keep everyone calm. 'But he definitely needs to go to hospital to be checked out.'

'Right, let's get him out of the car,' said Trevor, leaping forward and pulling at the driver door.

'No!' Sarah almost shouted, and then found herself having to apologise. 'He's had a head injury. It's very important not to move him until the paramedics can get here with a neck brace. We shouldn't touch a thing.'

'All right, all right,' said Trevor. 'Just trying to help,' he said, giving Daphne a look that suggested Sarah had lost it in a big way.

'Sarah's right, and she should know,' said Daphne stoutly. 'But thanks for stopping for us.'

'Look, we don't all have to wait. It would be better if you could take Daphne and Hamish home, Trevor, and I'll wait here with Charles for the ambulance. It shouldn't be long,' she said hopefully, looking at her watch.

'OK, but who's Hamish? Oh aye, right, your little dog. Fine. Come on then, Daphne.'

'Don't you think I need to get checked out too?' asked Daphne, seeming almost hurt that she was being left out of this medical emergency.

'Well, as you're walking and talking, I think you'll do,' said Sarah. 'Your knee might be a bit bruised tomorrow. We'll keep an eye on it. But you'd be better at home with a cup of tea, don't you think? And it's all a bit too exciting for Hamish. Will you be OK with him for a bit?'

'Oh yes, of course,' said Daphne, rising to the occasion. 'Don't you worry about a thing,' she said, adjusting her scarf and suddenly looking a lot more like her usual self.

A couple of minutes later, Trevor had driven off with

Daphne and Hamish, and Sarah was left alone at the roadside with Charles. As she went to check on him again, though, she got a surprise. His wide blue eyes were open, and he even managed a smile.

'Thank God,' she said, clutching her chest. 'Oh, I mean, good, you're awake,' she said in calmer tones.

'I came to as you were talking to Trevor, actually, but thought I'd lie doggo for a bit,' Charles admitted.

'Why on earth?' asked Sarah.

'Saw him at Frankie's. In the garden, messing around with the roses with that nephew of his. Didn't get a chance to say earlier. Bit odd, I thought,' Charles said with a wince, closing his eyes again.

'You probably shouldn't talk too much,' said Sarah, a hand on his arm. 'Try and just stay relaxed. An ambulance is on its way.'

'Oh, no need,' said Charles, trying to raise his head and then giving it up as a bad job.

'See?' said Sarah. To distract him from moving, she decided to see how much he remembered about the accident. 'Do you know exactly what happened? When we came off the road?'

'I remember Daphne shouting about Francesca being a killer. Bit ridiculous, I thought. Then the steering went loose.'

'Do you think... someone could have tampered with it?' Sarah asked, hesitating to come straight out with her theory that Francesca could have done it, when she nipped out to 'make the tea' and then failed to bring them any.

'Maybe... but who? Trevor can't see well enough to tinker with anything, and as for Frankie, she wouldn't know a camshaft from a carburettor,' Charles said, but his voice was sounding weaker. Sarah wanted to grab his wrist again to check his pulse, but somehow she couldn't, now her patient was awake. Just when she was deciding she had to be bold, and do it anyway, she heard a siren. Never had that wail been so welcome.

Five minutes later, Charles had been loaded into the ambulance, and Sarah, as an honorary healthcare worker, was hitching a lift up front with the team. The AA would be coming by to pick up the car later and tow it back to Merstairs. Charles was in a neck brace and was covered by a nice thick blanket, and she'd had her diagnosis of a nasty concussion unofficially confirmed. He'd been very lucky.

They all had been fortunate, in fact, Sarah reflected, as the countryside sped by. It could have been a fatal accident. Who wished them ill on that scale? Who wanted to see Sarah, Daphne and Charles out of action, and who was willing to see poor innocent Hamish mangled too, as collateral damage? Could it be Trevor, who'd been at Francesca's with his nephew? Or was it the lady of the manor herself, who'd been so mean about Sarah's dog?

One thing was for sure, there was someone very sick walking the streets of Merstairs. Sick and very, very dangerous.

FORTY-ONE

Once Charles had been seen, mercifully fast as was still the case with head injuries, and was established on an observation ward, Sarah sat by his side and took stock. Someone had found them a copy of the previous day's *Times* newspaper. Nominally they were doing the crossword, but in fact Charles had dropped off again and Sarah was taking the opportunity to mull over the facts of the case so far. The crashes and bangs and endless comings and goings of a busy NHS ward would not have been conducive to deep thought for most people, but for Sarah it was a soothing backdrop she had grown used to in her youth, and now associated with carefree times when all she had to worry about was an endless parade of exams, not an unknown miscreant who now seemed hellbent on wiping out her and her friends.

So, what did she know for sure? Really, only this – that two people had died. First, Gus Trubshaw, and then Bill Turbot. There was precious little linking the two crimes, apart from the fact that Sarah could not countenance a coincidence of this magnitude. There hadn't been a murder in Merstairs for nigh on fifty years, according to Daphne. What were the odds of two entirely unconnected killings cropping up hot on one another's heels?

On the other hand, what exactly were the links between them? Sarah totted them up. The two men had known each other; Bill Turbot, as she had seen for herself, was a regular in Gus Trubshaw's pub. She'd never seen them together, Gus having shuffled off this mortal coil before she'd first parked her Volvo in Merstairs. But by all accounts, Bill had long been a fixture, propping up the bar of the Jolly Roger – until Gus had barred him in one of his famous tempers. Who knows what secrets the two might have had, and discussed night after night?

But somehow, Sarah felt it was more a case of Bill having seen or felt something regarding the first murder, something he had unwisely let on about. That had been enough to cook his goose, she reckoned. What could it have been? A word, a gesture – something that had convinced the killer that he was onto them, with tragic results.

Suddenly there was a rustle from the bed beside her. Charles opened one eye. 'Ah. Um. What do you make of four down? I'm struggling a bit.'

Sarah squinted over at the paper, which was lying on Charles's chest. '"Crows flock to this, six letters." Hmm, tricky,' she said thoughtfully, though a gleam in her eye suggested otherwise. Charles's eyelids grew heavy again and, before she could put him out of his misery on the clue, he had drifted back to sleep. Once upon a time, the wisdom with concussions was that the person had to be kept awake at all costs. Sarah was glad the protocol had changed; this was a lot more peaceful.

She collected her thoughts again and cast her mind back to that time in the Jolly Roger. It had only been a few days, but already it seemed like aeons ago. Bill Turbot, she was sure, had been advancing towards her like a heat-seeking missile, then something had happened to throw him off course.

She could see it now, as though replaying a film in her head.

The door had opened... Daphne had walked in. Bill had turned tail. But surely that couldn't be right, could it? Her warm and chatty friend, scaring away this highly predatory man? What had all that been about, she wondered.

Then came a discreet cough at her elbow. While she'd been miles away, an attractive forty-something doctor with a sleek blonde bun at the back of her neck had approached on soft-soled shoes. 'I just wanted to have a quick chat about your husband's condition,' she said, furrowing her brow empatheti-cally at Sarah.

Immediately Sarah, a little pink about the ears, shot out of her seat and led the doctor away from Charles's bed. For some reason, patient confidentiality had never seemed so important.

'Oh, we're not... no, no,' she said, shaking her head.

The doctor raised a hand. 'It's none of my business, really. It's just I understood you're a medic, too, and I thought you'd appreciate a heads-up on your, er, erm, friend's condition.'

'Oh, oh yes,' said Sarah, willing herself to look as profes-sional as possible. 'Well, that would certainly be very useful.'

'As you know, head injuries like this do require careful monitoring, but we've now gone through the first few hours without any sign of convulsions or double vision, so I think we're through the worst. Has he been complaining at all of headaches? Any difficulties in understanding simple things?' the doctor asked.

Sarah thought briefly of the crossword clue, then dismissed it. She had no idea what Charles's benchmark level was with puzzles. 'No, he's been quite lucid, I would say. Sleepy, obviously.'

'Well, that's only to be expected,' the doctor said with the sort of briskness Sarah remembered well. It was plain the woman felt that Charles was as right as rain, and the sooner he could stop blocking her bed the better.

'Can I take him away now?'

The doctor thought for a moment. 'Normally, I'd insist he was seen by the dispenser and provided with the right medication and instructions on how to take it – but as you are in the trade, so to speak, if you are willing to take him into your own care, I think that will be absolutely fine. I must insist he is not left on his own for twenty-four hours, though,' she finished with a bright smile.

Sarah mirrored the smile, but as soon as the doctor had moved away to deal with her next case, her grin dropped. What had she let herself in for now? She felt very uneasy at the thought of installing a man in her house. It wasn't that long since Peter's death... it stirred up all kinds of feelings. Of disloyalty, definitely, and was that, could that be, a sort of excitement? No, definitely not. She wasn't sure she should even be talking to Charles, half the time, let alone looking after him. Besides, her cottage was hardly big enough for her, Hamish and the few remaining boxes. Where on earth was she going to put him?

FORTY-TWO

In the end, it seemed inevitable that Charles would end up
reclining on Sarah's sofa in her rather cramped sitting room,
with Daphne by his side, pouring him tea and generally making
a massive fuss of him. Hamish was sitting patiently at the foot of
the sofa, ready in case any crumbs of the cake Daphne had
brought round 'to keep Charles's strength up' – and mostly then
eaten herself – went astray. Daphne even tried to help him with
the crossword, though both remained totally stumped by four
down. Sarah resisted the temptation to put them straight.

'I'm glad you're settled in here, Daphne,' she said mildly.
'Because I wanted to ask you something. You know, about the
day I first went to the Jolly Roger—'

'Doesn't it seem like ages ago? It feels like you've been in
Merstairs forever, you're really part of the furniture now,' said
Daphne earnestly.

'Well, thank you, Daphne,' Sarah said. It wasn't the most
flattering description, but she did feel a little glow at the
thought. 'Taking you back to that time, though. Bill was coming
over to me, he looked really intent, and then you walked in, and

he veered right away and almost skulked off. Do you remember?'

'How funny,' said Daphne with one of her chuckles. 'I wonder if I spooked him! Maybe he saw something, something in the Beyond...'

'Hardly. If he had seen what was going to happen to him very shortly, he would have left Merstairs in a very big hurry, wouldn't he? Not gone off to another seat with his pint.'

'I suppose you're right, though it never does to take the mystical forces lightly,' said Daphne reprovingly.

Sarah tried to look suitably chastened, and then Daphne shot out of her seat, shocking Charles into wakefulness and making Hamish get up and bark for Britain. 'I've got it!' she said. 'I've remembered. There was someone coming in behind me. Well, a few people, actually. I stopped in the doorway, just scanning the bar, and then I saw you, remember.'

Sarah nodded impatiently. 'Yes, but who else was there?'

'All right, all right, wait a second, I'm just piecing it together,' said Daphne, putting her hands to her temples as she habitually did when a message was coming through from one of her otherworldly sources. Sarah sighed quietly to herself.

'Yes! That's right, I've got it now,' said Daphne again.

'Well, for heaven's sake, spit it out then, do,' said Charles rather weakly from his bank of cushions on the sofa. 'The suspense is killing me and Hamish.'

'All right, all right, but I just want to be sure of the order,' said Daphne with a shushing motion. 'It's very important that I get this straight.'

Sarah met Charles's gaze as Daphne went back into her semi-trance. His eyebrows rose and his blue, blue eyes brimmed with suppressed laughter. Sarah felt a lightening in the region of her heart, and then shot to her feet, bustling about and clearing up cups before clattering off to the kitchen.

'Do you mind, Sarah, I need complete silence for this,' Daphne remonstrated, one cross eye opening.

'Oh goodness, do get on with it,' Sarah grumbled, knowing her voice was more or less inaudible above the sound of the running tap as she refilled the kettle.

'Wait, wait, it's coming,' Daphne said in a curious half-wail. 'I've got it!'

Sarah returned with a tray loaded with a fresh pot of tea and obliged her friend by looking expectant. 'Yes?'

'It was Trevor Bains!'

'Trevor?' Charles half-rose from his languid pose, only to be told to lie back by both Sarah and Daphne. 'But listen, it can't be Trevor! He hasn't got anything to do with this. Anyone can see he's heartbroken about Gus.'

'It's true,' said Sarah. 'We were both there, soon after the news came out. He was inconsolable.'

'Well it was Trevor, that's all I know. With his nephew, too. Bringing in some of those big boxes of snacks from the wholesaler. And maybe Bill was one of those people who can't think of anything to say to the bereaved, so he avoided him,' Daphne suggested.

'Do you think that's in character, Charles?' Sarah asked.

'I wouldn't have thought so,' said Charles. Then he added more slowly, 'Although of course I didn't exactly see eye to eye with Bill myself.'

'Yes, why was that?' Sarah asked.

Charles fidgeted with his blanket. 'Well, if you must know, he was always flirting with Francesca. When we *were* actually married,' he said, frowning.

'Surely she didn't flirt back, though? He was awful,' said Sarah, remembering the man's lecherous ways.

'I think she wanted to make me jealous. Anything for attention, Francesca,' said Charles gruffly.

Sarah flashed irresistibly back to Francesca Diggory's suspiciously shiny eyes at her wonderful Georgian mansion. Her plan had certainly backfired. She was not a happy woman, and most of her angst seemed to be directed at her husband's departure from her life.

'Maybe something had gone awry between Gus and Trevor. Do you remember anything leading up to the time he "went away"? It was back in February. So in January, or around Christmas?' Sarah asked them both.

Daphne wrinkled her forehead. 'I'm casting my mind back... A cup of tea might help,' she said, a smile peeping out.

Sarah obligingly poured three mugs from the pot and set one before Daphne.

'The thing is, I'm hardly a regular,' Daphne began.

'Oh, I thought your book club met at the Roger quite frequently?' Charles said lightly.

'I suppose so... but we're always so busy discussing the books.' Daphne's expression was pious.

'In that case,' Sarah broke in, 'you're the only book club in the country that actually concentrates on literary criticism. And I'm not sure I can believe Pat is a really devoted reader – unless the group's choices are a bit saucier than most Booker Prize winners I've read,' she added with a smile.

'OK, well, I admit sometimes we do wander off-piste a tad... and now that I come to think of it, there was a time when everyone was saying Gus was looking peaky...'

'Yes, by Jove, you're right,' said Charles, almost spilling his tea in his excitement. 'He did lose a lot of weight, didn't he?'

'Around November? Yes. I was a bit jealous, actually, as I've been on a very strict regime for ages, and I can't seem to shift a pound,' Daphne said earnestly.

Sarah thought back to everything she'd seen her dear friend ingest over the last few days. 'Hmm,' she said, perhaps not quite as mystified as Daphne.

'I actually asked Gus how he was doing it, and do you know,

I remember he wasn't at all helpful? You wouldn't have thought he'd begrudge me a few tips, when I'm trying so hard.'

'Perhaps he wasn't trying to lose weight though... perhaps he was ill.' Sarah was all too aware of the sort of medical conditions that made a patient shed pounds like autumn leaves.

'That doesn't make sense, though. Why would he swan off to Canada, if he was ill?' Daphne looked puzzled.

'You're forgetting, Daphne, dear girl. He didn't mosey anywhere, did he?' Charles spoke up. 'He was in the trunk all the time.'

'Oh! Oh yes, how awful, I got confused for a moment. Poor dear Gus. So you think this whole thing could have been something to do with him being ill after all?'

Sarah, who was indeed beginning to suspect as much, sipped her tea thoughtfully. 'I think it might be worthwhile us popping to the Jolly Roger as soon as you're feeling better, Charles. Just for a quick drink,' she said slowly.

FORTY-THREE

The next morning, Sarah was very glad not to be woken up by Daphne banging on her door. But no sooner had she thought this than her mobile phone shrilled instead. It was Charles.

She'd been relieved when, at about 10 p.m. the night before, Charles had insisted he felt completely fine and would be going home immediately. Although she had felt strange about the prospect of having him under her roof all night, even if it was only for medical reasons, she was equally reluctant to let him go, in case he suddenly fell ill in the early hours. Concussions could be unpredictable. But he had been adamant, and eventually she'd wrung out the promise that he'd call her first thing. They'd said a slightly awkward goodnight on the doorstep, and she'd locked up with a curious set of feelings which might or might not have included anticlimax, a sense of reprieve – and possibly a soupçon of regret.

It was good to hear from him now, and be reassured that he was absolutely fine after all yesterday's adventures. 'Shall we stick to the plan, then?' she said brightly.

'Very much so. I'll see you and young Daphne there, in about an hour,' said Charles, ringing off.

Sarah spent an uncharacteristically long time gazing into her wardrobe, and wondering why on earth she didn't have an outfit suitable for the quite tricky situation they were about to blunder into. Eventually, she picked out some buttercup yellow trousers and a matching floral shirt, deciding she'd give Daphne a run for her money in the colour stakes today. But, when she knocked on her friend's door a few minutes later with Hamish in tow, Daphne was a blinding vision in jungle green and fuchsia and Sarah realised some battles were lost before they were even fought.

By the time they'd breezed into Merstairs proper, with Sarah marvelling anew at the amazing coastal views that were now a part of her everyday life, she was feeling quite nervous about what was in store. Seeing Charles leaning nonchalantly against the entrance to the Jolly Roger should have been reassuring, so it was hard to explain the slightly fizzy feeling in her stomach at the sight of his blue eyes. Probably just drinking her coffee too quickly before hurrying to fetch Daphne, she decided.

Daphne greeted Charles with a big fuss over his residual symptoms, which seemed to be minor as far as Sarah could ascertain without doing an examination, which was certainly *not* on her agenda. Sarah exchanged a quick lopsided smile with him and then they all trooped past the blackboard sign outside the Jolly Roger. Today it featured a drawing of a pirate's treasure map, featuring a shipwrecked boat – suspiciously like the one on the Ship and Anchor's sign – and the victorious Jolly Roger with its flag flying. The X shape of the skull and crossbones was emphasised, and chalked below it was the legend, 'X MARKS THE SPOT FOR GOOD BEER'. It looked like the fight between the rival pubs was ramping up a notch.

Charles held the pub door open for them gallantly. It was only just past opening time, so the plastic lobsters, sea urchins and fish had the place pretty much to themselves. Apart, that was, from Trevor Bains, who was in his usual station behind the bar, trusty tea towel in one hand and a sparkling glass in the other.

'Morning ladies and gent. What can I get for you?' he said, affable as ever, though when he looked at Sarah she thought she detected that slight droop of his mouth that showed his sadness. Or perhaps that was just what he wanted her to see?

'Did you know I was recently widowed?' Sarah asked him abruptly.

He shrugged, and blinked a few times behind his thick glasses. 'Might have heard it on the grapevine, I suppose. Aye, not much that isn't gossiped about in these parts. Charles, your usual?'

Charles nodded in Pavlovian response, but when Sarah glanced at him he shuffled his feet. 'Erm, no thanks, old boy.'

Sarah spoke again. 'Were you in the vicinity of Francesca Diggory's house yesterday afternoon, may I ask?'

Trevor looked from Daphne to Charles and back again. 'What's all this? Twenty questions?'

'I did actually see you in Frankie's garden, old boy,' said Charles ruefully.

'No law against it, is there? I was helping her with her garden, wasn't I? I drove Albie over. Gus always loved tending her roses, and I suppose... well, I suppose I've just been keeping the tradition on,' Trevor said, reaching for a tissue.

This time, Sarah was less sympathetic, suspecting as she now did that Trevor had been manipulating her fellow-feeling for the recently bereaved. 'When you were helping with the roses, did you by any chance cut through the brake wires on Charles's car?'

Trevor looked thunderstruck. 'What? Of course I didn't! What do you take me for?'

'That's a good question,' said Sarah ruminatively. 'I suppose we might be beginning to feel... we could take you for a double murderer? And someone who attempted to kill the three of us as well.'

Trevor gasped, and the tea towel dropped from his nerveless fingers. 'Are you crazy?'

'Not a bit of it,' said Sarah briskly. 'But you're looking very pale. Perhaps you should have one of your own shots, for medicinal purposes, and come and sit down over with us until you feel a bit better.'

Trevor meekly obeyed instructions, rattling a glass against the optics as usual, gulping down a quick vodka and then walking on shaky legs to Charles's favourite banquette. 'You've got it all wrong, you lot. It's ridiculous... I loved Gus. I would never...' Here, Trevor was overcome, and Sarah got up to fetch more tissues. As she went over to the bar, she caught sight of Albie Cartwright, carrying a crate of mixers up from the storeroom.

'Um, perhaps you could take over in the bar for a bit?' she said to him. 'Trevor's not feeling so great.' Albie, looking surprised, stepped out of the shadows. Her eye was caught by the twisting snake tattoo on his arm.

'What's up with Uncle Trev?' Albie asked suspiciously.

'Oh, nothing much,' said Sarah airily. Except being accused of murder, she thought to herself.

Albie walked forward a little reluctantly, and was just in time to serve a couple of customers who'd wandered in. Sarah went back to the banquette, where Trevor was looking a better colour, but still swivelling his head between Charles and Daphne as though he couldn't believe what he was being accused of.

'Feeling OK now? Shall I tell you what I think happened?' said Sarah, using cheerful but firm tones. 'Gus had started losing weight. I think he was very ill, wasn't he?'

Trevor looked at her as though she had two heads. 'How... how did you know that?'

'Never mind. So, he got a diagnosis, I presume, and things took their course?'

'Pancreatic cancer, they said.' Now Trevor fixed his eyes on the table. Sarah felt a jolt of recognition.

'Is that bad?' asked Daphne.

'Well, no cancer is great,' Sarah shook her head. 'But I'd say pancreatic is particularly horrible.' Despite herself, she was reminded of her own terrible months looking after Peter.

Poor Trevor's head drooped lower still. A large tear plopped onto the table. 'I don't know how you could think I'd, I'd *do* anything to Gus,' he wailed. 'I just wanted him to get better.'

'But you knew he wouldn't,' said Sarah inexorably. 'So you did the next best thing. You put him out of his misery.'

Trevor shook his head violently. 'Never. Never. I couldn't have done that, even if I'd thought of it. I wouldn't have had a clue how to go about it, even.'

'It's not that hard,' said Sarah, then coughed and went on quickly. 'And then, I suppose, Bill Turbot guessed something. He was one of your regulars, so he had plenty of time to observe you over the last few weeks. That day when I came in here for the first time, the penny suddenly dropped for him, didn't it? You were right behind Daphne, and for some reason he saw you in a different light. Something made him realise what you had done. Then he had to go.'

Trevor looked up at this, his eyes swimming, his expression confused beyond measure. 'I don't know what you're on about. Tell her, Charles. You know me. I'm not a planner, I've just been putting one foot in front of the other since Gus went. Och, he was the one who always had a strategy. When he left for his digital detox I... I just hoped, you know? I hoped he'd come back stronger, then we could face it together...' Here he broke down, but then blew his nose and carried on, his voice a little fainter. His voice was so plaintive, his expression so woebegone, that

Sarah had no choice but to realise the truth. Trevor hadn't done it after all.

'But the postcards from Canada. Didn't you realise they weren't in Gus's handwriting? That they were fakes? You'd been together for years, surely you'd have spotted they weren't from him,' she said insistently.

Trevor turned to look at her, his eyes still swimming. 'My sight, well, it's not that good,' he said simply, pushing his glasses further up his nose. She noticed the red mark on the bridge of his nose from the weight of the lenses. She remembered the odd way he felt his way around things, and a time when he had nearly gone flying, tripping over a bag he hadn't expected to be on the floor. Just now, he had served himself that shot by touch rather than by sight. He probably wasn't far off from being registered blind. 'Gus knew about my eyes; he always wrote to me in block capitals. He wanted to make things easier for me,' Trevor said, breaking down again.

'Block capitals... that reminds me,' Sarah said, a frown gathering between her brows. 'We passed the sign outside when we came in. It's been changed again.' She got up slowly but instead of looking at the sign outside, she went over to the bar. Albie was nowhere to be seen. After a moment's thought, she nipped behind it, took down a couple of the postcards and brought them back to the banquette.

'Ha, yes! Very funny, this morning's board,' said Charles. 'Your own work, Trev?'

'Och no,' said Trevor modestly. 'I always leave that to the lad. He's great at that sort of thing, very artistic,' he said, looking towards his nephew who'd just reappeared with a catering box of crisps. He got busy behind the bar, restocking and clattering around.

'Well, there's nothing like creative talent, I always say that, don't I Sarah?' said Daphne with a shake of her headscarf.

But Sarah wasn't listening. She looked up from a postcard

of a mountain range and stifled a gasp, as Albie Cartwright came over with a tray bearing three small glasses of brandy. 'Thought you lot might need a little pick-me-up,' he said gruffly.

Charles didn't need asking twice. He grabbed his. 'What a kind thought, dear boy. Your health,' he said, holding the glass aloft. The dark amber liquid caught the light. Was it Sarah's imagination or did it look a little... cloudy?

Albie Cartwright straightened up, his T-shirt as tight as usual over his biceps and the fangs of the snake tattoo, the serpent rings on his fingers gleaming. There was still a light dusting of chalk on his top, from designing the Jolly Roger's riposte to the Ship this morning.

Finally, the last piece of the puzzle was dropping into place for Sarah. Bumbling Trevor, just about making it through, keeping the pub going despite his sorrow and his sight – with the help of his devoted nephew, who did so much – serving, collecting glasses, even conducting the war of words with their rival pub. And who also, for apparently no reason at all, seemed to be devoured by anger. What could cause such irrational rage? Perhaps nothing less than being trapped in a situation of his own making.

Charles was just about to down the measure in one, when Sarah stuck out her hand and caught his arm. 'Stop!' she yelled, louder than she'd ever yelled before. 'Put that down. Don't touch a drop, Charles, Daphne, don't drink it,' she turned to her friend, who had her own glass in her hand and was looking aghast.

'What's going on, Sarah?' Daphne said tremulously. 'Why are you so shouty all of a sudden?'

'The drinks,' Sarah said. 'They're poisoned.'

FORTY-FOUR

It wasn't until the two constables had been and gone, taking Albie Cartwright with them for questioning by DI Blake in Merstairs police headquarters, that Mariella was finally able to sit down with Charles, Daphne and Sarah. They were still in the pub, but now the sun was long over the yardarm. Trevor Bains was lying down upstairs, and his other nephew, Jonty – who thank goodness wasn't a psychopath – was holding the fort in the bar.

The little group gazed at the glasses in front of them, to all intents and purposes identical to those that had nearly killed them earlier. Once they'd refused to drink Albie's shots, the look on his face had told Sarah all she'd needed to know. He'd often seemed grumpy and surly, but now it was as though he'd become the snake on his own arm – spitting with venom, writhing furiously as Charles leapt to his feet and laid about him with the drinks tray.

It had been a ridiculous last throw of the dice for him – he couldn't possibly have hoped to get away with poisoning three people in front of his uncle, as well as the rest of the pub. But Sarah could only assume he wasn't thinking rationally at all by this stage. He was just propelled by anger – a reasonless fury against anyone who spotted what he had done to Gus. It was the same rage that had sealed Bill Turbot's fate, when he had made the connection between the postcards and their author right in front of Albie. Sarah could have kicked herself for this alone – if she'd taken more notice of the handwriting when she'd first seen the cards, maybe Bill Turbot would still have been with them.

Thank goodness the police had not been far away, fruitlessly pottering around Daphne's beach hut in the hopes that a lead would bite them on their bottoms. So when Sarah had made her anguished call, Deeside and Dumbarton, otherwise known as Tweedledum and Tweedledee, had thudded almost instantly into the pub and done the necessary. Mariella had brought up the rear and was now contemplating her own shot glass.

'Do you reckon it's safe?' Daphne asked her and Sarah.

Charles picked his up. 'Only one way to find out. I need a drink, anyway.' He knocked it back, and they all watched, fascinated, for a few seconds. 'I was going to pretend to choke then, but I didn't think any of our nerves could stand it,' Charles said with a chuckle. 'So come on, tell us, Sarah, our puzzle-solving queen, when did you first make sense of it all?'

'Well, I'm hardly that,' said Sarah, trying to stop herself from glowing at the title. 'As you must have realised, I got it all completely wrong, and almost got us killed. And what that silly boy thought he was going to do with three more dead bodies, I don't know. You see, I thought Trevor was the guilty man. My idea was that he'd done it to, um, spare his partner any more pain,' she said with an inward wince, thinking back to her own grim final days with Peter.

The memory made her understand completely why someone might contemplate such a thing – but also why it must always be out of the question. Peter had begged her... and she had wanted to help him more than anything. But then, just as the temptation had grown almost too great, mercifully, his sufferings had come to an end without her involvement. She would always be grateful for that.

Then she collected herself and went on. 'But in fact, Trevor was completely in the dark, and he had nothing to do with Gus's disappearance.'

'But why would Albie kill Gus, then?' said Daphne, shaking her head. 'I always thought they got on quite well, though Gus teased him, of course. I just don't get it.'

'I think he did it to "help" his beloved uncle Trevor. Trevor was all he had – Albie had fallen out with the rest of his family. His dad, Dave Cartwright, told me that. Maybe he was actually jealous of Gus, or didn't like his ribbing, he seems pretty thin-skinned,' Sarah said. 'He was more or less frothing at the mouth earlier. But when he'd killed Gus, he got stuck supporting Trevor when his uncle couldn't keep the bar going on his own. He was trapped, having to write the postcards and continue the fiction that Gus was in Canada. Then Trevor fell apart even more completely when Gus's body was discovered. That's why Albie's been in such a terrible mood. He's been saddled with the consequences of his own actions.'

'But how did killing Gus help Trevor anyway?' Daphne's eyes were wide and her earrings swung as she shook her head in bewilderment.

'I suppose you'd have to call what Albie did a mercy killing,' said Sarah slowly. 'Watching Trevor agonising as Gus became sicker and sicker must have been intolerable for Albie. He thought he could stop his uncle Trevor's suffering by putting Gus out of his misery and pretending he'd gone away for one of his digital detoxes. I thought at first Gus had just been stran-gled, as the body showed the typical signs of—'

'Spare us, please,' said Daphne.

'OK, well,' Sarah continued more circumspectly. 'As it

turned out, Gus had been drugged first. He wouldn't have known what was happening and would have felt no pain. It seemed to me to be a, well, a caring death. That's why I thought it must be Trevor. But Albie is also capable of compassion, I suppose. He gave him something pretty strong—'

'We're working on the assumption that it was fentanyl,' chipped in Mariella. 'It's fifty times more potent than morphine. It's one of the drugs we think Albie's been dealing from the pub. There's a huge risk of overdose as it's so powerful, so it's not impossible that he just gave him too much by accident...'

'But he did also choke him to death,' Sarah pointed out.

'That's true,' said Mariella. 'Don't worry, we'll throw the book at him.'

'How ghastly,' said Daphne with a quiver. 'Of course, I always knew that boy wasn't quite the ticket. Pure evil, my spirit guide Pongo did warn me.'

'Shame you didn't mention that,' said Sarah.

'Well, I can't be responsible for everything,' said Daphne vaguely. 'So why did he put the body in my beach hut?'

'Well, mine – or rather, Francesca's,' Charles chipped in.

'I'm not sure why you're fighting over the honour,' said Sarah drily. 'I imagine he panicked initially, with the corpse on his hands. And then the hut just seemed easy, because everyone knew it was used to store stuff belonging to all the groups in Merstairs – the Mermaids, the Tai Chi lot, the Scouts, you name it... He probably thought it would take forever before the body was found.'

'If you hadn't needed to store Peter's suits, Sarah, it could have been there to this day,' said Daphne with a shiver.

'But even so, it was always going to turn up eventually,' said Charles.

'Yes. I suppose it was just another example of Albie's inability to think things through properly – killing Gus in the first place, not realising it would make everything worse, then stashing the body somewhere where it would eventually come to light. None of it was smart, really.'

'We know Albie was familiar with the hut, too. The high-vis jackets and boots in the box you opened were from the community service scheme, which Albie knew all about. He'd been made to remove graffiti from the beach huts when he was a younger lad,' said Mariella.

'Right. That's a proper link, there. It looks like the evidence is mounting up. And he's definitely strong enough to have stuffed Gus into the trunk. Gus would have been pretty frail by the time he died, and Albie has those enormous biceps,' Sarah added.

'Can't say I've noticed,' said Charles drily.

'Well, never mind that,' said Daphne. 'But how did Bill Turbot get killed?'

'I've thought and thought about this,' said Sarah. 'And the closest I can get to it is this. That time when you came into the pub, Bill saw Albie behind you. And then he looked at the postcards. They were still lying on the bar after Trevor had shown them to me. Bingo – he realised then what Albie had done.

'The penny dropped for me today just as Albie brought those drinks over. I suddenly realised that the letter X, from the kisses on the postcard Trevor showed me, was identical to one on today's sign. It had a tiny curly tail on it, quite distinctive. It must have been what Bill saw, too. That was careless of Albie, again. Maybe he'd got complacent – or forgotten that not everyone's eyesight is as rotten as Trevor's.'

'Do you really think Trevor didn't recognise the writing at all?' Daphne asked.

'Well, no,' Sarah answered. 'Poor Trevor's sight is abysmal. His glasses are as thick as milk bottles. The cards were all written in capital letters – Trevor thought that was to make it easier for him to read, but in fact it also made it simpler for Albie to disguise his writing. Bill had no eye problems, though. I think he had a sudden flash of recognition, like I did. Albie saw his expression – and his death warrant was signed. And he realised we were getting close to the truth earlier, so that was another three fentanyl cocktails he knocked up.'

'What about the stamps on the postcards, though?' asked Charles. 'Wouldn't everyone have noticed they weren't authentic?'

'Ah, but they probably were,' said Sarah, trying not to sound smug, though she was rather pleased she'd tied up this particular loose end. 'Albie's dad told me he used to be a stamp collector. Nothing simpler than sticking on a Canadian stamp and mocking up some sort of postmark, maybe blurring it with a bit of dirt or water to make it look as though it had been on a long journey.'

If only Albie hadn't gone to the bad, Sarah thought. He could have put all that ingenuity and energy into something worthwhile.

'But how did he do it? How did he bump Bill off?' Charles asked.

Sarah grimaced. 'It's hard to piece it together, and unless Mariella gets a confession we may never be sure... but I imagine Albie either arranged to meet Bill over by the beach huts, or just waylaid him there on his morning walk. He probably injected him with some fentanyl to make things easier but didn't get the dose right, as Bill struggled terribly when he was being strangled. Sorry, Daphne,' she added, as her friend grimaced. 'Mariella, I'm not sure if a puncture wound showed up in the post-mortem, but it might be worth asking the pathologist...'

'It was found,' said Mariella quietly.

They all sat in silence for a moment. Sarah couldn't help shaking her head. There was such terrible evil in the world. Albie's initial impulse had probably been largely a twisted sort of altruism, but his bid to spare Trevor from Gus's suffering had inflicted pain on so many and set off an irresistible chain of events.

Suddenly Daphne sat up a little straighter. 'So, when we went to Francesca's, it must have been Albie who cut the brakes?'

'Yes,' said Charles. 'I saw him in Trevor's car, waiting outside the house...'

'He had experience with cars,' Mariella chipped in. 'He did an apprenticeship at the garage, until he jacked it in to help out at the pub. And he sometimes helped Francesca with her car at a cut-price rate, she's admitted as much.'

'Did he really? I suppose if I'd known that I might have put two and two together... but by that stage I'd started wondering about Trevor. Albie never once crossed my mind,' said Sarah.

'That baby face of his! I'm kicking myself. It helped him get away with so much. But he was trying to tell us about his real character all the time – why else get a tattoo of such an evil-looking serpent, not to mention all his snake jewellery? That's the real Albie. I just got everything the wrong way round.'

'Well,' said Mariella. 'That's not a problem. After all, it's not your job to solve crimes, is it? Any of you,' she added, looking round the table sternly.

'No, no, it's not,' said Sarah a little wistfully, when Mariella had got to her feet. 'But I have to say, it is quite absorbing as a hobby.'

'A hobby,' said Daphne, outraged, waving to her daughter as she headed back to the police station. 'You heard what Mari just said. Investigating killers isn't a game. And besides, it's not like there'll ever be another case like this. Will there?' she said fiercely, and Sarah found herself shaking her head mutely.

'Good, I'm glad you agree,' Daphne went on. 'If you want a hobby, you should stick to crosswords. And by the way, you never did tell us the answer to that clue.'

'Four down? "Crows flock to this"? Can't you guess?' Sarah looked from Daphne to Charles.

'She's always been insufferable when she's got a clever secret up her sleeve,' Daphne confided loudly to Charles. 'Come on, out with it, girl.'

Sarah put her head on one side, in a very Hamish-like gesture. 'It's *murder*,' she said. 'A *murder* of crows.'

While the others groaned, Sarah thought hard. After a long career devoted to preserving life and doing no harm, Sarah felt as strongly as anyone that killing should be avoided, in all ways, at all possible costs. But having the odd little mystery to solve – missing cats, stolen bicycles, that sort of thing – well, that was a different matter, wasn't it? She was sure there would be plenty to keep her busy in Merstairs – and there were Peter's things to deal with now she felt stronger – but if any puzzles came her way, well, that could be fun, too...

'Let's drink to it,' said Daphne exuberantly, holding her glass aloft. 'A totally crime-free Merstairs!'

'And all who sail in her,' said Charles, winking at Sarah.

Sarah smiled round the table, at friends old and new, and realised how comfortable she already felt in Merstairs, despite the terrible events of the last few days. She raised her own glass, and clinked it against Daphne's. 'Yes, let's drink to that.'

But Hamish, sitting contentedly chewing his tennis ball, noticed his mistress crossing the fingers of her other hand surreptitiously under the table. He wondered what that meant. Oh well, just as long as they were together, having lots of fun by the sea – with plentiful chips and bacon too – then he was perfectly happy to be here, in this funny little place called Merstairs.

A LETTER FROM ALICE

Welcome to Merstairs!

Thank you so much for reading *Murder at an English Pub*. I hope you've enjoyed it as much as I loved writing it. I've always adored the English seaside and I grew up going to the Kent coast for bucket and spade holidays. It's something I still love to this day, so it's been a treat to set a series in this wonderful part of the country. Sarah, Daphne and Hamish had a life of their own as soon as they popped into my head. I hope you'll join them on their next adventures. If you'd like to find out what they're up to, please sign up at the email link below. Your email address will never be shared and you can unsubscribe at any time.

www.bookouture.com/alice-castle

If you enjoyed this book, I would be very grateful if you could write a review and post it on Amazon or Goodreads, so that other people can discover Merstairs, too. I'm also on X, Facebook and Goodreads, often talking about my own cats, who thank goodness are not quite as naughty as Mephisto!

Happy reading, and I hope to see you soon for Sarah Vane's next outing.

Alice Castle

KEEP IN TOUCH WITH ALICE

Alicecastleauthor.com

 facebook.com/Alicecastleauthor
x.com/AliceMCastle

ACKNOWLEDGMENTS

A big thank you to my fantastic agent, Justin Nash of KNLA, my wonderful editor Nina Winters, and all the team at Bookouture, for their faith in Merstairs.

PUBLISHING TEAM

Turning a manuscript into a book requires the efforts of many people. The publishing team at Bookouture would like to acknowledge everyone who contributed to this publication.

Audio
Alba Proko
Sinead O'Connor
Melissa Tran

Commercial
Lauren Morrissette
Jil Thielen
Imogen Allport

Cover design
Tash Webber

Data and analysis
Mark Alder
Mohamed Bussuri

Editorial
Nina Winters
Sinead O'Connor